THE
GRAVE
OF THE
Fireflies

ALYCIA DAVIDSON

THE
GRAVE
OF THE
fireflies

TATE PUBLISHING & *Enterprises*

The opinions expressed by the author are not necessarily those of Tate Publishing, LLC.

Published by Tate Publishing & Enterprises, LLC
127 E. Trade Center Terrace | Mustang, Oklahoma 73064 USA
1.888.361.9473 | www.tatepublishing.com

Tate Publishing is committed to excellence in the publishing industry. The company reflects the philosophy established by the founders, based on Psalm 68:11,
"The Lord gave the word and great was the company of those who published it."

Book design copyright © 2008 by Tate Publishing, LLC. All rights reserved.
Cover design by Stephanie Woloszyn
Interior design by Jonathan Lindsey

Published in the United States of America
ISBN: 978-1-60604-644-9
1. Fiction: Fantasy; Short Stores
08.11.17

I want to thank my savior for blessing me with
this wonderful opportunity, and my
parents for taking the time to read this book.

THE GRAVE OF THE FIREFLIES

Chapter One:

THE HOUSE IN A FIELD

"IT'S SO HOT IN HERE!" Kenny moaned, wiping a bead of sweat from his forehead in an overdramatic way. He slouched in the dusty old leather seat and sighed out of boredom. Robert rolled his eyes and went back to watching the dirt road, not that there was anything to really pay attention to except the rolling clouds above. The old truck glided across the rocks with little grace. Kenny moaned as he was tossed from side to side.

"Oh, put a cork in it," Robert snapped. Kenny rolled his eyes in reply and looked away and complained more under his breath, making Robert grip the wheel tighter in anger.

These two were roommates and brothers. Though not bound by blood, they shared a bond that couldn't be broken, even by all their bickering. Seventeen-year-old Kenny, AKA Kenneth, Mathis was the complainer of the two. He was an honor student, with perfect grades and a bright future ahead of him, having graduated high school a year early. But he lacked common sense, and his head was always in the clouds. He had hair that was platinum blonde and caramel-colored eyes that, in bright sunlight, looked like raspberries that had been freshly picked in the warm summer and a slight batch of freckles were planted on his face. He was quite a daydreamer, always believing in some imaginary world he'd never be able to see. It got him into a lot of trouble sometimes, but he didn't mind; he knew Robert would be there to bail him out of it.

Speaking of Robert, the eighteen-year-old sitting next to him with his bored eyes still on the road, he was a soft-hearted guy with short, pure black hair that curled at the ends and gentle silver-toned eyes. At times he was known to have a short temper whenever it came to Kenny's crazy ideas. "He's always getting himself into so much trouble," he would say, "and I *always* have to get him out of it." And even though he complained about it, he didn't mind, gave his dull prep school life a little kick of excitement every now and again. Robert was more laid back and less adventurous than his young friend. A man of Italian heritage, and a lover of the arts and fine music, he held a degree in classical music and was known throughout his hometown as a genius of Beethoven's caliber. He held the last names of Drake-Lionel, he wore them proudly, he was more on the realistic side, and he was never one to believe in fairytales, unless they were those he created with his music.

These two were starting their lives as young graduates, like they had done everything before; together. Best friends forever they'd always say. They were getting out of the house and living on their own for the first time, not to mention trying to start a business of some sort, at the moment undecided, and make a reasonable living. Robert and Kenny had known each other for as long as they could remember, they could read each other like open books. Both hoped to make good pay and maybe expand their business into a famous chain (that is if they could get along for three minutes without getting into a fight).

Kenny playfully bumped Robert in the arm with his elbow, making him lose grip on the steering wheel. He hissed and looked down at Kenny who innocently looked out the window of the old, dirt-covered Chevy pick-up with his tongue sticking out like a dog.

"It's so hot!" he moaned again. Robert slammed on the breaks, almost throwing Kenny out the window. And he groaned, setting his head on the steering wheel with a heavy sigh and angered eyes turned toward his young friend.

"What'd you do that for?" Kenny asked, trying to stop his racing heart.

"Stop whining or I'm going to toss you out and make you walk the rest of the way," Robert replied calmly yet in a very harsh tone.

"Throw me out? Please, we're in the middle of nowhere. You'd get in so much trouble with your mom if you did that," Kenny said, cockily grinning while crossing his arms. He chuckled triumphantly. "Besides, you don't have the heart to toss me out of here."

Robert rolled his eyes again and started to drive once more down the dirt-covered street. He knew Kenny was right. After opening her home to Kenny for the past few years, Robert's mother had raised him like her own, and she would hang Robert if he left her poor baby out on the street.

"You're lucky she likes you, or you'd be walking right now," Robert said un-enthusiastically. The rocky road tossed them all around the car; Kenny kept hitting the roof with a loud thud, one after another. He shouted every time, Robert just mumbled under his breath, "I told you to tighten your seatbelt, but no, you didn't want to listen."

The trip seemed long, and Kenny was growing bored, the radio signals were screwed up due to low frequency in the countryside, and the batteries in his CD player had died hours ago. He looked over at Robert who looked equally bored and tired, but at least he kept his complaints to himself.

Poor guy, he's been driving almost non-stop since yesterday morning, Kenny thought as he looked to the clock next to the radio, *and it's almost seven o'clock.*

"Hey Rob," Kenny asked.

"What now?" Robert moaned, not removing his eyes from the road.

"I can drive if you need a break," he said kindly.

"Uh... let me think. No!"

"Wait, why not? You're so unfair!"

"One; I don't trust you, two; you don't have a license, and three; I don't trust you."

Kenny crossed his arms again and huffed angrily. Robert slammed on the breaks again. He threw his hands out in front of him to stop himself from being tossed into the dashboard.

"What's wrong? What did I do now?" Kenny asked in confusion. Robert turned the car off and opened his door. Kenny looked out in front of him, *Are we here, finally?*

A small house stood in the middle of his vision, old flowers that had wilted, and overtime, broken and scattered in the wind, lay all across the lawn. Weeds were growing freely all around the green field. The house was the only thing that didn't look as though it had come from a horror movie. It was made of manila-colored tile, a few of the windows on the second floor were broken, but that could easily be replaced. They looked as if they belonged to the attic level anyway, and Kenny always hated attics. The roof was the color of fine red wine and the shutters were of the same tone. The porch was in need of many repairs as well, a few old chairs and a table stood on the dusty surface in front of an olive green colored door.

There was an old dog, a Shetland, wearing a rosy red collar, lying on the welcome mat sleeping, that is until the car pulled up and the headlights flashed in its eyes.

Down a ways stood an old water well, it had a rose plant blooming around its surface. A ways off in the distance stood a small stream running down into a forest. A small, oak wood gazebo was sitting near the edge of the rock-filled body of water and tiny droplets of the cleanest liquid Kenny had ever seen bounced from the rocks all over its surface. Also, a few miles down, you could see a small town, not much was really to be seen of interest in it, only a few houses and shops, but Kenny guessed this was the closest thing to civilization out here. The last thing noticeable was a blur of white, like a small shack, hidden deep within the forest behind the small old manor in front of him.

A white fence lay across the path leading down into the town, blocking entrance onto the estate from the outer fields.

The sun was gently shinning down onto the setting. The river looked ablaze in the heavenly light. It was unreal, you could smell the crisp autumn air and how pure and uninhibited the area was, and you could almost taste a familiar memory of visiting your grandparents when you were younger when you breathed.

Robert opened Kenny's door, he snapped from his trance and turned to his older friend.

"You okay?" Robert asked quietly.

Kenny nodded. "It's kind of, what's the word, surprising... that's all. I'm fine."

True he was entranced by the magical setting, but he never was one for creepy houses in the middle of nowhere. Especially if it belonged to Robert's family, either side for that matter, they were all strange people, and they always seemed to be hiding something from him.

"Okay then, get out and help me unload," Robert demanded. Kenny nodded, wanting to wake up from this slightly bizarre dream. He slipped out of the car and grabbed his suitcase from the back of the truck. Robert was already on the porch unlocking the door by the time Kenny closed his car door.

"W-wait up, Rob!" he called. He pulled the heavy suitcase out of the truck bed and carried it over to the porch. The dog growled as he went by. He crept over to the opposite side of the doorway and slipped inside the dark area.

The wallpaper was a disgusting green color with gold trim, the smell of mothballs reigned inside, and cobwebs roamed freely. It was a lot different looking than he'd imagined.

"Ew, it smells like grandma!" Kenny said, curling his upper lip in disgust. Robert rubbed his tired eyes and walked down the stairs.

"That's because it is," he replied.

"You mean this house is made of old people!" Kenny asked, backing up.

"Idiot, this was my grandmother's house. Everybody in my family on my mom's side since coming over from England when the colonies were first made has lived here. It's like our estate. After my grandpa passed away, she started one of those Red Hat Society things, and she had a lot of old friends over." Robert said coldly. Kenny sighed, *I don't want to stay here anymore. I don't do well with old places like this at all!*

Eventually he sighed and looked at Robert who was staring blankly at him. He was sitting slouched over on the first step of the creaky staircase which was covered by a tacky green, burgundy rose and gold vine-patterned runner that was tattered on the sides.

"Where am I staying?" Kenny asked. Robert moved his eyes from the floor up to Kenny and stood, using the squeaky old mahogany railing to stand. He pointed his thumb up the stairs and looked at Kenny with his tired eyes.

"Robby, are you okay? You look pale," Kenny stated as he headed toward Robert. He stood next to the raven-haired teenager and looked at him with big brown eyes. Robert nodded and headed up the stairs to the dimly lit hallway with his hands in his pockets. Kenny followed him closely. The floorboards would creak under him as he walked. He stayed mere inches behind Robert, feeling very fragile and scared from all the noises. Every single step he took he felt another set of eyes on him, like something was watching him in every panel of the wall. But it was only his imagination playing tricks on him.

Before he knew it, he was standing at the top of the stairs, staring into an old painting of a fairy sitting on a vibrant, pink lilac flower. She had bright auburn hair, two pools of emeralds stared at him, her long eyelashes splashed (so lightly it was almost transparent) with light white paint like they were wet with dew. Her skin was a rose-gold color, and her lips were pale white, her outfit the same color as the lilac. Everything else was done in rich greens and gentle whites. His eyes glanced to the bottom of the picture where lay hidden the signature, A. Drake.

"Robby," Kenny began, "who painted that?" He pulled his eyes from the painting toward his friend.

"My grandmother, Alberta Drake," he replied, looking at it.

"Drake? But I thought this house belonged to your dad," he questioned.

Robert laughed. "I don't know who told you that, but no," he replied.

Kenny nodded a little as Robert urged him into the hallway to his left (seeing as the other way was nothing but a dead end) that was filled with more portraits, none which he found to be as *enchanting* as the first. Kenny looked once more at the painting, only to see the fairy in it wink at him. He gasped heavily and rubbed his eyes, trying to convince himself it was a hallucination. When he re-opened them, the picture stayed still.

"Come on, Kenny!" Robert called. Kenny nodded and followed him closely.

Eventually Robert stopped, turned to his left again, and opened a door. "You can stay here, and I'm right across the hall. Go ahead and unpack, I'll see if there's anything that isn't moldy for dinner," he said as he turned.

Kenny went to say something only to see him already gone. He shrugged his shoulders, knowing his question wasn't of importance if he didn't stop him, and he breathed a sigh. He looked at the hallway, only seeing the door across from him and what appeared to be another hallway at the very end of the long corridor. With a deep breath, he turned and entered the dark room.

It was average-sized, a daybed stood near the windows in the far back of the slightly odd rectangle-shaped room. Along the right side of him stood two bookshelves filled with old diaries and sketchbooks that were all dated back to the 1940s. To the left of the bed stood a small bedside table made of mahogany. A very old oil lamp and a photograph stood in a broken frame near the edge. And lastly, to his left, stood an old mirror, and under it lay and old, oddly eerie chest.

The windows were slightly open. The white lace curtains were blowing around in the soft breezes, and the last remaining sunlight from the outside gently lit the room.

"Guess I should unpack," he whispered, shrugged his shoulders, and he entered the old room.

Chapter Two:

THE MIDNIGHT CONVERSATION

LATE THAT SAME night, Kenny rolled over onto his side and opened his eyes, his stomach churned as he got out of bed. He pressed his hand against his mouth and moaned. "I think that *food* was bad," he whispered as he walked to the door. He peeked outside and looked down the hall. Robert's light was on, and his door was slightly open, which meant an open invitation, so Kenny walked over to the door. *Why's he still up? It's like three in the morning or so.* He slid his head into the room and smiled.

Robert looked up at him in question. "What's wrong?" he asked, removing his reading glasses from his face. He had some color back into his face, and he looked rested, plus he didn't snap at him, which meant he got some sleep.

"Why are you up?" Kenny asked.

"I got some sleep, but I guess I wasn't as tired as I thought. I woke up a few minutes ago," he replied.

"Can I come in?" Kenny asked kindly. Robert shrugged his shoulders and went back to reading a book he had in his hands. The dog was lying at his feet, looking at Robert with a happy grin on his face. But it growled at Kenny as he entered, his body tensing in fear a bit as it kept its eyes on him.

"That dog *has* to go," he spat.

"Leave him alone. He's old and misses grandma," Robert replied, rubbing the dogs head. "Isn't that right, Leroy?" he said childishly.

Oh give me a break, Kenny thought, looking over Robert's room as the dog barked happily. Robert continued to pet him as Kenny's eyes wandered. The room was set up like Kenny's, it was about the same shape, a normal twin-sized bed was placed up against the back wall, but he had no windows. He had a candle lit and set on the bedside table near his head. Both walls were packed with bookshelves that were handmade and embroidered with small dragons and fairies. They were filled with more diaries and papers.

"What's wrong?" Robert asked as Kenny sat down on the edge of the bed.

"I feel a little...sick," Kenny whispered in reply.

"There's nothing in this house that's going to hurt you," Robert said kindly, yet a bit of amusement was in his voice.

Kenny looked at him in question. "What?" he asked.

"My entire family has lived in this house and no one else. Like I said, some settlers that came from England built this entire town, and this house has been in the Drake family line for generations, and there aren't any ghosts or monsters, just a few bugs, so relax," Robert said kindly.

Kenny nodded and stood. "Thanks," he said, still unconvinced.

Robert swung his legs over the edge of the bed and walked over to Kenny. "Stay here," he demanded as he vanished behind the door. Kenny stayed there, watching as the dog eyed him angrily. He backed away a little bit toward the door and shuffled his feet in disarray as he waited for Robert to return.

The door re-opened and Robert walked in, he placed an old, tattered peach-colored bear in Kenny's hands and smiled. Kenny blushed deep crimson. "I don't need a doll to sleep with!" he shouted.

"I know, you're an adult, you don't need these things anymore, but I thought he might help. I've had him for years, and he's never let me down once." Robert cut in with a smile. "Besides, you don't have to act tough around me anyway, it doesn't work."

Kenny looked at it and played with the loose button he had for an eye, watching the seams glisten in the candle light. He held it close, remembering memories of his childhood as Robert placed his hand on Kenny's shoulder.

"Get some sleep," Robert said. Kenny nodded and walked off toward the door with a sigh. He looked down the hallway as if he were planning on going downstairs.

"Where are you going?" Robert asked, stopping him at the top of the stairs. Kenny handed him the stuffed bear and heaved a heavy sigh.

"I need some fresh air. I *really* don't feel too good," Kenny moaned. He had his hand pressed against his mouth again and his other hand over his stomach.

Robert stood up straight and rubbed the back of his head, trying to think of what he could do to help Kenny. He gently leaned in toward Kenny and looked at him.

"The bathroom is downstairs. Just go through the kitchen, into the back hallway, second door to your left, okay?" Robert whispered. Kenny nodded and swallowed hard.

Kenny blinked a few times. *Downstairs, in the dark?* he asked himself as he headed to the door.

"Goodnight Kenny," Robert said as he went back into his bedroom.

"Goodnight Rob," Kenny replied, watching Robert close the door. After, he sidled his way down the hall to the stairs, the floorboards started to get on his nerves with their constant creaking and cracking. He used the railing to guide himself down the stairs into the dark, the only light coming from the moon outside.

"First thing we add to this dump is light fixtures," Kenny said to himself as he set foot at the landing. He turned to his left and headed past the small living room to the kitchen.

There was a small green loveseat in the middle of the room

and a brass and mahogany coffee table set in between it and a large portrait of a man. Kenny, paying more attention to the painting than his surroundings, tripped on the small olive green rug and landed on the couch. Dust flew up around him, getting into the seams of his clothes and his eyes. He pushed himself off of the couch, rubbing his eyes furiously as he tried to clean them out. He landed on the floor with a loud thud, letting out a moan of agony.

"Everything okay down there?" Robert called from above.

"Yeah, I just tripped," Kenny replied, moaning loudly as he stood. Above he heard Robert walking back to his room, chuckling lightly as he went. Kenny stood and walked into the kitchen, the large windows above the sink showered everything in the moonlight.

Kenny unbuttoned the top button on his pajamas, seeing as he was incredibly hot, and walked over to the window. He ran his finger across the window pane, leaving trails in the dust. His eyes wandered outside to the gazebo and the creek, then the small flickering lights that kept appearing everywhere. Kenny leaned in closer and gasped in wonder. *Wait, are those fireflies? This late in the fall?* he asked himself, looking at the small bubbles of light outside.

Kenny slowly crept to the back door, near the hallway where he was originally going to enter. He opened the door and went to jump down into the grass below when he saw a shadow looming over him. He closed his eyes, swallowed hard, and turned around.

"I didn't do it," he said.

Robert chuckled and placed his hand on Kenny's shoulder. Kenny laughed innocently, closed the door, and smiled guiltily.

"All right, you caught me," he said laughing.

Robert pointed his thumb back to the living room. Kenny sighed and walked toward the musty, smelly old room.

"Go out to the porch, I'll meet you out there in a second," Robert said.

Kenny looked back at him in question. "The porch?" he asked.

"Yeah, the porch," he replied.

Kenny nodded and walked back into the living room, making sure to step over the rug this time. He looked back at Robert who was grabbing a few cups from the cupboard, then continued onward. Before he knew it he was standing in the fresh air, letting the gentle breezes brush his skin as he sat in one of the chairs.

Kenny sat for a few moments, staring out into the field that was still packed with fireflies. They illuminated every blade of grass, all still wet with rainwater from a light shower that had rolled in a little while earlier. Robert walked out onto the porch, holding two glasses in his hands. He handed one to Kenny, who gladly took it, then he sat down in the opposite chair.

"Why are there fireflies out here? It's so late in the year," Kenny stated as his gaze moved over to Robert.

"I don't really know, but my grandmother did," Robert said quietly.

"Can I ask you a question? What's up with all the fairies and dragons in that house?" Kenny asked. "I thought your family was all religious and junk, you know."

"On my father's side. My mother's side, The Drake's, which family this house belonged to, loved fairies, mythical creatures, and dragons; that sort of stuff. Of course I don't believe in any of it, but there was that one story. My grandmother used to tell me it every summer when I'd come down here during the summers while you were at camp."

Kenny swirled the cider around in his cup and looked at Robert.

"Really, what was it about?" he asked.

Robert looked at him. "Well, you see, late nights like this I'd sit out here, a cup of this cider in my hands, kind of like we are now. She would tell me, 'Gaze out there my dear'."

Kenny watched as Robert pointed out into the field, his eyes gazed out there as well. They locked onto a swarm of fireflies that were floating near the well. They looked as though they were dancing in some tribal ritual.

"Beautiful, aren't they?" Robert asked.

Kenny nodded and looked back at his friend who had a small smile on his face. He looked relaxed and peaceful, usually he was so stressed because of school and work he never got time to just sit back and rest. There was rarely a time Kenny got to see Robert smiling like this.

"She said," Robert started, "'What do you see?' I would look and look.

"'It's a field Grandma.' I would reply and she'd laugh.

"'Look closer,' she would say.

"I blinked and looked. 'Fireflies,' I would reply again.

"'Those aren't fireflies, my dear boy,' she would say, 'Those are fairies.'

"And then, for the first time in the conversation, I'd laugh. Fairies I thought, fairies! I'd look at her and raise my eyebrow. She always said I had a cocky grin on my face, 'Did you forget your medicine again?' I asked. She would shake her head and tell me of a legend about a place called the Grave of the Fireflies, the land of the fairies hidden deep within the forest. She then told me to catch a firefly, right then and there.

"And so I did, well I tried, but I could never catch one, ever. No matter how hard I tried. I would chase them to the creek, then to the fence, but they'd always get away from me, and I was told to always, *always* stay in the fenced area. It got annoying after a while; it was like they were taunting me.

"Then I'd return, muddy and grass-stained, and sit down in this very chair. Grandma would laugh again and say one final thing, 'Did you ever chase one until it stopped? All the way, until it returns home?' she asked."

Kenny sipped his cider and looked at Robert, who had breathed a heavy sigh after his explanation. The night was slowly turning into day, and the fireflies were going back to their homes.

"And?" he asked.

Robert looked at him in question. "And? And what?" he repeated.

"Did you ever chase it all the way until it stopped? Like she had asked?" Kenny said, his voiced filled with a small bit of anticipation.

Robert broke out into fits of laughter, gently shaking his head in response. Kenny cocked his head gently to one side as Robert looked up into the sky.

"Oh dear, look at that," he said. Kenny looked up into the air in question, staring blindly into the newly spotted sun.

"The sun, wow it's that early?" Kenny asked. Robert nodded, stood up, and pushed his chair in.

"I guess so, time flies by here fast," he said quietly. He stretched as Kenny stood, grabbed his mug, and watched as his friend yawned heavily. *Still, you didn't get much sleep. You're going to be just peachy tomorrow.* He thought, blinking a few times to adjust his eyes to the lighting.

"You go on inside. You haven't slept in almost two days. I'll clean up," Kenny said smiling. Robert raised an eyebrow in question as Kenny snatched his cup away. He winked and headed inside without another word. Robert smiled and looked out into the sky again.

"I never did follow one all the way," Robert said in an apologetic tone. "Sorry, Grandma."

Chapter Three:

THE HIDDEN ROOM

IT WAS LATE morning, about noon or so, Kenny had just awoken from the heavy sunlight bursting down onto his face, hissing so loudly that he couldn't go back to sleep. *I guess seven hours of sleep isn't so bad,* he thought, looking out the window at the high sitting sun. Eventually he rolled out of bed, changed into a pair of jeans and a light tank top, and hobbled down the stairs, faintly smelling food coming from the kitchen.

"Robert?" Kenny asked, rubbing his head. He looked in the kitchen with a smile on his face and wonder in his eyes. He slowly crept toward the musty old kitchen slash dining room. He poked his head inside, his smile faded, and he sighed heavily in disappointment.

"Where'd you go, Rob?" Kenny asked. He walked inside, the floorboards creaking under his feet again, not as badly as the stairs had but enough to make him jump. He walked over to the table and snatched a note from its surface. A chair was already pulled away from the table. The white flower padding was worn and had over time become a yellow color. He sat down and skimmed over the note.

Kenny,

Gone out for groceries; be back in a little bit, check out the house and get used to your surroundings. DO NOT go past the fence behind the creek. If you need me, my spare cell phone is on the table, you know my number.

Robert

KENNY LOOKED AT the note. *I wonder when he left.* Eventually he yawned and looked at the old oil stove, a batch of pancakes stood on an old china plate. Kenny stood and walked over to the pancakes. He pressed his finger against the top of the food and sighed.

"Oh man, they're cold," he said in anguish. He picked up the plate and walked over to garbage. As soon as he threw them away, he walked out into the living room and headed to the stairs. He was somewhat getting used to all the twists and turns in the house. He trekked up the creaky stairway again, wishing he hadn't wasted his energy on coming down in the first place. His eyes were still fixed upon the painting of the fairy.

For the first time he noticed her transparent wings; they were barely visible. Done in a slightly darker pink but brushed so lightly against the canvas that you could barely tell any difference. As soon as he was at the top, he gently touched the canvas. He liked to feel the paint on his fingers almost as much as he loved to feel the texture of the paper of books on the tips of his fingers when he was reading.

"I wonder if Robby likes to paint on top of the whole violin thing? Artists," Kenny spat. "I'll never get them." He scratched the back of his head and turned the corner to the rooms in the back. He had nothing better to do than sit back and relax until

Robert came back from the town. He had looked all over his room and couldn't find anything of interest, and everything in Robert's room would probably be the same, so checking out his room would probably be a waste of time as well. He walked to the end of the hallway, a little frightened since he was never shown what lied back there beyond their rooms, only to find another small flight of stairs leading up and to the right. He guessed it was the hallway he had vaguely seen the night before.

Kenny swallowed hard and walked up the stairs, trying to put little pressure on them as to keep the noise down, for fear that something was following him. He was quite a paranoid person, always afraid of something behind him (but mostly that was Robert's doing, seeing as he was constantly playing mean jokes on him when he least expected it).

The flight of stairs was smaller than he expected. At the top was a small door; it was different than the others in the house. It was olive green, and it had gold trim around it with embroidered leaves, all of them individual. Small bugs were printed on it as well, and again the most easily spotted thing was the fairies. *Talk about obsessive compulsive disorder*, Kenny thought with a small laugh. He reached out for the door handle with a trembling hand. It was gold as well and had an oddly shaped keyhole beneath it. As soon as his fingers touched the exterior of the handle, he heard a knock on the door downstairs.

He pulled his hand away from the door and sighed. *It's probably nothing*, he thought. Again he went to grab the handle when the knocking began again. Kenny sighed, he ran down the small flight of stairs back into the main hallway. He skidded across the long rug that covered the floor (it had the same repulsive design as the rest did), slammed into the wall, and fell flat on his face.

"Kenny, open the door!" Robert called from below.

"I'm coming, hang on!" Kenny replied as he stood. He headed over to the stairs, slowing his pace this time so he wouldn't run into anything and walked down the stairs.

Robert's silhouette appeared through the cypress colored stained glass window on the door. He was holding heavy grocery sacks, his hand jiggled the door handle, and his eyes were fixed upon the growing outline of Kenny.

Kenny raced to the door and opened it. He quickly grabbed a grocery sack before Robert dropped it. The paper bag was so large it covered his face and muffled his loud grunt as he caught the last paper bag. Robert laughed and pulled down the top part of the bag.

"I knew you were under there somewhere," he said with a smile.

"Robby! Back so soon?" Kenny said laughing. Robert patted Kenny's head and walked passed him into the kitchen, feeling relief on his shoulders from the heavy weight taken from him by his younger friend.

"You should've waited to go shopping until later, you didn't get *any* sleep, and I probably could've helped carry some things," Kenny said, stressing the word any as much as he could as he followed him into the kitchen.

"It's okay, I'll take a nap later," Robert replied. Kenny sighed and set the sack down on the counter. He began unpacking random items, anything from apples to ice cream and everything else in between.

"We don't have a fridge," Kenny stated, holding up a small bottle of milk.

"We have an ice box in the basement," Robert replied.

Kenny looked up at him in wonder, questioning where the entrance to this basement was. "We actually have a basement here?" he asked, setting down another box.

"It's required; see we get a lot of tornados around here. We need somewhere underground to hide away if we do get hit sometime," he replied, rubbing the back of his head. "Anyway, did you get to look around?" Robert asked as he continued unpacking.

Kenny shook his head in reply. "No," he said, no louder than a whisper. He pondered the thought of keeping his little discovery to himself, but then again what would Robert really say if he found out about it later and dragged it out of him? The thought hadn't occurred to him that Robert may have already seen it. He was too mystified to think of much else.

"Kenny, is everything okay? You look troubled," Robert stated. Kenny looked up from a box of cereal and stared at him in question.

"Uh, yeah, everything's all right," he replied quietly.

"Can you do me a favor?" Robert asked out of the blue.

Kenny still had his eyes fixed upon Robert. "Sure," he replied.

"Would you go through the books in your room, see if there is anything that isn't used?"

"Why?"

"There's an old craft store downtown, I ran into the owner, and she asked, since Grandma passed away, if we could go through her books and see if there are any still of use, sketchbooks and diaries, that sort of stuff."

Kenny nodded and turned, giving Robert a small smile of reassurance as he left. Robert chuckled a bit. *Almost thirteen years I've known him and he never changes.*

"Hey, Rob, where do I put the books that are still usable?" Kenny called.

"Just set them in a pile outside your door," Robert replied.

"Sure thing!" he said, turning around and running up the stairs. He picked up his pace a bit to get up quickly so Robert wouldn't think something was wrong. *I shouldn't tell him, not yet.*

Chapter Four:

THE BOOK NAMED UNTITLED

THE NEXT FEW hours were spent cleaning the house and going through the old books. By three, the bottom floor looked brand new (though it still kept its old-fashioned look) and spotless. Kenny felt like the hours became twice as long, going through the old books in the room, half of them weren't ever open and the others were torn and unusable. He was growing bored. Robert checked on him every so often, offering to help him, but he would kindly refuse and order him to get some rest.

Kenny ran his finger across the rim of the next book, this one looked like it was from Ireland. It was a dark evergreen color with gold embroidery (much like the door he had found earlier), and it had no name on the side. This was no sketchbook or diary like everything else he had previously seen; this was a book.

He pulled it from the shelf and sat down on the chest under the mirror. A book with the word *Untitled* printed into its cover. He carefully opened it, knowing just how easily old books could fall apart if opened recklessly. The beginning of the book was blank, as were the next few pages. He slowly looked over all of the pages. It was written in some odd language that he guessed was ancient and forgotten, seeing as it didn't look familiar to him.

The ink was a real light black and parts of the letters looked faded. *Most likely it was done in a feather pen*, Kenny thought. He slowly flipped the page, and there it was, the illustration that signaled the start of it all. It was a Celtic cross, done in a dark green ink. In the middle of it appeared to hold a picture of what looked like crescent moon, but he wasn't sure, it wasn't overly big. Kenny leaned in closer. Something looked as if it had flashed for a moment when the small ruby stones on the curtain's tassel swept through the sun.

"So strange," he whispered. Robert knocked on the door and let himself in, he had a small smile on his face. It faded when he saw Kenny hadn't moved.

"What on earth are you doing?" he asked.

Kenny finally looked up. "Look at this!" he shouted, standing up quickly. Robert's eyes widened in shock, and then he slowly walked inside. Kenny rushed to his side and handed him the book. He took it and looked at it carefully.

"It's just another drawing, Kenny. Definitely not grandma's, but still," he said, quite coldly.

Kenny shook his head, grabbed the book out of Robert's hand. He pulled him over to the bed, made him sit down and take the book. He sat there in shock, holding the book loosely in his hands as he watched Kenny scramble to one of the book-shelves again.

"That drawing, the ink is green," Kenny stated.

Robert laughed. "Yeah, I can see that," he replied sarcastically.

Kenny shook his head. "No, no! Look closer, tell me what it reminds you of," he stated, looking carefully through the bookshelves.

"It looks like the ink they use for money," Robert said plainly.

Kenny nodded. Robert shrugged his shoulders in reply, not catching onto what Kenny was trying to tell him.

"Tell me, what have you seen all over this house?" Kenny asked, not taking his eyes from the bookshelves. He was coughing heavily from the dust flying up all around him, wiping it constantly from his eyes. Robert watched Kenny rush around the room for a while as he thought about Kenny's question. *All around this house?* he asked himself, looking slightly confused. His eyes gazed across the book he held in his hands as Kenny looked back at him. Robert lifted his head up from the book and shrugged his shoulders again, not knowing what to say.

"Think, Robby! They're everywhere, in the statues, the picture frames, the door handles even!" Kenny shouted. Robert sighed heavily and thought hard for a few moments. Soon he lifted his head up again. He had an 'I'm sorry' look on his face.

"Rubies, Rob, rubies!" Kenny stated. "Look they're in the bookshelves right here, right in front of your eyes!" he said. He pointed to the rubies in the dragon's eye on the side of the shelf. Robert stood up, and he looked at the dragon closely, realizing now he was right.

"Yeah, my Grandma's birthstone was ruby, it means nothing," Robert replied. Kenny broke out into fits of laughter, and he smiled like a child. He pulled out an old jewelry case from behind a batch of books he had put back. He opened it and pulled out a pendant, very regal with a large ruby in the center, it was at least six inches in length and maybe a little over four and a half inches in width. Kenny moved back over to the bed, he held the gold chain in his hand as he lifted it up into the sunlight and instantly the room was showered in an aurora of colors. Robert looked at him; Kenny smiled.

"Did you ever notice what happens when the light of rubies in the sunlight reflects onto green ink?" he asked. Robert raised an eyebrow in question. He felt eager to know what Kenny was explaining and rushed over to the bed near his young friend.

"Hold the book up with the front facing the window," Kenny commanded. Robert did just that, Kenny grabbed the bottom of the pendant and directed the rays of light onto the cross. Quickly, for a mere second, Kenny saw words run across the top of the cross, but Robert quickly slammed the book shut. Kenny looked at him in question.

"What's wrong?" he asked kindly, but a bit of anger was in his voice due to Robert's action.

"That is just *too* weird," he replied.

"Come on, Rob, let's see what it says," he said smiling. Robert shook his head in disagreement, quietly whispering the word no under his breath. His scared eyes moved over to Kenny as he placed his hand on his friend's trembling shoulder.

"It's okay, I just want to see what it says, please?" he asked childishly. Robert sighed and eventually opened the book again and turned it toward Kenny so he could look. Kenny held up the pendant, the book's page basked in the light of the ruby. Across the top of the cross, embedded into the form of the symbol lightly pressed into the surface of the page itself, even in the bindings it stood.

A small poem, seemingly able to overtake one's vision as it was such an intriguing and somewhat fear-creating statement. Such an oneiric sort of state they were in. It was surreal and undeniably questionable. And if the boys would even utter such a thing, taboo. They didn't want to speak it, they felt they had too, but could they really speak such an intriguing little tale, why, of course since it was only a little fable, but what if it wasn't, what would they do then? Oh, how their minds became foggy from the dozens of questions in their heads that emitted from this.

From the heavens beyond the vast lands of sea,
Through thicket, vine, and within every tree
A house, a home, a humble abode
That is what you Mortals are told.
Will you dare seek?
Will you dare follow?
Follow them into the overshadowing hollow;
A treasure, a myth, a legend you will find
Hidden deep in the fiery land of vine.
Go seek it, embrace it, find it, and then

You shall be given the treasure of Men.

NOW IT WAS getting hard to bear, Robert threw the book down on the floor, knocking the pendant out of Kenny's hand onto the floor with it, almost bringing him down too. Kenny looked in terror at Robert, who had his hands over his ears. He was quietly whispering, "Please go away. I didn't want to read it. I didn't mean it, honest."

"Robby, what's wrong?" Kenny asked.

Robert hugged himself, trying to calm himself down and cease his shaking. He was never one to handle things he couldn't understand. Kenny looked back at the book for a moment. He wondered why certain words pertaining to mortals were highlighted or underlined. Everything slowly, painfully, hit Kenny when he heard Robert crying. Quickly he fell down onto the floor, closed the book, and tossed it under the bed. Then he stood, walked over to Robert, and placed his hands on his shoulders. He had to kneel down to look into his eyes (beings he was shorter by at least four inches) and gently wiped away a tear or two.

"You need some rest, come on," Kenny said. He stood, grabbed Robert's hand, and pulled him into his bedroom. Robert was still weeping, still whispering to thin air that he was sorry. Kenny's eyes kept moving back toward Robert to make sure he was all right, even though he knew he wasn't.

"Everything's going to be okay, Robby," he said kindly. "I promise."

Chapter Five:

THE DISCOVERY

LATER THAT AFTERNOON, Robert had been lying in bed, asleep, for hours. He had stopped crying and was relaxed, his head sunken into his pillow and eyes closed lightly.

As for Kenny, he was back in his room, looking over the book and trying to make sense out of this whole unfortunate accident. He never meant to hurt Robert in any way, and he didn't think reading something would make him flip out like he did. It was puzzling.

I should've listened. He said he didn't want to read it, and I forced him into it, he thought, letting his head rest against the glass on his window. He kept the right window open to get some fresh air, and he wanted to look for fireflies again since it was growing dark. They made him smile.

Kenny pondered the riddle a bit. "A house, a home, a humble abode," he repeated. *I know that is the key part of the whole story. It was right before the sentence containing the italicized word mortals, which was a clue, seeing that it was done darker for a reason, and it's obviously connected to the underlined word men. That meant it wasn't referring to humans, but maybe some sort of magical creature?*

"A creature, some sort house, and a forest filled with hollow trees. Hollow...trees aren't hollow though. Maybe that's a clue too...hollow, a hollow, a forest maybe? Bah! I don't get it, why am I blowing my brains out trying to figure out a stupid little riddle like this?"

None of it made sense, but he went along with it anyway, jotting down every new idea he got in an old diary he had become fond of while cleaning. He was bound and determined to figure this out, even if it was driving him mad. *Maybe re-reading it would help. Guess it's the only thing I can do*, he thought, scratching the back of his head.

Kenny hung the ruby pendant from a hook that was nailed into the wall above the window, for who knows what reason, perfectly aligning with the vanishing sunlight. He held the book up and re-read the fable, not catching anything that differed from the last time. Under his breath he mumbled the clue, he ran his finger across the page to see if any fresh ink would rub off, possibly revealing something, but no matter what he did nothing changed.

Eventually he began to grow tired and went to close the book, until a heavy gust of wind blew it from his hand. He scrambled after it as it headed toward the small crack in the wall. It wasn't big enough for much to go through, probably not even one of his bigger notebooks, but it *was* big enough for the book to just barely slide in.

Come on, don't do that to me! Kenny thought as he dove after it. He landed on the floor with a loud thud, sliding across the rug on the hardwood, surprisingly slick, floor. He landed head-first right into the wall just as the book slipped away from him down into the foyer beneath.

Kenny sat up, rubbed his head, and sighed heavily in failure. "Dang, I almost had it," he whispered, pinching his nose in agony. The door squeaked as it open, signaling Robert had just awoken from the loud catastrophe Kenny had caused. *Oh, dang, now I'm going to get chewed out for this*! he thought.

"Come on, Kenny, can't you stay out of trouble for three minutes?" Robert asked with a small laugh. He poked his head inside. Kenny looked up with an apologetic look on his face as Robert gasped.

Kenny became dumbfounded at the sudden look of shock he had on his face from entering. He raised an eyebrow in wonder.

"Look out!" Robert called. Kenny looked at him and then back up to the wall just as the bookshelf he had almost crashed into tumbled down. Everything happened so fast. All Kenny could register was the falling book case and Robert's screaming, then before he knew it he was being tossed to the floor by a blur of black, knocking him out of the way from the furniture that was tumbling down onto him.

Kenny's head smacked against the hardwood floors as the bookshelf hit the ground. The impact shook the house, and the remaining books were scattered everywhere. Dust flew up from the rug and bookshelf, creating a haze around the room. His vision blurred for a moment. He saw Robert on top of him, shielding him from the danger. Robert's terrified eyes were hidden behind thick locks of black hair, and his teeth were clenched so tightly that Kenny could hear them grinding together. And as far as Kenny could register, he was panicking, but it all went blank after a moment.

Robert opened his eyes and looked at the unconscious Kenny lying under him with worried eyes. He quickly shot up and looked at the bookshelf, seeing that he had just barely gotten out of the way. The thick wood top was maybe a half an inch away from his foot, at most. Where it once stood was a door, unlike anything Robert had ever seen. It looked like a portal. If he believed in such things, he would have called it that, but it was only a door, nothing more and nothing less.

Robert looked back at Kenny and gently shook him in attempts to wake him up. He slid his hand under Kenny's head as he tried to lift him into his arms, when he slowly let a few tears slip down his cheeks. Not from the large bump he felt, but from the small drips of blood on his fingers. Kenny's scruffy blonde hair was dyed red, and Robert's grip began to loosen a bit as he realized what had happened.

"Kenny, wake up! Wake up!" Robert called. Kenny remained silent, breathing slowed and eyes tightly closed.

Kenny breathed out. "Dang, that hurts," he mumbled. Robert gasped and shook Kenny's body lightly.

"Hang on! I'm going to get help! Just, just hang on!" Robert shouted. He laid Kenny's body on the floor, patted his shoulder reassuringly with his nervous hand, and stood up. *Hang on!*

Chapter Six:

THE DEED

ROBERT STOOD OUTSIDE of his own bedroom, hands in his sweatshirt pockets, and eyes wandering up and down the hall slowly. He was waiting, impatiently at that. Luckily, he remembered the local doctor's phone number and called him hastily. He remembered his voice sounding strained and terrified, which was most likely why help had come as quickly as it had. But it was taking too long, it should have been ten, maybe fifteen minutes at the most, but almost an hour was long enough.

The door opened and the doctor walked out; he was a little odd-looking and intimidating, but he had a smile on his face none the less. He remembered Robert as a young boy and smiled reassuringly.

"He'll be all right. He has a slight concussion from falling, but he should recover quickly," he said. Robert stood and looked at him. "And the blood was?" he asked.

"His skin tore from sliding across the floor, most likely it got caught on a loose nail," he replied, handing him a bottle of medicine. Robert looked at it, breathing a heavy sigh of relief.

"Give that to him if his head begins to hurt," the doctor said. He closed his bag and went to leave when Robert stopped him.

"How much?" he asked. Though he was hesitating, usually house calls were expensive, and he didn't bring a lot of money with him when he came out. He knew he needed to ask.

"One pill, make sure he eats with it so it doesn't affect his stomach," he replied.

"No, how much do I owe you?" Robert asked, sounding slightly worried.

"It's on me," The grey bearded man stated with a nod.

And with that he left, leaving Robert in the hallway by himself. Soon he turned and looked into his bedroom. Kenny was sleeping, lying on his back, his head was bandaged, sunken into the pillow, and he looked relaxed, which made Robert shoulder's sag in relief and security. He watched as Kenny rolled over and he giggled, happy to know everything was okay.

Robert sighed heavily and rubbed his head, trying to relieve some pressure from his aching temples. Then he put the bottle of medicine into his pocket and closed the door fully so Kenny would remain undisturbed.

He leaned on the door for a moment and listened to Kenny's breathing, just to make sure he was all right. For a moment there was nothing but silence, and then he heard a knock. *Who on earth could that be?* He asked himself. The knocking came again, louder and faster than before. He headed to the door, again very quietly to make sure he wouldn't make any noise as he walked. A man stood outside the door; he was tall and had a curly moustache. He was wearing a top hat and had a very pointed nose.

O'Reilly, Robert thought, hissing. He walked down the stairs to the door. The man turned when he heard him coming, his silhouette appearing to be laughing as Robert hurried down the stairs.

Robert slammed open the door and looked at the repulsive, cruel man in disgust. He breathed out heavily and clenched the doorknob tightly.

"Robert, my dear boy, look at how you've grown!" O'Reilly said in a fake tone.

"Cut the crap, O'Reilly, what do you want?" Robert asked coldly. He crossed his arms and stared the elder man down.

"Your tongue has grown sharp, boy," he hissed as he pushed his way past Robert into the house. "Come," he said, walking into the kitchen. Robert closed and locked the door then followed the elder man into the newly cleaned kitchen.

"If it's the house you want, forget it. For the last time, you're not getting the house, the land, or anything in it," Robert said coldly.

O'Reilly laughed and turned to face Robert. With a swift hand, he lifted up his cane and pressed it against the underside of Robert's chin to make him stare into his devious black eyes.

"Of course it's what I want, foolish child," he said coldly.

"Like all the rest of the times you tried, you're not getting it," Robert replied smugly, eyes filled with anger.

"Oh, I am, this time I am," O'Reilly said with equal cockiness in his voice.

Robert slapped away his cane and hissed coldly. *He's bound and determined to get this house, why?* He asked himself. He heard footsteps above him now. His eyes narrowed. *Stay up there Kenny, this isn't something you need to get involved in.*

"Robert?" Kenny called shrilly from above. O'Reilly looked out into the living room then back at Robert. He smirked and raised an eyebrow as if to ask 'anyone I know?' as he pulled a note from his pocket and set it down on the table. With a chuckle, he patted the note and gave Robert a devious look before walking back into the living room; Robert followed.

"What is that?" he asked, pointing to the note.

"Open it and see for yourself," O'Reilly replied.

Kenny walked down the stairs quietly. He looked at both men in confusion, unable to get a good look at either. Robert ran over to Kenny and pushed him behind to hide him from view, never knowing what O'Reilly would try to do. Kenny grabbed Robert's shirt.

"What's going on?" he asked. Robert hushed him and then looked back at O'Reilly, who was twisting his moustache.

"Good day, gentlemen," he said, tipping his hat. Robert

watched as he headed to the door, he unlocked it and walked outside, leaving the door wide open.

Leroy was hiding on the porch; he barked at O'Reilly as he came into the old dog's view. Both boys heard O'Reilly scream and watched as he jumped in fear. He slipped on the welcome mat and tumbled down the stairs. Robert laughed a bit, watching O'Reilly scramble to his feet, Leroy nipping at his heel. The old, reliable dog chased him all the way to his limo.

Robert looked back at Kenny before he headed to the door. He snapped his fingers and the dog quickly ran back to him, barking loudly. It was happy and quite energetic for being such an old dog. Robert kneeled down and petted the dog on the head. "Good boy," he said kindly. The dog licked him and pranced up the stairs as if nothing had happened.

Kenny looked at Robert in fear and confusion as he closed the door then re-locked it. With tender eyes, Robert looked at Kenny.

"You okay?" he asked, completely ignoring what had just happened.

"What's going on?" Kenny asked. "Who was that?"

Robert sighed, knowing he couldn't hide what just happened from Kenny's prying eyes.

"His name is John O'Reilly, he's a big shot millionaire, and his family has been after this land for almost a hundred and fifty years now," Robert replied as he headed over to Kenny. He placed his hand on his head and rubbed it gently. Kenny looked up at him, worry all over his face.

Robert cocked his head to one side and smiled. "Don't worry about it, everything's okay, I've got it handled," he said kindly.

Now, that letter of his, he thought, narrowing his gaze toward the envelop sitting on the dinning room table. He walked inside without saying another word. Kenny followed him closely, not wanting to fall over seeing that he was still dizzy from getting up too fast.

"You should go back to bed," Robert demanded kindly, not looking at his young friend.

"Nah, I'm okay now," he replied smiling, even though he was lying.

Robert nodded slightly, not wanting to agree, but he just let him be. He sat down and took a heavy breath. Kenny sat down next to him and looked at the letter. Robert opened it, he tore the envelop open, not caring if he ripped it since it came from O'Reilly (which usually meant something was up).

"What does it say?" Kenny asked.

Robert read aloud:

To Whom It May Concern:

You have unpaid dues that, since the passing of Alberta Drake, shall be passed down the new owner. If not paid by the eve of Friday, October 31st 2008, the property shall belong to John M. O'Reilly.

Your dues are fifty thousand dollars. Please have the check payable to the County of Heather Field.

Have a nice day.

William H. Kerry, Mayor of Heather Field

"HE'S TRYING TO evict us, and the county is agreeing...I can't believe they would do that!"

Robert gripped the paper tighter in his hand, a thick line of anger appeared on his forehead. Kenny rubbed his shoulder and took the note.

"The thirty first, this is the twentieth, there's not enough time to get that much money," he whispered.

Robert brushed back his bangs and shook his head. "That man," he whispered. "He's the living devil."

Kenny took the note and set it down. He sat there for a moment, watching as Robert sat in deep though. *Fifty thousand...fifty thousand, that's so much*, Kenny thought, rubbing his cut head. Robert looked at him and saw him struggling to focus, and then he sighed.

"You should get some rest, it would be best for you so you

don't get a headache. The doctor said you should sleep," Robert said. Kenny looked at him and nodded in reply, he stood up and placed a gentle hand on Robert's shoulder.

"Everything's going to be all right, I promise," he whispered. Robert looked at him and then back at the note. Kenny sighed, not knowing what to say to comfort him. He felt his body tremble as he removed his hand.

"Goodnight," Kenny whispered.

"Goodnight," he replied quietly.

Soon after Kenny was already upstairs asleep, or so Robert thought, he couldn't sleep after hearing what he had just heard.

Robert didn't know what to do. This house was all his grandmother had, and this was his family's most precious belonging. What was he to do?

"I don't think there's anything I can do, I really don't," he said shrilly. "I can't believe I'm going to lose the most important thing this family has to that...that man!"

Chapter Seven:

THE CLUE

THAT NIGHT SEEMED endless and nothing seemed to calm Robert down. He tried to do everything he could think of; painting, playing his violin, even reading one of Kenny's childish fantasy novels, but nothing could get his mind off of O'Reilly's sick scheme.

Leroy was sitting next to him on the couch in the foyer, glistening with a solemn light. He had the fire on to make sure it was working if somehow he miraculously found enough money to keep the house. He needed to have some way to keep himself and Kenny warm in the bitter winters.

He gazed into the inferno. You could see it in his eyes that he was worried, and the raging light only ignited the feeling. Kenny came down the stairs, holding the rims of his robe together with his shaking hand. Robert didn't move, as if he hadn't heard the creaking and cracking of the floor.

"Robby, are you okay? You haven't moved since I left," Kenny stated quietly. Robert lifted his head up and turned to face him.

"Yeah, I'm okay, just trying to think clearly, that's all," he replied. Kenny walked down the stairs to the landing and smiled gently. His eyes were still trying to get a good fix on everything. Robert didn't move. He just kept gazing into the fire. *He really does love this house*, Kenny thought with a sigh. He turned around and headed for the kitchen.

Robert said nothing. He just stared into the fire, confusion, anger, and hatred consumed his face.

A few moments later Kenny crept around to his right, back into the bright blue foyer. He saw Robert had found *Untitled*. He had it in his hands and was still gazing quietly into the fireplace. Kenny handed a cup of tea to Robert. Robert looked at him as he took it. "What's this?" he asked.

"You didn't get any tea today," Kenny replied. "You get cranky if you don't have it, that and you haven't had any sleep for a while, not a good combination."

"You never think of anything but my health, do you?" Robert asked with a small smile.

"I just don't want you getting sick. I hate seeing you get sick, it scares me. You know how weak you are," he replied. After, neither said another word, all fell silent except for the howling winds outside.

There were two large windows on both sides of the brick fireplace. They creaked and cracked heavily in the winds. Some books were set in the middle of the mantelpiece on top of a long white lace fireplace scarf. That was all that was to be seen, that and the entrance to the hallway in the back. It was kind of bland and not very welcoming, which made Kenny sit down in an uncomfortable manner next to Robert and slouch over with a load moan. Robert looked at him with a smile on his face.

"How's your head?" he asked.

Kenny smiled back and laughed. "It hurts but I think it's getting better," he replied, pointing to the book in Robert's hands. "I'm sorry I made you read that."

"Huh?" Robert asked. He lifted his head up and looked at him.

"That poem thing, I didn't know it would freak you out, you sounded like a crazy person."

"Ah, it's nothing. I guess I was just a little too tired to be reading eerie things you randomly find. So, what's this stuff you've written here?"

Robert handed him the book, he looked at the notes he had written before his unfortunate incident. Kenny smiled guiltily, "Oh, I was just trying to figure what that saying meant, nothing important," he replied.

"Did you get anything out of it?" Robert asked.

"Well, mortals and men are the key words, meaning this isn't referring to a human or man, but an animal or a magical creature. So, we know it has to do with a forest, and it also talks about a house, and I have a hunch, I saw some sort of structure in the forest when we first arrived, like a little house or something," he explained.

Robert looked at him. "That house used to be my grandfather's research house," he replied.

"Research...like what kind?" Kenny asked.

"See Heather Field has an old legend, I don't know *exactly* what it's about, but they used to believe that there were underground tunnels running all through the forest, like some secret channel that supposedly used to belong to the natives. The entrance was hidden under the largest tree that was said to be... hollow," he said, Kenny's eyes widened as Robert began to speak again. "But a lot of the trees were cut down when they built the town. According to the story, the entrance was hidden purposely. They say those catacombs went as far as the forest itself, but no one really confirmed it because it was so far to the end, I believe they said all of them connected the original thirteen colonies.

"But at the end it is said that there was a room piled to the ceiling with treasure. My grandfather would go down there every day to chart maps and figure out incredibly difficult puzzles. He stored everything he found out in that house in the woods," he finished.

Kenny smiled before he yawned and let his body fall to his right, his head rested on Robert's shoulder. Normally Robert would find this odd, seeing as Kenny wasn't an overly touchy person. He was one who let his words explain his feelings. But he knew his head was probably throbbing, and he needed a bit of comfort.

Leroy laid his head on Robert's lap and licked his hand, making him lose grip of the book. He just let it fall onto the floor. Kenny looked on into the fire. He could still, after this long, feel Robert shaking from fear and holding in tears.

"Hey, Robby, it's going to be okay," Kenny said quietly.

"You don't know that ..." he replied.

"Why's it called 'The Grave'?" Kenny asked, cocking his head harshly to the side, "Do they go home to die?"

Robert laughed, "Old legend, Kenny. Supposedly their king was buried there after he died, and the fireflies go back to watch over him while he sleeps. They think he'll wake up if they watch him and protect him while he rests."

"Like Egyptians...awesome," Kenny smiled. "Just a crazy idea, but what if tomorrow we go look at your grandfather's notes, find that entrance, and go get the treasure."

"I think you need more sleep."

"I'm serious."

Kenny sat up and looked at him in shock, never thinking he'd say something like that so quickly and calmly.

"We need the money," Kenny stated. Robert laughed, tossed his arms over the back of the couch, and let his body sink into the couch. He let his head rest on the back of the couch, and he let his body relax.

"You know I don't believe in fairytales, Kenny," he said.

Kenny sighed and yawned. "Well, why don't we just get the money from your mom?" he asked.

"No way, are you crazy!" Robert boasted. "We came out here to prove to mom that we were capable of being on our own without help! What would she say if we came crawling back asking for money?"

"What would she say if we came crawling back for a home?" Kenny spat.

Robert's eyes widened at his quick remark. He wondered if he had hurt Kenny just then with what he said. The anger just melted off of his face, like a snake sheds its skin, and was replaced with nothing but question. Robert hadn't looked as confused as that in ages.

Kenny scratched his head and slid off of the couch onto the floor. Robert's eyes moved down to him slowly, he raised an eyebrow in question, still confused. Kenny ran his finger across the pattern on the rug. He felt his fingers weave in and out of the floorboards, like he was gently stroking a harp. He picked up the book and looked at the picture carefully.

"Hey, you know we were supposed to be out here making money, opening a business or something. What've you been thinking about for a career path? What's been going on in your head?" Robert asked.

Kenny laughed. "Maybe I want to...nah you'd laugh!" he boasted cheerfully.

"Oh come on, you know me better than that! What do you want to do?"

"Okay, okay, I've always wanted to be a surgeon."

Robert looked down at him with pride in his expression. This was the first time he had heard him say anything as grown up as that. Usually he wanted to be a pro wrestler or something insane, but this was a completely new statement for his ears.

"A surgeon, Kenny I'm proud of you, that's a major thing!" he laughed, Kenny only changed the subject as quickly as he could. He felt embarrassed.

"Do you like to draw, Robert? I know you took a lot of art classes back in the city, but I've never seen you *actually* create anything," Kenny asked. Robert brought his hands back down slowly. He petted the dog on the head and yawned.

"Paint, I like to paint," he replied after a moment's hesitation.

"Really?" he asked, looking up at him.

"Yeah, that portrait of the man in the living room, I painted that, it was my father...or at least that's what mom said when she handed me his picture."

"With all the years we've lived together, I've never heard a word about him. After he vanished so suddenly, it's like Olivia just erased him from existence. He was very brave-looking, in the army?"

"Yeah, mom's funny that way. I keep asking about him, what was he like, what kind of father was he, but she just ignores the question and says he's all memories now. It's kind of bizarre, even for her.

"But yeah, he was in the Marines, a General. Mom said he had to be shipped off somewhere while we were...recovering that night. He was sent out on a mission and vanished, they never found him."

"You must be proud, though. I don't even remember mine"

Robert watched as Kenny's smile faded; he hugged his legs and set his head against his knee caps. Robert slid down the couch and sat next to him. He rubbed his shoulder and looked at him with compassion. He knew how much Kenny's past haunted him. Not much fazed Kenny for long periods of time. But his past conjured up a different level of un-comfort. He rarely talked about it.

"It's okay," he said quietly.

"I envy you, Robby, I really do," he whispered.

"You couldn't stop it, things like that happen. You were only four when it happened," he said quietly. Kenny nodded, he breathed in heavily and began to cry, thinking back upon the night he hated most. Robert patted the back of his friend's head and lifted his gaze up to the fireplace.

From this angle he saw something he hadn't noticed before. It looked as if words were embedded into the fireplace scarf, the light solemnly making them visible. He shook Kenny's shoulder. Kenny looked up at him and then to where he was pointing. Both scanned the words carefully.

Kenny stood up and walked over to the runner, but as soon as he got there, the words vanished from the white cloth and appeared now to be actually embedded in the small rose vine carvings across the face of the old wood.

"Robby, do you have a match?" Kenny asked. Robert nodded and stood, he fished through his pockets until he pulled out a partially used set of matches. Kenny took them and went to light one, but Robert snatched it away.

"I don't think you should be handling a match. Get that book of yours and write this down," Robert said. Kenny nodded, feeling a little useless and sidled back over to the book.

"What does it say?" Kenny asked as he kneeled down to pick up the green bound, brittle, yellow page filled book.

"The light is strong in the dark, follow the path to the ark," he replied. Kenny looked at him in question, wondering what exactly he was talking about. *Some sort of light and an ark, huh? That doesn't make much sense*, Kenny told himself. He blinked a few times then wrote it down on an extra page in the book, not really putting too much effort into figuring it out much. It'd come to him eventually, what was the use in racking your brain if the answer was going to hit you in the face one day? That's how he looked at most everything.

Robert licked his fingers and put the match out then carefully looked at the scarf and the fireplace front. After all, the years he had visited this house he hadn't ever noticed them before. He wanted to know how exactly these words suddenly appeared, and how they could've stayed so well hidden through a transparent lace scarf. It was all very puzzling.

"Did you get that, Kenny?" he asked. He turned around and saw Kenny asleep on the floor, mouth agape and breathing sped. The dog looked down at him from the top of the couch and then looked up at Robert with its tongue hanging out. *I told him he needed rest; he probably passed out*. He thought with a worried smile.

Robert called the old dog down off of the couch to his side. It gladly hopped off and sat down near Kenny, nudging the sleeping boy in the arm. Robert picked Kenny up and set him on the couch, he barely moved except a small flinch every other ten seconds or so. He pulled a quilt down on top of Kenny and watched as he relaxed and stretched.

"You blonde-haired bum ..." Robert whispered childishly. He picked up the book from the floor and made the dog heel as he headed upstairs. It was quite dark up there, and the howling winds outside made him all the more uncomfortable. This wasn't the most pleasant night of his life.

Robert decided since he was still wide awake that he would clean up the bookshelf in Kenny's room. It kept bugging him that things were scattered all over the place, and everything wasn't kept tidy like he liked.

The door was still open, and so was the window, the books were scattered across the floor, and the bookshelf had remained where it had fallen. Robert's eyes moved over to the newly discovered door slowly, his gaze narrowed as if he could feel something wasn't right. He gasped as a pair of glowing orange eyes vanished and the door slammed shut. Dust blew from the creases out into the air from the impact. He rushed over to it and grabbed the handle. He pulled as hard as he could, but it refused to open again. *Please tell me those were not eyes looking at me just then*, he thought, pounding on the door. *Maybe it's just my imagination, yeah probably just my imagination and nothing more. I need some sleep, that's all.*

After he went over to the books and began piling them up neatly in two separate piles (one for used books and ones that weren't used) in front of the still upright bookshelf, he didn't have the strength then to pick up the one Kenny had knocked down. His hands were shaking from fear, and his eyes kept darting back to the door, praying he wouldn't see the eyes again. But in a strange way, he almost wanted to.

"What does it mean an ark?" he asked himself. He shook his head to bring his mind away from the story. That was just Robert. He hated not being able to understand something. It made him feel inadequate and he always hated that. He needed to know everything about everything he could possibly take in. His thoughts brought him back to what Kenny had said. And then he thought of his father, the brave man in the portrait down below him. And again of what Kenny had spoken of, his deep envy and anguish and guilt of what had happened all those years ago. After that night, Robert was never the same and neither was Kenny, no matter how far away they tried to run from the truth.

"I'm sorry, Kenny, I really, truly am, I just don't know how to help," he said in a whisper. "What can I do? I can't bring back what was taken from him, but I can't take away what was given to him. I'm so lost."

Chapter Eight:

THE NIGHTMARE

THE NEXT MORNING, Kenny smiled as he set his fork down on the table. He wiped his mouth with his sleeve and smiled wider. Robert was slowly eating his small salad, looking over the newspaper. He was sitting across the table this time, near the open window and the busted stove standing behind him, creaking and cracking from just being used for the first time in some while. Kenny drank an entire glass of milk in one go then sighed in happiness.

"What's wrong, Rob? I know you don't eat anything but the greens anyway, and you're sick of it, but come on! You're usually not *that* depressed!" he said.

Robert pulled his reading glasses off and set them on the table. He folded the paper and set it to the side. With his hands clasped loosely together he leaned forward, using his elbows to support his hands in the air. He looked sickly and pale.

Kenny looked at him in worry. *I knew it! He's so sick of me eating all the good stuff and him being stuck with the nasty veggies and fruit he's finally going to murder me!* He thought, swallowing.

Robert sighed, a few more seconds passed, and then he yawned heavily. Kenny laughed in relief.

"Are you that tired?" he asked smiling, relieved he was only tired. Robert rubbed his eyes and nodded in reply.

"Yeah but I am sick of eating all this crap, you know you could contribute a bit and try to at least eat sweets when I'm not in the room," Robert said cockily.

"Not my fault you up-chuck if you eat anything but vegetables and fruit, that's just your weird stomach!" Kenny rolled his eyes playfully. He stood and pushed his chair in. Robert laid his head on the table and watched as Kenny started to clean up.

"I'm still hungry ..." Robert mumbled.

"Sorry, I probably shouldn't eat pancakes and stuff like this in front of you. What's it like going through life on a strict vegetable, fruit, herbal tea, and tofu diet? Your whole life on mother nature's other white meat?" Kenny asked. Robert only looked at him with an almost 'are you serious' look on his face.

"Well, on another note, how'd you sleep?" Robert asked.

"Well," Kenny said, standing up straight after dumping a plate into the sink. "Aside from the dust inside of the couch's seams, the dog licking my feet, face, and hands, his breath is horrid, and the springs sticking into my back, the two hours of sleep I got were just peachy!"

Robert broke out into a fit of laughter as Kenny rubbed his aching lower back. Typical Kenny, he was always complaining about something. He was such a child, never seeming to act responsibly when it came to anything.

"And you?" he asked sarcastically.

"Not well," he replied. Then Kenny stopped laughing, his face flooded with worry. *Could it have been the bed? No, he had only a few hours of sleep in his room but that bed was like a cloud. Maybe I was snoring? Maybe he's got the flu? Oh no! He cannot get sick! He could die! Or maybe it was a ...*

"A nightmare, that's all," Robert said, interrupting Kenny's internal rant. Kenny looked at him sincerely.

"A nightmare?" he asked.

"Yeah, it was nothing, seriously," he replied.

"Sure, if you say so. So what are we going to do today?" Kenny asked, slamming his hands down on the table in excitement. Robert's milk glass shot up in the air, and he watched as it went tumbling down onto the floor. Landing with a loud crash, it shattered. Kenny gasped and looked at it with worry in his eyes. "Sorry," he said, grabbing a rag. He wiped it up, not sparing another look to Robert.

"I can get it," Robert said kindly.

"No, you don't look too good. You've been working too hard. I've got it," Kenny replied. Robert let his shoulders sag in disappointment as he knew that Kenny wouldn't let him do anything if he felt his health was at stake. That's the way he had always been, and he supposed that's just a brotherly instinct as well. Robert closed his eyes and breathed in heavily, letting his aching body relax until Kenny shouted.

Robert's head shot over to him. Kenny was holding his hand tightly. A piece of glass had cut his skin a little bit while he was cleaning, but just enough to trigger Robert's photographic memory. A memory flashed from one frame to the next of a horrible night from his past, one he had thought he locked away for good.

A rainy night, one with no light at all and clouds filling the sky like a cold blanket of despair. Two crushed vehicles in the middle of a rocky road, wheels slowly coming to a stop, covered in thick layers of mud. Two unidentifiable bodies bloodied and bruised. A scarred boy, covered in glass, hidden by thick rain-covered grass. And unstoppable tears of torment that haunted him like a ghost.

And then Robert screamed, his hands were over his head as he stood up, knocking over his chair. Kenny stood up and quickly grabbed Robert before he knocked anything else over or hurt himself.

"Calm down, Robby!" he called. Robert ran into the stove and slid down onto the floor, his hands still over his ears. Kenny, with regrets no doubt, slapped Robert. Time looked as if it had slowed as his face turned to his right, the entire left side of his face turned red and his eyes widened in shock. Kenny looked away rubbing away a few tears of fear from his own eyes as Robert's common sense returned and he began to calm down.

"I'm sorry, Robert," Kenny whispered as he wiped beads of escaping sweat off of the confused Robert's forehead. Robert looked out into space, still trying to calm down fully. Kenny continued to cry. "Everything's okay, everything's all right, Rob," he whispered, laying his hand gently on Robert's trembling shoulder.

"How sweet," a voiced bellowed from the door. Kenny lifted his head up and looked at the owner of the voice. O'Reilly stood there, grinning deviously. Kenny moved to the left side of Robert, concealing him from view. He hadn't even been in the same room with O'Reilly for more than a minute, and he was already terrified of him.

"Now he's having his girlfriend protect him," O'Reilly mumbled under his breath.

"Leave him alone, he's not even coherent...Wait 'girlfriend'? You sick son of a-dude! I'm a man!" Kenny shouted. O'Reilly hissed, "Well now, I would've never guessed!"

Kenny's face was overcome with a bit of embarrassment and anger. *I don't look like a girl*, He told himself, blinking a nastily smug look from his eyes.

"Why are you here anyway?" Kenny asked, remembering exactly who was ticking him off.

"Ah, right, actually I just came to see if you had my money yet," he said, cutting him off.

"It's too early, slither back into your hole for a little while."

"Sharp tongue on you as well, you must've gotten in from his mother! Spending too much time with her can ruin a good mind."

O'Reilly walked inside, his boots knocking against the floorboards. He lifted his cane in the air to hit Kenny, not even thinking twice about his actions. Kenny closed his eyes and looked away. He heard the wind rushing against the wooden stick and felt the impact begin to grow. And then it stopped.

Kenny opened one eye slowly and saw a hand on the cane, restricting it from moving any further. He traced the hand up to the arm and then towards Robert's head. His eyes were bouncing back and forth, trying to get a good view on things. He obviously was still out of it. His hand was trembling and his grip was weak. He wasn't in good shape.

"Get out," he spat. "Get out now!" With that, he snapped the cane in two, O'Reilly backed away in fear, dropping his half of the cane on the floor. Kenny gasped in fear and excitement. He didn't know Robert had that sort of strength.

"Y-you heard him! Get out!" Kenny snapped. He grabbed the pointed end of the cane and began to swing it hastily at O'Reilly, trying to scare him off.

"All right, all right, fine! But be warned, I'll be back!" O'Reilly snapped. He turned and ran out of the house, leaving the old snake-like cane on the floor. Kenny quickly looked back at Robert, who was breathing heavily, but he had a smile on his face, a smile of relief and of triumph. But he still looked horribly out of it.

"How'd he get in here?" he asked, still not quite coherent.

Kenny shook his head. "No, no! Don't say anything! You don't have the strength! A-are you okay?" he asked. He kneeled down to Robert's level and brushed back his sweaty bangs.

Robert nodded a bit, moaned, and released his grip on the piece of wood and embraced the frightened Kenny. His brown eyes widened, the sun dancing all across his face, turning his irises a deep raspberry color. Robert's eyes were as soft as two river stones and his skin as pale as porcelain. Shimmers danced across the kitchen floor from Robert's tears, certain parts show-ered with more color than the rest.

Kenny looked at those spots, those tears that came drizzling onto the ground like raindrops, his eyes fixed upon them alone now. Robert was crying, and his grip was tightening. It looked like a portrait done by a lonely artist, a picture that Robert had seen long ago, identical.

"Don't worry, Robby, I'm right here, I'll always be here," Kenny whispered.

"I'm sorry, I'm so sorry," Robert whispered. "It was my fault, my fault."

Kenny closed his eyes, not sure of what he was referring to, but he returned the hug. He tried to let this moment sink in for Robert's sake, but it was hard with the sound of sobbing constantly filling his ears.

I don't know what you mean, Robert. But I forgive you, He thought, looking at Robert. *You don't need to cry, not while I'm here.*

Chapter Nine:

THE WOMAN IN THE PHOTOGRAPHS

"ARE WE THERE yet!?" Kenny moaned, wiping a bead of sweat from his head.

Robert laughed and shook his head. "City kids," he mumbled, looking back at Kenny. "You do realize we've only been walking for two minutes."

"That's long enough!" Kenny shouted. The house hidden in the forest seemed far away, and Kenny was curious about the Robert's late grandfather's research and notes. He pleaded his heart out to have Robert take him out there. And so he agreed, thinking it might take his mind from his troublesome memories.

Robert led the way into the thick patches of trees that surrounded most everything the boys saw. The old white house they were going to was decaying. It was covered in moss and spider webs, so Robert described.

"Do we really have to go inside?" Kenny asked warily.

"You're the one who made me drag you out here," Robert said angrily.

Kenny laughed innocently and looked away with some smugness in his facial expression. Robert rolled his eyes and slipped his hands in his pockets. The leaves were crunching under their feet, and it was beginning to feel like fall instead of summer unlike it had been the last few days. The breezes were growing cold, and the trees had quickly become bare.

"So what exactly are we looking for?" Kenny asked. He zipped up his jacket as far as it would allow him, the black leather racing jacket clung to his body like cellophane wrap.

"You tell me, you're the one who wanted to come," Robert said through chattering teeth. Kenny looked at him and nodded, remembering why he was bearing the cold to come up to this abandoned place.

"So, why are we coming out here?" Robert asked, snapping Kenny out of his trance. He wasn't one for mysteries, especially when those mysteries came from Kenny's mind.

Kenny breathed in heavily. "We need to look for a map of some sort. If we find one then we can find the entrance to the... "

"No way, are you crazy!" Robert cut him off. He sharply turned around and glared at Kenny. "We are not coming *all* the way out here to find a map that may or may not exist to go to some *magical world* hidden somewhere under the earth to bust my butt off and put *my* life in danger to find some *treasure* hidden deep in the mystic catacombs underground that will supposedly save my family's most precious belonging."

"Oh come on, it only sounds bad when you say it like that!"

Kenny and Robert looked at each other for a moment before Robert let his shoulders sag.

"Fine," he mumbled.

Kenny laughed and clapped his hands together with a small grin of triumph. Robert turned around and headed to the house again. Kenny picked up his pace until he was walking side by side with Robert. He was always a few inches shorter than him; no matter how old they got he was always taller. He looked down upon him like a cat to a mouse.

"Are you feeling better?" Kenny asked. He looked up at Robert with a small smile.

"I'm a little dizzy, but I'm better," Robert replied. Kenny nodded and fell silent, not wanting to invade Robert's privacy. If something was wrong he would tell him. Robert looked down at him with a bit of wonder in his eyes. Usually he wasn't this quiet, this calm.

"Are *you* feeling okay?" he asked.

Kenny nodded quickly in reply, still smiling widely. Robert just looked away afterwards. He too knew that if something was up, Kenny would tell him.

The rest of the walk was silent, all but the rustling of the winds in the oak trees above and the crunching of the leaves below.

Before both could register, they were standing in front of the old white house, its windows were dust covered and moss was covering the entire left half of the building. Robert urged Kenny inside, nudging him in the back. The door creaked and cracked as he open it. Dust blew up around them, both coughed heavily as they walked inside.

It was dark, musty, and smelled of camphor. The floor was covered in old, tattered papers, and the walls were covered in sketches of magical creatures and old diagrams of what appeared to be passageways. The windows let little light inside, spiders scurried away as soon as they heard the door scratch the surface of the floor.

"Where do we start?" Kenny asked coughing.

"Look in the back rooms, anything of importance most likely was hidden," Robert replied. He brushed some dust from his shoulders and looked at Kenny with a bit of boredom in his eyes. He looked back up at him with a smile.

"Go home," he commanded, pointing back to the house.

"Wait a second, what...why?" Robert stammered.

"This isn't a good place for you to be, not with your...*condition*. All this dust will probably kill you."

"I'm not leaving you by yourself."

Kenny stuck out his bottom lip as far as he could get it to go.

Robert looked at him in confusion and shook his head. Kenny crossed his arms stubbornly and snapped his head away. Robert gasped.

"You didn't just give me 'the look', tell me you didn't!" Robert said in shock.

"I said go!" Kenny snapped.

Robert grew angry with his stubbornness but calmed himself, knowing Kenny hated to see him mad. He pulled out his cell phone and set it in Kenny's hand. In shock, he turned to look at him.

"The spare cell number is in the contact list," Robert stated.

"Which one, I'm not familiar with these numbers," Kenny stated, scrolling through the numbers.

"The one that says 'spare cell phone' in front of it, obviously," he replied.

Kenny laughed and slid the cell phone in his pocket. He patted Robert's shoulder and smiled reassuringly. Robert swallowed hard and looked at Kenny once more, trying to convince him to forget this whole crazy idea of staying alone, but he refused, kindly explaining his fear for his friend's safety.

"Go, I'll be okay," Kenny said once more. "I'm a big boy, can tie my own shoes and everything."

Robert nodded in agreement. "Call if you need anything, but no text messaging your buddies back home and no long distance calls, emergencies only. The only place I can re-charge it is in the city, and I don't want to be wasting precious money on gas for your pleasure," Robert said.

"Right, got it, no calls, no text, and emergencies only, you sound like your mother, you know!" he said happily. "See you in a while."

"And make sure you come home as soon as the sun begins to set, strange things happen here at night, things people shouldn't ever see. I don't want to come by tomorrow and find only your foot in the house."

With that, Robert left, giving Kenny a cocky look and a large smile. *Oh, that's a lovely thought to leave me with,* Kenny thought laughing. He waved to Robert then closed the door.

"Now, he said the back rooms would most likely have the important stuff, so let's get going!" Kenny said in delight. He walked into the hallway, concealed by a large curtain hanging from the wall. He pulled it aside and looked in the long corridor where rooms were standing left and right. Most were empty.

The one he found of most interest was the third door on the right. It was painted black and filled with dozens of old cameras, it was indeed a black room, a very outdated black room. There were old pictures hanging all over the walls of anything you could think of, a slug on the sidewalk to a bunch of kids at a county fair.

All of them are in black and white; they're old, Kenny thought as he slipped inside. He enjoyed the pictures of a very old chapel the most. They had a mysterious feeling to them, like they were taken for a very specific reason. And seemingly, in every picture there laid a small blur, never quite in the middle or to the direction of one side or the other. It was just there, like a gust of wind so heavy it was visible to the naked eye. But not so much as to call it a paranormal photograph; it was too small to be a ghost.

Kenny looked at the desk placed in the middle of the room where more pictures stood. These were worse, the blur looked smeared and the focus was off terribly. *Earlier works*, he thought, setting a picture down. He sat in a creaky old chair and began going through the drawers, hoping to find something of use. More and more pictures, trying to focus upon the same thing, resulted in failure. All were just wastes of space.

Except one, one he found familiar and somewhat beautiful. The shot was perfect, everything was so clear. The blur appeared as a...*Could it be?* A fairy, yes, it was indeed a fairy. And not just any particular fairy you would see in books or children's drawings, it was the fairy in the house. The one in the painting he loved so much.

Kenny looked at it, knowing now why Robert's grandfather wanted to take such a wonderful picture of such a beautiful creature. She was amazing, breathtaking, and if Kenny would dare say it, dreamy.

He had fallen in love with a figment of his imagination. It

wasn't easy to say no, to deny a feeling as deep as the one he was enduring. It made his chest hurt, his eyes struggled to stay open. The pain was horrible, but it felt so good and so new.

"I-I-I," Kenny stuttered. "I'm going to find her...this woman in the photographs."

Chapter Ten:

THE RUNAWAY

IT WAS LATE night, sometime around ten. With no windows and no clock, Kenny had lost track of time. He hadn't even thought of checking the cell phone's clock every now and again. He had found everything he needed, from a few maps depicting the entrance and half of the passages below like he was looking for, to a detailed diary that held all the knowledge of the traps hidden in the catacombs.

Kenny was dashing toward the house, drawing an extra map in the untitled book (just in case he lost the original) as he went.

Robert is going to kill me! He thought, swallowing hard. The lights in the house were still on and shadows were moving around in the foyer.

Shadows?

Multiple human shadows, three he hadn't ever seen before. And upon a closer look he realized one was O'Reilly.

"No, no! R-Robert! Crap, Robert!" Kenny shouted as he fumbled around a tree. *Somebody broke in; he's by himself! He didn't call...wait, what if he couldn't? What if he...what if he couldn't!*

Kenny gasped. "Robert!" he shouted. He picked up his pace and ran as fast as he could, stumbling and tripping over tiny rocks, almost losing his papers and books. He heard nothing, nothing but the rustling of the trees, no voices inside the house, no floorboards creaking as the shadows moved.

Now he saw it clearly, O'Reilly *was* lurking in the light of the moon, standing halfway in front of the window. Robert appeared to be tied to a chair. Kenny watched for a second, not moving, until O'Reilly raised his cane. He shot it down onto Robert's head, and he let out an ear-shattering cry of pain. His body slumped forward in the chair and remained there, unmoving. Kenny let all of the papers he had slip from his hands, and he darted toward the house, praying he could stop whatever O'Reilly had planned next. He stumbled up the porch stairs and slammed the door open. His eyes darted around for a moment before he ran into the foyer.

"Robert!" Kenny shouted. Then he was tackled to the floor by two large men. He struggled to get free, but they only tightened their grip. O'Reilly walked over to the two brutes that had Kenny smashed against the floor. He slapped his new bronze cane in his hand and stared at Kenny with his beady black eyes. Kenny looked up at him, small trickles of blood ran down his lip from colliding with the floor. He hissed angrily at him. O'Reilly did nothing except smirk and slammed his foot into his face. And with a snap of his finger, he ordered his men to tie him next to Robert.

Only a few minutes passed before Kenny was tied up in a chair, back to back with Robert, whose head was still hung low.

"Hey, Robert, are you okay?" Kenny asked. Robert remained silent for a moment. Kenny turned as far as he could in Robert's direction, trying to look at him. His shoulders were tense and his hair was mangled and wet with sweat. He wheezed as he tried to breathe and cried in agony. But he was able to build up the strength to respond.

"Yeah," he said quietly.

Kenny listened to his voice, the strain-filled chorus that fluttered from his lips was heavy.

"Dang, they didn't hit your throat did they? If they did, I swear—"

"No," Robert interrupted. "They didn't touch me."

Robert closed his eyes in thought, hoping he sounded convincing enough through his scratchy voice. His throat was bruised badly. O'Reilly knew Robert had lung and throat problems. It was the perfect way to get him to talk.

"Now boys," O'Reilly said as he walked in front of the two boys. Both of their eyes moved over to him; Robert had trouble focusing. But once the tall villain was in his sight, he hissed in anger. Then he coughed and screamed in agony. Kenny's eyes grew wide in terror, and O'Reilly smiled deviously.

"Where is my money?" he hissed.

"Filthy snake ..." Robert mumbled.

O'Reilly raised his cane to hit him again but decided against it; he chuckled coldly. Every hair on Kenny's neck stood up, his eyes welded shut from the horrid, malicious laughter.

"We...we don't have your money. Give us more time!" Kenny cried out, almost in tears.

Robert's eyes grew large for a moment before he closed them gently.

"What makes you think I would possibly even think about giving you a few more days? If you want to forget about the whole deal, you can just hand over the house now," O'Reilly said.

"What is your obsession with this house?" Robert asked. "It's falling apart and there's nothing even worth anything in this old place."

"You, boy, of all people should know. The Grave of the Fireflies, of course," O'Reilly replied. Robert's eyes narrowed, and he turned his head slightly toward the old man.

"You believe in that crap? That's the *only* reason you've been hounding my family for years? Is for some fake treasure?" he asked coldly.

"Aren't you *way* too old to believe in fairytales?" Kenny asked.

O'Reilly laughed. "Fairytales, it isn't a mere fairytale, foolish child," he explained.

Kenny looked at him in question, wondering what was going through his unpredictable head. He believed in the story, he believed with all his heart, but to hear that this walking, talking broomstick believed it too came as a shocker.

"What do you mean?" Robert asked.

"Don't play dumb, boy, you've seen it. The orange-eyed monster, staring at you through the veil of darkness, shrouded in the shelter of the door," O'Reilly said. Robert swallowed hard, it was so quiet in the house you could hear it clearly. Sweat tumbled down his face, his breathing sped to a gasping-like pace, and his eyes struggled to stay open. He was terrified.

"They just stare at you until you can't bear it any longer," he continued.

Robert gasped heavily, Kenny's eyes widened in shock.

"S-stop, he can't breathe, you're going to kill him!" Kenny shouted.

O'Reilly laughed. "Its pure black, pebble-like pupils fixed upon you. They wouldn't remove themselves from you, they couldn't."

That was all the more Robert could take, he fell forward a small bit, letting a moan of pain escape his throat. O'Reilly snapped his fingers and the two brutes untied him, they dragged his limp body over to the wall near the old grandfather clock. Kenny watched in terror as O'Reilly brought a pistol from his pocket.

"Give me the key, boy," he ordered.

Robert said nothing, his eyes weakly looking up at him. Kenny struggled to get his hands free from the tight ropes, bruising his wrists more every time he pulled harder.

"I don't have it," Robert whispered.

"Then perhaps, you have it? Hand it over, or should I kill your little friend here?" O'Reilly asked, turning toward Kenny, his pistol still aimed at Robert.

"I don't know what you're talking about!" Kenny shouted.

O'Reilly hissed angrily and pulled the trigger, and Kenny's eyes welded shut to block out the sight. The gun went off and then all fell silent; the sound of the ticking grandfather clock was all that remained.

Kenny opened his eyes a small bit and looked over to Robert. He was shaking, his eyes wide with fear, and a small scrape was across his left cheek, the same half of his face was covered in gunpowder. A huge bullet hole was in the wall next to his head. Kenny was sure he was going to be hard of hearing for a while.

"Five minutes, you have five minutes and no more time to give me the key," O'Reilly commanded. "Untie the boy."

"But, what if he goes and runs off?" one of the men asked.

"I trust the blonde will stay, for if he doesn't, I shall shoot the other," O'Reilly said firmly, staring at Kenny while he spoke. He turned and walked into the hallway. The two large men dropped Robert and headed over to Kenny. They untied him and pulled him to his trembling feet.

They towered over Kenny; he felt weak and frail. Robert was sitting on the floor with his head hanging down, not moving even the slightest inch. One of the men tossed Kenny aside and then left the room, the other snarling angrily behind him.

Kenny waited for a moment before he turned to face Robert. His eyes were filled with tears, and he was hesitant to check if he was still alive. But he knew Robert needed help, so he quickly rushed to his side and looked at him. He gently, carefully, and tenderly shook him, trying to make sure he wouldn't feel any unnecessary pain, but he didn't move.

Kenny sat down on his knees and placed his hand on Robert's shoulder before he pressed his ear against his paralyzed friend's chest. He waited and listened for a steady heartbeat, praying he was all right and only unconscious and that the bullet did miss him. Robert coughed a small bit and blinked a few times before he closed his eyes fully again. Kenny felt his shoulder dampen. He looked at the puddle of blood Robert had coughed up all over him.

"R-run," he whispered. Kenny's eyes widened in shock, tears dripped down his cheeks as he tightened his grip on Robert.

"Not a chance, I'm not leaving you alone, not with that...that *man*," he replied.

"Please, Kenny, run as far away as you can and don't look back. Promise me you won't look back ever again," Robert demanded.

"No, no, no! I won't leave you. I swear I won't let you die here."

"Trust me."

Kenny's grip slowly released itself, he sighed heavily, thinking hard for a few moments before he pushed himself off of Robert. He looked him in the eyes, Robert had the most reassuring, most trusting smile on his face. It was hard to tell him no again.

Kenny gasped. "Don't make me," he whispered. "Please don't make me."

"Run, run away and don't look back. I trust you; you can make it on your own for a while," Robert said smiling. Kenny wiped the blood from Robert's cheek away with his sleeve and looked him over.

"You're body, you won't last three hours in this condition," he said, mostly to himself.

"Don't you trust me, Kenny?" Robert asked.

Kenny was in shock. *Of course I trust you*, he thought. Trying to speak these words was not as easy as thinking them.

O'Reilly and his men were coming back, two large cronies' voices booming throughout the house and the heavy cracking of the floor. Robert looked warily at Kenny, nodding one more time. Kenny nodded before he hugged Robert, trying to withhold his tears.

"Stay strong, I'll be back," he whispered in his ear. And with that, he left, heading into the hallway through the kitchen and out the back door, not looking back a second time, just as Robert had asked of him. That was all he could do now.

Once outside he looked around a small bit, not sure where to go. A flint of light caught his gaze. He turned to the right near the well and let a small smile creep across his face. A firefly was dancing across the surface of the brick structure.

"Did you ever chase one, all the way?" he asked himself, thinking of Robert's story. It was the only thing keeping him sane right now. He swallowed hard and ran after it, trying to stay out of the mud and places his footsteps would appear. *Hang on, Robert, just a little bit longer, I promise I'll be back.*

Chapter Eleven:

THE PATH THROUGH CEMETERY

A FIREFLY, A bug with a light attached to it, no more than a small animal, barely noticeable in the daylight, and at times invisible in the night air as well. Hard to believe something so small could have such power or that much stamina. Kenny was already sweat-drenched and covered in mud, chasing the small insect through the trees, past the fence to the forest, behind where Robert had forbid him to go right off the bat, then through the historical-looking town with no living creatures in sight. He was now in an old, deathly frightening cemetery.

Kenny's body went pale as he climbed over a small mound. The moon shimmered above him, slightly tilted to his right, which illuminated a large statue to his far left. It was a woman. She looked like a nun with her arm outstretched, reaching up to the sky. In her other hand she held a lamp that was swaying in the wind.

He watched her for a few moments. Then she turned her head, Kenny's eyes widened in shock and his lip trembled in fear. *The statue moved! Impossible!* He thought watching her. She smiled and nodded then turned back to where she was originally perched.

Kenny blinked a few times, trying to focus his bouncing gaze upon it, when he realized the firefly was still going, still flying away into the crisp autumn air. The rustling of the leaves in the wind sounded like voices, which pulled him toward an area far away from the only source of light, the fleeing firefly. But it always seemed to somehow pull him back, away from the darkness, and the thought of O'Reilly following him.

Kenny panted as he began to run again, his body felt weak, so very weak, but he knew that this was no coincidence that O'Reilly decided to show up, that Robert had ordered him to flee, and that there was only one tiny firefly in the entire valley. Not a coincidence at all, but his destiny. He didn't have time to think about it though, not while Robert's captor may be in hot pursuit.

The moonlight showered every gravestone in a shimmering blanket of silver, some were small and almost unnoticeable, and others were tall and overpowering. The crosses were the ones that made him shiver, for their shadows appeared to be a man with outstretched arms looming over him.

Why are you so scared? he asked himself. *They're only pieces of stone, and all you can hear is the wind.* He sighed heavily and continued on, wanting to find the end of this path and get some rest which he selfishly knew he deserved. He wanted to keep his mind fixed on Robert, that way he could find the courage to keep going, but it was impossible to think straight with the howling of the wind.

Kenny found himself lost in the labyrinth of tombstones, the ground kept shifting underneath him. The path would stray upward and then tilt down and then it would begin anew. He felt dizzy for a few moments. All this up and down motion was making his mind swerve. He started blinking rapidly to try and clear his vision. The firefly danced ahead then vanished behind a tree.

Kenny breathed in heavily and began to walk again, feeling like he would never get a break from this nightmare he was tossed into. He yawned, pressed his hand against the trunk of the tree, and moved around it to look at his surroundings before he went on.

In the middle of a blank field stood a mausoleum-like building, half of the entrance was crushed and the inside was visible. A few old, empty coffins were lying on the floor. The firefly was inside, hovering above what seemed to be a trap door in the ground. Kenny hesitated, he wanted to follow, and he knew he had to but he didn't feel secure. The firefly bounced up and down in a furious-like motion, like it was angry he had stopped. Kenny looked at it in question, wondering if he should just turn around or follow.

"I know he's here!"

That's when Kenny felt he had to go; O'Reilly *was* following him. *I didn't leave any footprints, how did he find me?* He looked back and saw O'Reilly and his men's shadows dashing across the tombstones behind him. Robert was with them, tied and forced to walk. Kenny turned to go but felt called to the light again. He turned and headed toward the mausoleum, still struggling to gather courage.

At this point he began to feel terrified, inside the winds howled, and the handle on the trap door clacked against the wood paneling beneath it, shadows bounced all around the walls, and to top it all off, he could still hear the men's voices. It was like living in a horror movie.

Once inside though, the firefly dashed into a small crack in the old, rotten wood of the trap door. He reached out for the handle and pulled it open. It made a large creaking sound, which he knew had given him away. He quickly slipped inside and closed the door.

It was dark and musty, the only light coming from the firefly that remained still now, unmoving. Even when he began to walk it slowed down to make sure he could see.

Above he heard voices, unwelcoming voices and one innocent one. He listened for a moment, staying still with his hands outstretched to his sides so he could feel the wall underneath his fingers.

"We lost him, boss," one man said.

"I see that, you imbecile!" O'Reilly shouted. "Fan out, he couldn't have gone far!"

"But boss, there ain't nowhere else he could've gotten to," the other man stated.

"Just look!" O'Reilly snapped. Above he could hear them walking around, twigs snapping under their feet, and the angry mumbling of O'Reilly filled the night air.

"What's that?" one man called. For a moment after, silence filled Kenny's ears, all but the sound of dripping water.

"Eyes, those are eyes!" the other man called.

"It's the Gohma!" O'Reilly stammered. Kenny's eyes widened. *What on earth was a Gohma and why does he sound so happy to see one?* He turned around and watched the shadows dance above through the cracks in the wood door. Then Robert screamed in terror. Kenny went to run when he felt a hand on his shoulder. It was oddly familiar, like it was someone he knew. He turned behind him and saw a tall, black figure. It grabbed his hand and forced him down into the darkness. No matter how much he struggled, the creature refused to let go and would tighten its grip until he was forced to do as it wanted.

The shadow fell down into a small pit, not far from where he was previously standing. Kenny had to follow. Water splashed up around Kenny's pant legs, soaking him thoroughly from the knee down. The muck-filled liquid splashed up into his eyes. He tried to rub them, but the man continued to run down the path, not sparing a moment of rest.

The path seemed endless. It just kept going and going. Kenny hit his head on vines and kept slipping on wet stones. He fumbled around, trying to keep a steady footing, but it was almost impossible to do so in such a situation.

Kenny had read books like this, where someone would come and rescue the hero from the villain then pull them away into the darkness, straight to where they needed to be, or the kidnapped sidekick, who would be pulled along by the villain until he grew so tired he just collapsed, and when he awoke he found he was safe near his partner.

But he knew neither of those things were going to happen. This *thing* was going to continue to drag him away until it found it was safe then do away with him.

Soon he saw a light ahead of him, growing larger and larger, basking everything in a radiant glow. He hoped to catch a glimpse of the creature before it killed him, but the light grew too quickly. He shielded his eyes with his free hand and continued to walk until his eyes were forced shut from the power of the light. It felt like the brightness was calling him toward it, and the moment he set foot into this aura, things would never be the same.

Chapter Twelve:

THE INDIGO CITY

KENNY FELT HIS arm being pulled, and before he knew it he was tossed off of a cliff. Not long after, his body felt bursts of water explode around it. His eyes shot open and scanned the underwater utopia he had entered. Fish of all colors vibrantly swam away from him, and another dim lighting in the distance blanketed everything in an odd glow.

Kenny, amazed by the strange sight, quickly forgot he couldn't breathe. His mind had slipped away from him as had the little air he had in his lungs. The bubbles that escaped from his lips lifted from the water and rose to the riverbed's surface in small numbers.

Kenny quickly felt himself gasp for air and a much needed wake up call from his boggled brain told him he was drowning. He needed to resurface as fast as he could. He looked up and swiftly swam to the seemingly far off river's top, using a nearby rock that had formed from the floor to give him a boost. His clothes had become heavy as the water that filled their seams. This made this trip a little more difficult than it needed to be.

Soon, Kenny became visible from above only seconds before he burst out of the water, taking a large breath as he brushed his hair back out of his eyes. He coughed once or twice and looked at the new area he had been forced into.

Indigo colored buildings with gold trim and large, destroyed doors made up a ruined city. Not a soul was to be seen. Only a few lamps and many streams of water that ran through the city's floors were to be labeled as moving and or alive.

"The legend was right. This seemingly *normal* little country town does have a lot of passages underneath," Kenny whispered as he pulled himself to shore. He groaned as he pulled himself up onto solid ground, and his eyes gazed up to the ledge above. The man had vanished. Kenny realized that whoever it was had probably saved him by tossing him in the water. It was a long drop, and without experiencing it for one's self, most would probably believe persons to be killed when tossed in. If O'Reilly looked down below, and Kenny was out of sight, he would assume Kenny was dead. He also realized, painfully, that this journey was just beginning, and he had a long way to go before it ended.

Once he felt ground beneath him, he breathed a heavy sigh and stood. The houses made up a maze, leading deeper and deeper down into the dark. He saw now he was inside what looked like a tree. The highest branches formed a large dome above him. He had entered from a ledge behind him, which was sitting in the far corner of the tree. Vines blew from the wall and spread anywhere they could get to. The light was surprisingly blinding here for being underground in the middle of the night, but Kenny didn't mind. He liked the light.

The floor had half an inch deep tunnels in them which water ran through, making markings across the floor, telling a story from a language long forgotten. High above moonlight swiveled in through the cracks of the vines that had formed together.

O'Reilly was far behind, probably unaware of where Kenny had hidden. He prayed Robert would be okay, that maybe O'Reilly wasn't completely heartless and would allow him to rest a bit. He almost had to; killing off a hostage would be like throwing his entire plan away.

"What an odd place," Kenny whispered, wandering down the alleys. The buildings were made of an odd material like brick but also like plaster and metal. And they were naturally indigo color, the gold trim was made of an old mineral that had probably been lost years ago.

It was so quiet inside. Even the sound of water rolling down a leaf in the distance was clear like a waterfall. Kenny's combat boots clacked against the floor, and the sound echoed far across the room. Kenny didn't favor this, not at all.

Since *it* had happened, he never favored being alone. He would even, at times, sleep in Robert's room and leave before he woke up because he felt so scared. The place was well lit, it was easy to see everything, but it always felt like someone was there.

Everything was beginning to look the same. Every building was destroyed and indigo. The area was easy enough to get lost in and almost impossible to find a way out of, as if it was made for that sole purpose. The lake he had been tossed into was long gone. Most likely he wouldn't find it again even if he tried to.

The one thing that kept getting Kenny's attention was on the remnants of the broken doors, even the inside doors, stood a small, glass, indigo emblem which looked like a small teardrop. He saw a different reflection every time he walked passed one, not his own but someone else's. It was a blurry vision, a vision of someone he knew, someone long forgotten in his memories that had vanished, that had been swept away in the winds.

The glass teardrops were even pressed into floor. They were hanging in front of windows and were placed in the walls, the pots, the windows, even the doorknobs! Another thing he began to notice was the words and symbols that were painted on the wall were done in the same green ink as the cross in the book.

Kenny reached into his soaking wet pocket and pulled out a drenched sheet of paper. The map he had sketched was smeared and unreadable. He folded it, almost tearing it in two a few times, and slid it back into his pocket. Then he began to walk again. His mind was racing, trying to think of what he could do to find his way out of this mess.

Kenny's body rocked side to side as he walked. He was growing tired now, his eyes blinked a few times, trying to regain focus. His mind was boggled on top of it all.

"Where do I go? Everything looks the same," Kenny stated as he stopped walking. He was lost inside the indigo colored city, probably alone on top of it all. No matter how much he tried to stop his mind from returning to the screams of Robert, it always did.

Kenny, lost in his thoughts, soon found himself standing in front of a black corridor. It was dark but it was inside a house, so maybe it wouldn't be too bad to go in and get some rest just in case predators were somewhere. He thought that a set of stairs would be in the corridor, seeing as every other door he had seen was filled with a large set of stairs.

A small bit of water had dampened the smooth downward slide. Kenny's foot slipped from under him and sent him downward. Again he was tumbling, rolling around, and hitting his head on things and all he could really do was pray there was something besides rocks to break his fall. Once he regained his footing, he went down feet first with his back pressed hard against the slick flooring beneath, and he kept his hands and forearms pressed against the floor to keep his body balanced.

A bright light came from an exit far down below him. Kenny bit his lip hard and tried to close his eyes to keep the wind out. He embraced for any painful impact that he would encounter if he landed wrong. Through his squinted eyelids, he could tell he was getting close as the light became harsh and larger. Plus the rapid sounds of water told him as well.

This is it, he thought, swallowing. The light engulfed him, and the sounds of water burst his eardrums. He plunged into the light, hoping for a painless fall as he continued to fall, losing all feeling and sense of security.

Chapter Thirteen:

THE HOLLOW

KENNY OPENED HIS eyes slowly. His eyelashes were damp with water, making his vision even more blurry. He felt cold and his body was trembling, across his skin he could feel small drips of water splash onto him every other second. *Where am I?* He asked, swallowing hard.

Once his vision un-blurred, he found he was lying near a small river while the rain poured down onto his body. He felt grass beneath him and saw nothing but small holes appearing then disappearing on the surface of the riverbed. Using his shaking hands, he pushed himself up a small bit. Once he was sitting on his scraped open knees, he clutched his shirt together to keep himself warm.

He looked out into the distance, seeing nothing but a wide field of grass. He began to feel so weak and helpless, unable to think straight on top of it all. He stood, his body still trembling, and looked far off into the distance, still seeing nothing but wide open space drenched in rainwater. He started to walk off toward an area showered in little light, the only place he felt safe enough to go to. The ground was muddy, and most of the time he found himself knee deep in muck, which proved difficult to get out of.

Why do I keep getting myself into these messes? Kenny asked himself, shivering from another cold breeze that rushed passed him. The ground was soft beneath his feet. The grass was tall and heavily basked with rain.

Kenny felt warmth run down his cheek. He stopped walking and blinked a few times. *Am I crying?* he asked himself, touching his ice cold flesh. He felt the hot liquid on his fingertips. His water-stained eyes gazed over to his trembling hand. He gasped heavily. *Blood?* He wiped more of the liquid away, only to feel more rushing from a sore area under his temple. Droplets entered his eyes, making them burn. He rubbed it away, which resulted in failure as his hand was covered in the blood too.

Kenny felt lightheaded. He stumbled a small bit as he walked off toward the shallow area ahead, now barely lit. Below him stood another wide field, placed within a twenty foot deep crevasse in the shape of a circle. One very large and very old tree was placed near the opposite wall from where Kenny was standing. A deep, crystal clear pond was centered within the area. Small blue crystals grew from the wall and equally bright bubbles floated around the area.

That's the light, he thought, blinking. He went to take another step toward the edge, not realizing the earth stopped beneath the place he had perched himself. He fell down inside, rolling against the dark blue stone, cutting his body up even more.

Before the fall had even seemed to start it was over, and Kenny landed hard in a patch of grass near a circle of rocks. He moaned loudly, lying completely still for a moment. His body felt incredibly frail, and he turned his head to look off into the distance. Everything was showered in a navy blue pigment due to the odd lighting, except one spot, deep within the shadows of the large oak.

A small, gentle orange bubble of light sat floating in midair. Kenny blinked a few times and watched (as best he could with the blood in his eyes) as the light turned toward him.

"Do you mind?" a small voice called.

Kenny rolled over onto his stomach. "Huh?" he asked.

"*Do. You. Mind*!? I am trying to read!" it called again.

"Oh, my bad, I didn't realize ..."

He heard the voice moan in a repulsive way. He pushed himself up and slowly walked over to the light, using the wall to stand up. He slowly hobbled over to the large tree, feeling the wet bark under his hand as he looked around the oversized trunk.

A small girl looked up at him; in her hands she held a small lamp, no bigger than a quarter.

Kenny smiled a bit. "Sorry about...Ack, you're a—"

"A girl?" she spat.

"A...a...f-f-fair-y?" he stammered.

"Well, duh! Isn't that what you are?"

She stood up, closing a very small book as she did. She slid it under her arms and turned to face him. She floated up off of the small leaf she was sitting on and held the lantern up to Kenny's bloody face. She let out a yelp of terror, realizing he was bigger than she was.

The tiny woman dropped the lantern and her book and fell to the ground, landing in a small puddle of water. Kenny watched on in wonder. She looked like a small bug from where he was standing, being no bigger than five inches.

"Oh, now look what you did," she moaned.

Kenny kneeled down and picked up her small lantern. He handed it to her with a small smile.

"Sorry," he said kindly.

She stood, ringing the water from her pink blouse and matching puffy skirt, and then she grabbed the lantern and looked up at him in question.

"Are you going to eat me?" she asked.

Kenny broke out into a fit out laughter. "No, no, I'm not going to eat anyone...although I am hungry," he replied.

She breathed a sigh of relief and tried to fly up toward him, only to fall back down. Kenny extended his hand for her. With a small smile on her face, she grabbed his finger.

"Need a lift?" Kenny asked kindly.

"Yes, I'm afraid I can't fly when my wings are...Oh my!" she stopped "Look at all that blood!"

Kenny slowly pulled his hand away, clenching it into a fist. He pressed his bloody hand against his chest and looked away, feeling slightly guilty.

"Sorry. Uh, this hand isn't bloody," he explained, extending his other hand.

She climbed up onto his wet hand. She barely even fit in his palm. Kenny watched as she walked over to his wrist and then began to climb up to his shoulder.

"You're just soaked with blood! Were you in a fight?" she asked.

Kenny swallowed hard. "You could say that," he replied.

"Are you all right?" she asked again.

"Yeah, I'm fine, uh ..." he replied. Kenny grabbed the small fairy girl and set her down on a leaf. She watched as he picked up her small book, gently brushed the water from the cover, and handed it to her. She gladly took it and held it close, the lantern in her other hand.

"So, dear, what are you doing in my neck of the hollow?" she asked.

"Oh, I just kind of wandered in here, you see, I was lo-uh... hollow? Did you say 'hollow'?" he asked.

She nodded. "Why, duh, silly, of course," she said with a small giggle.

"Y-yeah, I just forgot, that's all," Kenny said. A nervous laughter followed.

She smiled, stood, and looked over Kenny's body. He was in deep thought for a few moments, staring blankly into a small pond in the distance.

"Are you all right, dear?" she asked.

"I'm okay, just thinking. Uh, Miss, would you mind sparing a few moments to take me somewhere so I can stop the bleeding here?" Kenny asked, pointing to his bloody head. "I'm not quite all here right now, you know, because of the loss of blood?"

She gasped. "Why didn't you say so?" she shouted.

Kenny laughed a small bit, shrugging his shoulders gently.

They felt heavy due to the rain in the seams of his jacket. His vision began to blur, and he shook his head a little bit. The water that had melted together with the blood flew off of his forehead. He fell a bit and grabbed onto the tree trunk to keep himself upright. He let out a moan and clenched his teeth.

Kenny laughed a little. "I...kind of...for-ugh ..."

His body fell limp, his eyes faded out, and he fell back toward the long blades of grass where rocks hid themselves as if they used the green earth's children to shelter themselves from the rain. His head collided with the ground. His hand unclenched, revealing his blood stained skin. The rain tapped on his pale flesh, slowly washing the blood away. His eyes were barely open, catching only a small glimpse of a shadow in the distance resembling Robert. The last thing he heard was someone calling his name and then all fell silent.

"Rob—"

Chapter Fourteen:

THE PAST FORGOTTEN

ROBERT WATCHED AS O'Reilly walked over to him. They had tied and gagged him again after the group had searched for Kenny endlessly for hours on end but found he was long gone. Now they were in the back of one of O'Reilly's stores, near the old chapel in the town. Robert was tied to a chair across the room from O'Reilly. He had his head against the wall, eyes turned down to the ground, and his body slouched in the chair.

"Just give me the house, boy, it isn't worth your life," he said as he stood. He fixed the rims of his suit and walked over to Robert, who had pure hatred in his gentle eyes. O'Reilly pulled his cigar from his mouth and blew the smoke in Robert's face, making him hack and wheeze horribly. The elder man untied the cloth so Robert could speak.

"Oh dear, the little boy can't breathe," O'Reilly said coldly, slight amusement in his tone.

"You're a monster," he hissed.

"Why, for attacking someone who is completely defenseless?

For attempt of murder to two boys who have never hurt any-one?" he asked.

Robert coughed heavily again, feeling more pressure on his lungs. Every time he felt the urge to relieve the pain by cough-ing. O'Reilly smiled deviously.

"Let's make a deal. You give me the house, and with all the money I'll get from finding the Grave of the Fireflies, I can get you the medicine you need to make sure this little case of the coughs doesn't turn into something *bigger*. Face it, dear boy, you have no other choice, your lungs are collapsing as we speak, you won't last the night," he said.

"A deal with you...Like I'd sell my soul to the devil ..." Robert mumbled, looking away.

O'Reilly hissed, and he grabbed Robert's face and turned his head harshly to make him look into his eyes again. Robert felt his body go limp a bit, feeling terrified from the look he received. Again his mind flashed to a distance place, somewhere long hid-den in his memories.

A tear slipped from his eye. It tumbled down onto O'Reilly's hand. The evil man just smirked and wiped it away.

"Having a nightmare?" he asked coldly, realizing Robert was in some sort of trance.

The blank stare that consumed Robert's face was horrifying in some ways, cold and unwelcoming, yet in others it was weak and misunderstood as if he was calling out to someone, someone who could save him.

O'Reilly removed his hand. Robert's head fell down, tears still slipping from his eyes, and then O'Reilly gagged him again. A thought jumped into his head, a memory that was triggered by that devilish stare of the man who was torturing him, and his mind slowly was consumed by it. He was reliving a dark memory once lost to him for years and not liking it one bit.

RAIN AND HAIL poured down onto the large cityscape, not a soul was to be seen, and all the lights in the houses and buildings were turned off. It seemed eerily familiar to the young Robert, at the time only fourteen, who was running through the storm on a Saturday evening. He used his forearm to block the rain and hail from hitting his head. The sound of his boots on the pavement was silenced from the heavy howls of the ferocious wind.

Come on, where did he go? Think, think you idiot! Robert thought to himself, ducking into the shade of a large tree. He leaned on the trunk, grasped his chest for dear life, feeling his heart vibrate under his fingers, and breathed heavily. The torn seams on his coat undid themselves as he breathed, the cloth rubbing against the thick bark continued to rip his only means of warmth.

"Come on, Kenny, where did you go?" Robert shouted. He looked off into the distance, seeing nothing but a light fog rolling in and the continuous rain. His thick bangs kept getting in his eyes, making his vision even worse.

Where could he have gone? I've looked everywhere; the tree house, his school, my school, the house...Where did he go?

The young Robert breathed in heavily and rushed off toward the opposite side of town, near the beginning of the old country road that, after about a thirty-eight hour drive, led down into Heather Field. The moment he escaped the shelter of the tree, he was pounded with hail. It bruised his head in numerous spots, but he didn't care. The only thing on his mind at the time was Kenny.

He ran for almost two hours, finding himself deeper and deeper into the countryside and further away from his home until he found a large shadow in front of him. He turned around and saw another, he couldn't figure out what these shapes were, and it was starting to bother him.

Robert gathered some courage and headed toward a tree in the distance, needing to get out of the rain for a few moments. This place looked familiar, certain things he could pick out and name, but it was almost impossible to say just where he was with the heavy storm. He was covered in mud and soaked completely, and his body felt heavy and stressed.

Robert soon found himself looking at the back of someone; this young enigma was sitting on the ground, looking at two tombstones. He was shaded by the tree, though he was still soaked with water and shivering in the cold. Far in front of him was a rocky road and high grass. *I know this place...it's so familiar.* He walked closer, seeing that the man he was staring at was a boy, a teenager no older than himself at the time.

"Tell me," the man said, his voice sounded like a whisper even though he was shouting. "Why did I have to be the one to lose them, Robby?"

Robert's eyes widened.

"Kenny?" he asked, placing his trembling cold hand on the boy's shoulder. The young man looked up at him, his eyes were sorrowful. It was indeed Kenny, but he looked different, not from the sad expression on his face, but from something else. The young Kenny, whose hair was scruffy and face immature, held a face filled with confusion.

"Come on, you can't just sit out here in the rain," Robert said.

"I...I ..." Kenny stammered.

"It's time to go home," Robert snapped.

"I can't...I'm sorry."

Robert felt Kenny's shoulder slip from his grasp, and he watched as his body tumbled down onto the ground in between the two tombstones. Lighting flashed, illuminating everything. The names on the graves read 'Lily Mathis and Kenneth Mathis'. Robert backed away in fear as he saw Kenny's body become almost transparent. Robert quickly kneeled down next to Kenny and lifted him into his arms. He held him there, seeing his body through his friend, like he was a ghost. Robert knew where he was now, and he felt scared.

"How did he find them?" Robert asked himself, looking at the graves. His gaze moved down to the unconscious Kenny in his arms.

"He's so cold...he's as cold as the graves," he whispered.

Kenny shivered from an ice cold wind that flew by them. Robert shielded him from the hail and the rainwater as best he could. He heard thunder in the distance and saw lighting flash behind him. He buried his face into Kenny's hair, whispering to him words of comfort. He knew how much Kenny hated lightning.

A crackling, hissing-like noise started to grow loud over Robert's head. His eyes quickly snapped up to the tree above, and it was set ablaze and sent tumbling down toward him. He let out a yelp, clutching onto Kenny as hard as he could, shielding him from the falling tree and dove toward the ground.

Both fell into a large puddle of water. Robert watched as the tree came closer and closer, until its shadow consumed everything.

Robert screamed in agony, clutching onto Kenny's body fiercely with his trembling hands.

He gasped. "Kenny!"

ROBERT'S EYES SHOT open, and he breathed in heavily and looked around for a few moments, realizing he was back in O'Reilly's store. He had awoken, and he was all right now.

Just a dream, it was only a dream, only a dream. You're fine. You're perfectly fine. Get a hold of yourself. His breathing went from a heavy gasping like pace to a gentle, calmer state as he realized he was all right and not in trouble. He felt his lungs sting with pain as he continued to calm himself.

His eyes closed gently and his hands unclenched. As his fingers unfurled, he felt a sharp pain burst into his palm. He groaned heavily and welded his eyes shut, his body recoiled a small bit in attempts to get away from the pain.

Shoot, he thought, letting another moan slip from his dry lips. He looked over his shoulder and saw a nail sticking from the wall. It pierced his tender skin. Realizing he could use this to his advantage, he grinned smugly a small bit and curled his pointer finger up toward the sharp end of the nail, realizing this may save his life. His hand winced hastily, feeling a shock of warmth burst from his finger. With his bloody finger, he began to write a message on the nearby wall. He wrote, 'O'Reilly, Murder, Drake, Help,' down on the wood planks carefully, the rough feeling of the old wood brushing against his skin was odd, his shaking finger made the writing look horrible, but it would make it more effective.

After he had finished he let his head fall down a small bit and he took a deep breath, and he began stomping on the floor, driving his heel into the back of his boot as he tried to slide down a small bit, this left huge dents in the soft, warped floorboards. The back of his shoes cut his heels, though he refused to stop kicking and moving his body around.

He continued to slide down gently until he felt his wrists connect with the nail. He quickly began to saw the ropes apart, trying to avoid being cut again with the rusty nail. Soon after the ropes snapped apart, he felt his wrists untie and his chest expand as he was freed. The ropes slid down his abdomen down onto the floor.

Robert's body shook a small bit as he slid off of the chair, his head collided with the wood that was, just moments ago, underneath his feet. His eyes closed gently and his breathing slowed to a soft pace for a moment, he had a small smile of relief on his face as he un-gagged himself.

"Finally, it doesn't hurt anymore," he moaned, rubbing his chest. He used his hands to push himself up a bit before he stood. He wobbled a bit as he wiped the sweat from his head.

"Now, to find Kenny," he whispered, walking over to the door and to his freedom.

Chapter Fifteen:

THE FIREFLOOD

IT'S SO COLD. *Why is everything so cold? I can't stop shaking. I...I...I want to wake up now, I really want to wake up now, Robert.*

Kenny's eyes fluttered open a little bit, and he saw the outline of someone flash and disappear quickly. His head was still pounding. He could feel the blood continuously slipping from his open wounds. He let a small moan escape his throat as he tried to roll onto his side. The grass was cold. It lightly brushed against his skin as the wind blew each blade around, one in a slightly different direction than the one next to it. Small rain drops cascaded down onto him. It was a light shower, like the heavens were washing his sins away slowly.

Kenny's brown eyes gazed up above, seeing a shallow orange pigment rolling across the sky. Shades of purple and yellow danced with red and blue ones, combining to make a gentle sunrise high above.

"Am I dead?" Kenny asked himself. His eyes closed, they refused to stay open any longer due to the stings of pain from the still flowing blood entering his irises. He used his trembling hands to push himself up a little bit, his entire body shivered as he tried to stay upright. He saw he was alone, still in the small area he had passed out in, but the small fairy girl had vanished, most likely she had flown off to try and get him help.

How long was I out? He asked himself, looking toward the sky. He could see faint sunlight rush above his head, glistening through the clouds lightly.

Once he felt all right, he stood and looked around. He was trapped, the only way out was up above, but he was in no condition to climb up the rock wall before him or the tree next to him.

"Why me?" he moaned, brushing back his bloody bangs. He rolled up his baggy, still wet sleeves and rung the water from his heavy leather jacket. Then he marched off toward a wall that was showered in blue rocks and crystals on the other side of the tree. It seemed to have a different feeling to it than the other areas, something continued to draw him toward it.

Kenny yawned and rubbed his eyes. The sore muscles strained themselves to see once the blood began to drip into them again. He rubbed his arms, trying to keep warm as he continued onward. Surrounding his feet was a heavy fog. It basked everything in a very eerie grey glow. This walk seemed to go on forever to him, he knew this was his only hope of getting out alive, but it seemed hopeless once he thought of the things he would have to deal with *if* he ever got back to Heather Field.

Once at the wall he stopped, realizing there were pictures carved into the rock. It depicted small humans with large butterfly wings being chased around by a large spider with one very giant eye. Everything was done in a deep blue or green except that eye and it was bright orange, almost red. It just seemed to stare off into the distance.

Kenny placed his hand on the wall slowly and cautiously. He carefully ran his finger across the old canvass beneath and stared at the spider with soulless eyes. No emotion was anywhere to be found anymore. As if this picture was somehow draining him.

"Why is this...familiar?" he asked himself as he blinked. The moment he re-opened his eyes the spider on the wall began to move. Kenny brought his hand away in terror and watched as the fairies and the spider began to crawl across the rock. His eyes widened as he saw the spider eat a fairy that looked as if it had tripped. It was like a horrible nightmare that he couldn't wake up from. The creature just continued to snatch up and eat the small fairy drawings, rearing its head back in triumph. He could almost hear it screeching.

Then it turned, its eye staring at him hungrily. He backed away a small bit in terror. The creature began to pry itself from the wall slowly with its front legs, using its one very large back leg to support itself. Kenny stumbled backward, tripping over a small stone as he went. He landed on the ground with a loud thud.

This creature just continued to grow and unlatch itself from the wall until it was standing in front of him, towering over him like a cat to a mouse. Like when paper books are turned into movies, the depiction was hastily turning into reality. Kenny tried to push himself away from the creature as it grew closer and closer. It lunged at him, roaring loudly like a lion. Kenny brought his hands above his head in attempts to shield himself but knowing his luck he wouldn't make it out of this in one piece.

He screamed in terror as the overpowering shadow of the spider consumed him. The black essence began to swarm beneath him, forming a large circle around his body. Dozens of small web-like strings shot from the ground beneath, grabbing onto him like hands. No matter how hard he struggled they wouldn't let go. One grabbed his neck, another grabbed his waist, they pulled him down into the shadow below until nothing but his head and arm were visible. He reached out above, holding onto thin air for dear life as he felt it become hard to breathe when the dark entities pressed against his chest. *I can't do it, this is it for me, I'm so sorry*, he thought with anguish.

Soon only his wrist was all that remained visible, and he felt a warm hold on his trembling fingers and then his hand. Someone had seemed to grab him. He could almost hear the small fairy girl screaming in the background. This person's fingertips were hot like lava, and it burned Kenny's flesh and felt like fire, but he grasped this enigma's hand back, knowing it was only a matter of time before he would be devoured if he let go.

Kenny's vision went blank after a moment, and his grip released on the person's hand, but whoever it was refused to let go, and it refused to let Kenny give in. It continued to pull him up, higher and higher, until his face was revealed. He gasped heavily, feeling a little bit of relief, but he dared not open his eyes for fear of the creature looming over him consuming his thoughts.

"Pull yourself together, Kenny!"

Kenny's eyes shot open. *How does he?*

Above him stood a man, not much older than himself, with fiery auburn hair as thick and soft-looking as any woman's and eyes as red as two freshly discovered rubies. Under those eyes lay two black spades facing down toward his mouth. On his face stood a soft smile; one that Kenny seemed to trust.

"Hang on!" the enigma cried out.

Kenny tightened his grip on the man's hand. He began to pull him from the pool of darkness. Kenny struggled to pull his other hand from the darkness. He became sweat drenched from fighting the pressure of the creature. And this strange person's body appeared to almost be made of fire, like his blood was made of lava.

At last! Kenny thought as he pulled his other hand free from the darkness. He reached up to the man and quickly grabbed his lower arm to pull himself up. He could hear the large creature roaring and snarling, but it was gone. Its large form concealed in the heavy shadows and out of sight.

Kenny felt his heart beat in his throat, a sting of pain hit his head, and he lost his grip. The strange man grabbed his hand tightly, groaning loudly as he continued his attempt to free him.

"Don't give into the darkness, don't let it consume you! You're stronger than this!" he shouted. Kenny blinked a few times and looked at the man with seldom hope in his eyes.

"It's no use...I can't do it, I'm not strong enough," he whispered. He felt the hands dig into his skin. He let out a cry of pain as his body began to drift down into the black hole that was swallowing him.

"You *are* strong, your friend needs you to be strong, and he needs your help!" the man shouted.

Kenny's eyes widened. *R-Robert*, he thought. His eyes narrowed a bit and tried to pull himself up again. The claws that had dug into his abdomen tore his skin as he continued to escape their hold. The man nodded and tightened his grip again, using all of his strength to help.

Only a few more moments passed and Kenny was freed. He grasped his chest in his hands, feeling his heart beating rapidly beneath his fingers, and fell to the ground in exhaustion. The other man stood. He looked down at Kenny as he walked over to where he had fallen. He kneeled down next to him and looked into his tired eyes with compassion. The little fairy girl flew down to Kenny's side.

"I told you I'd get help!" she said, placing her hands on her hips.

"Thank you," the red Elvin man said to the small woman. "You may take your leave."

The fairy nodded and waved to Kenny before she flew away. Kenny looked up at the red pigmented man who had a small smile on his face.

"How did you know my name?" he asked. The man smiled and placed a finger lightly on Kenny's wounded forehead. He winced a bit, feeling sharp pain run through his body.

"Hush, child. All will be told in due time," he said, his voice sounding so clear now. He stood and started to walk off when Kenny grabbed his pant leg to halt him. His grip was terribly weak, but he wasn't going to be left alone, at least not without some answers. He gazed over his shoulder and stared at him with question in his auburn eyes.

"Who are you?" he asked. He turned the upper part of his body to face Kenny, a smile planted on his pale face.

"Fireflood," he said calmly. A few strands of red and yellow light, like long vines with thorns on them, danced around his body, and before Kenny could register, he had vanished. The area was as it was, upon the wall stood the same pictures in the same spot he had found them to begin with.

"Sleep, child," a voice boomed, the sound reigned throughout the morning.

Kenny's vision bounced a small bit before he sprawled out onto the floor again. His eyes closed gently, and he curled up in a soft patch of grass like a child searching for warmth in the cold nights of winter. He had a smile on his face as he drifted off, feeling safer now than he had ever felt.

Chapter Sixteen:

THE CHAMBERS

KENNY SHOT UP in a cold sweat. A very annoying sound caught his attention. It sounded like beeping, a constant thump of noise every other second. He fished through his pockets, searching for the host of the noise, until he found Robert's blue cell phone. Surprisingly it had withstood the gallons of water Kenny had been thrown into. Kenny flipped it open and looked at the number. He didn't recognize it but he answered anyway.

"Hello?" Kenny asked.

"K-Kenny," a soft voice called.

"Rob...Robert!? A-are you all right? Where are you? Are you hurt? W-what's going on?" he stammered. For a moment all he heard was Robert's heavy breathing and a small laugh.

"I can't move anymore. Can you come get me?" Robert explained.

Kenny bit his lip, trying to find a way to say no. He wanted so badly to tell him yes, to give him reassurance, but he was never a good liar.

"If you can't, it's okay," Robert said through heavy strained breaths.

Kenny's eyes widened, "Oh, Robert, I want to, but ..."

"It's okay, you aren't hurt are you? Where are you?" Robert asked.

"I don't think you would believe me if I told you," Kenny said quietly as he stood. He continued to listen to Robert breathe, paying more attention to that than anything else. He heard heavy winds in the background and rain tapping on old wood paneling and what sounded like glass.

Kenny swallowed hard. "How much longer can you last by yourself?" he asked.

Robert burst into a small bit of laughter. "Maybe another few hours, if I'm lucky, my lungs aren't working well and...I think I'm dying," he replied, trying to stop himself from crying. He was terrified.

Kenny felt his heart stop beating from Robert's words. He let the phone slip from his hand down onto the wet grass. Everything went so slowly, no matter what he did he couldn't catch a breath or even blink.

He stood still for a moment, shivering in the cold winds that continuously rushed in and out of the small area he was in. Robert was hacking in the phone. Even with the phone being down on the ground, buried in the grass and muffled in sound, it was clear as daylight. He wondered how long it had been since he last took a breath. He bent down and scooped the phone up in his trembling hand. He could picture Robert sitting in some rotten old barn, drenched in rainwater and blood, shaking horribly. Grasping the phone for dear life, he thought, *At least I can say goodbye.*

"Robert, please listen carefully and do exactly as I say," Kenny demanded. Robert said nothing. Kenny swallowed hard, praying he was still alive. "Lie down, tell me where you are, exactly where you are, shut off the phone, close your eyes, and go to sleep... Robert, please answer! Robert!"

Kenny listened for a moment, hearing nothing but absolute silence. He pressed the phone hard against his ear. His eyes were closed tightly, tears slipped from his eyes, rolling down his cheeks heavily.

"*Robert!*"

His voice burst throughout the area, and it showered everything in the heavy echo of his screaming. He dropped to his knees, the phone slipping down onto the ground again. He had his hands over his head, and through his heavy gasping he cried out Robert's name.

"This is *not* happening. Please, dear God in heaven, tell me this isn't happening!" Kenny prayed, shouting to the heavens for an answer to this madness. He felt heavy stings of pain burst into his side and head.

"I shouldn't have left, dang it, I shouldn't have...I should've...I...I...oh man!" Kenny stammered, grinding his teeth angrily together, feeling guilty for leaving. He wiped a tear or two from his eye, picked up the phone again, and pressed it hard against his ear.

"If you can still hear me, Robert, I'm sorry," he whispered. "I shouldn't have left. You can only blame me for this. You probably would survive if I hadn't left."

Kenny stood in silence, the phone gently pressed against his ear.

"What are you babbling about?" Robert asked. Kenny sat there in shock. "You aren't dead?" he said gleefully.

"Do you want me to be?" he asked sarcastically.

Kenny laughed and wiped away more tears, gently rubbing his eyes with a small smile on his face.

"Robert, please lie down and get some rest," he demanded kindly.

"Ok, take care of yourself, try to get back here as soon as you can," he replied.

"It's a promise. You take care of yourself too."

"I will."

Kenny listened as Robert ended the call, then he closed the phone and gently pressed it against his forehead, whispering a thankful prayer under his breath. Then he slid the phone into his pocket and walked back over to the wall, now seeing the outline of what looked like an entrance. He tapped his hand against the rock wall, listening carefully for any hollow sounds or echoes from somewhere inside. For a moment the only thing that happened was Kenny's hand bruised. Then he heard something click once he pounded on a loose stone. He pressed his ear against the wall only to hear what sounded like cogs spinning.

"Did I hit some sort of switch?" he asked himself, pulling away from the wall. He watched as a small area in the wall tumbled inward, dust burst from the cracks, showering everything in a heavy gale of smog. As soon as the small area of stone wall was in merely six inches, it began to slide toward the right, slowly vanishing behind the rock wall. Kenny smiled a bit in joy. "My lucky day!" he shouted, heading over to the entrance.

Kenny slipped his head inside cautiously. It was a dark and musty old cavern that headed only one direction. Every ten feet or so was a lamp, but the flames were almost gone. There was sound of dripping rainwater that filled the air and the sound of spiders scurrying up the side of the wall and howling winds bursting around inside. The ground was moist and brown, like mud but not quite as soft, and it smelled like a rainforest inside, damp and hot.

Man...awful dark in here. Maybe I shouldn't...no, Robert needs me! Kenny thought with determination. He stepped inside, hearing the sound of his footsteps echoing throughout the tunnel. He slowly began to walk inside, stepping in a few soft patches of what seemed like wet clay more than mud, leaving a long line of footprints behind him. The cave looked like an old mine, the further down he went the darker it seemed to get. The lights began to fade away, leaving nothing but darkness and the nervous sounds that Kenny made.

Everything is okay; there's nothing behind you. Kenny said to himself as his eyes nervously gazed behind him. He breathed in heavily and exhaled slowly, seeing a fog-like substance appear in front of him. He rubbed his eyes, wiping away a few tears that had slipped from his tired eyes. Even after resting for that short period of time he was still so tired, and he was becoming parched. His dry lips began to peel. He bit the loose skin and tore it off, letting his mind wander around freely as he blindly walked into the dark.

"Why me?" he asked again. "Why is it *always* me who has to do all the walking in these stupid predicaments? Robert always ends up getting to sleep for a week, and I have to walk a billion miles to find him."

The walls were soft and Kenny's hands smashed the surface of the cavern's sides. His body was soon covered in mud and gunk from running into the invisible walls and strange formations in the dark. He was as blind as a bat and his senses failed him.

Kenny stepped down on a twig, it snapped, and he jumped back in fear, letting out a small scream of terror. He tried to study the broken twig for a moment before bursting out into a fit of laughter. He smiled and placed his hands on his hips. "You're such an idiot," he mumbled to himself. That was something Kenny had always been able to do, laugh at himself when the chips were down. After he rolled up his sleeves and marched down the pathway, slouching forward a small bit in agony. He was beat, and all he wanted was a good night's sleep in a warm bed. Maybe a little of Robert's 'special drink' he would make whenever Kenny was sick would be nice too.

Chocolate milk with drizzles of caramel sauce; he would fill it up so far that most of the time it would overflow and Kenny's fingers would be a sticky mess from holding the cup too long. And he could never forget that tiny little bit of coffee Robert added every now and again. He was hyper whenever he was sick and wouldn't go to sleep, so Robert began to sneak a small bit of his mother's coffee into the drink when she wasn't looking to help him relax. It always did seem to have an adverse effect on him, making him very calm and tired.

Sly devil, at least he doesn't drink it himself, Kenny thought, brushing back his bangs. He didn't even want to imagine Robert on caffeine! The poor man could barely handle a small bit of sugar in his cider without becoming a maniac. As Kenny continued to walk down the pathway, lost in his precious memories, he failed to realize the ground stopped. Stumbling with little grace as he tried to keep his balance, he fell off of a ledge, tumbled down a small ramp, and landed in a large pile of mud.

Kenny struggled to get his face free. From his neck up he was a half a foot deep in mud. He had nothing to grab onto or use to push himself up with, nothing but weeds and clay-like substances. He shoved his arms down into the mud, praying that there was some sort of stone plate beneath him. *Me versus mud, not exactly the match of the year here, come on Kenny!* Luckily there was an odd metal object beneath his left hand. Once he had a good grip, he used all of his abilities to thrust his upper body toward the sky. After a hard struggle, he burst from the pile of mud, gasping for air. He calmed himself down a little and rubbed the mud from his face, cursing angrily under his breath.

"For the love of," he grumbled, spitting the horrible tasting mud from his mouth. He stood up quickly and backed away from the pile of sludge. His heel smacked against a large stone, and he stumbled a bit and fell down into another pile of dirt and rock. Dust flew up around him. He coughed and waved his hand in the air, trying to blow some of the dust away. *Robert was right, I am a klutz. Born graceless, die graceless, I guess.* Kenny thought, sighing. He let his body fall forward as he placed his elbows on his knee caps and let his head rest in his hands. He thought for a moment, pondering the question of why there were so many dirt piles. It was odd, usually in places as lightless as this that hadn't been used in some time, the dirt would form a blanket on the ground, not set in piles randomly on the floor. He wiped some more mud from his face and dusted his knees off before he stood. His back was soaked with mud, his jacket felt heavy, and his shoulders became heavy.

"Somebody was here, not long ago either. The mud is fresh," he said to himself, carefully walking around a large pile of mud. He trekked down further into the darkness, avoiding as many mud mountains as he could. Soon he found himself running into weeds and large vines that shot from the wall, water was surrounding his feet now, he was knee deep in the muck and gunk. It amazed him just how quickly the environment changed in this 'hollow' he had entered.

The liquid was bitter cold; it felt like ice. Small crystals seemed to form on his pant legs as he waded through the river. He shivered from the heavy bursts of cold air that blew around him, and his skin felt bitter, and his eyes seemed to freeze together if he kept them shut too long.

"The temperature just dropped like twenty degrees," he said through clattering teeth. He rubbed his arms, feeling colder and colder with every step he took. Sometimes, he could see the moon shimmer above him through cracks in the ceiling, which revealed all the strange things at his feet. Flowers were growing in the waters, bright pink and orange colors sparkled in the moonlight, and their long vines twisted in the rushing stream. It was beautiful.

To keep himself sane, Kenny watched the ground instead of what was in front of him. And he walked straight forward into the unknown for about a half an hour or so. Kenny was barely above water anymore. It hit his chin, he had to swim through the passage most of the time, but the water was so contaminated that he could barely see. It was getting harder and harder to breathe and with every passing second he found himself growing weaker and weaker as if this filthy water had some sort of hold on him.

Dang, he thought, taking a deep breath. He went to dive when he felt the area around him shake and rattle. He turned around and saw a long black arm shoot from the water. Like the shadows had some sort of mind of their own, they sprung at him with animal instinct. He gasped and watched it come toward him. The hand grabbed his face and pushed him down into the water. He tried hard to get away, kicking and flailing around in the contaminated liquid. Every movement he made the less air he had. It all slipped from his lips in almost one go. His eyes widened as he began to feel his lungs ache in pain from lack of air.

Before he knew it, he couldn't feel his body anymore, everything fell limp. His eyes faded out, and the hand threw him down into a tunnel. The only thing he could feel was the water brushing around his body. The dirty liquid flowing into this new area was being pulled down fast like a wind tunnel. His body was flailing around like a rag doll, hitting everything within sight.

For a few moments his body just floated down further into the tunnel, and Kenny's only thoughts consisted of sorrow and regret. It seemed that the tunnel wouldn't ever stop, and he would never get a moment to feel his body again, to catch a small breath to let an apology slip from his lips with. He gasped, feeling water burst into his lungs, and he slowly reached up to grab his throat, realizing this was it.

I didn't want it to end this way, he thought, closing his eyes. *I won't let it end this way*!

Chapter Seventeen:

THE SAVIOR

KENNY OPENED HIS eyes; a bright white energy surrounded his body. *Am I...dead? Is this what heaven looks like?* The sharpness of the aura burned his salt water stained eyes. His limp body seemed to be floating in the middle of the pure white area, though he was lying completely flat on his back.

In a small place high above laid a black crescent shape. It rotated slowly in a counter clockwise motion. A small area next to it housed three half circles that spun around in spherical motion, the tips touched each other just enough to have them connect. Far below stood another circle that continuously spun in circles within itself like barbed wire, though it depicted thorns on a rose vine, and it was jagged in strange spaces like a child cut it from paper. It felt like he was staring into the inside of a grandfather clock.

Underneath that stood a giant cog which seemed to spread at least twenty feet above his head, just rotating ominously like clockwork. More pure black, incredible designs seemed to keep appearing the longer Kenny floated in this white room. He felt like he was trapped in a clock, all the ticking noises and mechanisms confused him. He reached out toward the sky, almost in a trance, his fingers outstretched toward the bright ceiling, trying to pull himself up.

The shapes all began to expand until they became long chains of black, even though they seemed far away, they were close. They hovered down toward him at a rapid pace.

"I don't want it to end like this," he whispered. Reaching up further, Kenny slowly felt his body begin to sink down into the ground, and he saw the white he was lying on consume him hastily. Tears burst heavily from his eyes, and his mouth opened up wide. Water spewed from his mouth, drenching his previously dry, rough lips. He felt air slip into his lungs into the water that floated in a stream above his head now. It was like the black objects had formed themselves into the stream not moments ago he was floating in.

"Please, don't let it end like this!" he shouted. He felt gravity suddenly pull on him. Like hands wrapping around his form, they surrounded every inch of his body. And before he could even realize what had happened, he was sent hurdling down into the pure white abyss below. He didn't cry out in fear or call for help, there was no one to hear him. He just felt his body tumble down further and further until his shadow became visible on a field of white.

As his body hit what he thought was the bottom, the ground shattered beneath, water burst from the hole in the shape of his body. Kenny slowly fell down into a dark, pitch black river. He slowly looked up, seeing the white light shimmering down into the water slowly fade away.

Kenny, hand still outstretched toward the rays, floated downward quickly. The dim salvation of the pure white land high above had vanished. The darkness had overtaken the valley of water, leaving him alone to fend for himself again.

I don't want this to be the last thing I see, he thought, reaching out toward the light again, trying to regain lost hope. He floated down, further and further into the pitch black of the night. His fingertips trembled. His eyes struggled to stay open. His body felt frail.

The further down into the darkness he went, the less feeling he had in his body. Before his tired mind could even think of a reaction he was unconscious, just floating in the abyss of pure dark. The only thing that, during this long time he was just hurdling into nothingness, really boggled his mind and made him flinch was that he was still breathing, still able to see what lies above him.

"Can I...wake up now?" he asked, speaking clearly, as if he were only witnessing a simulation. His voice echoed throughout the area, it rang like church bells for a moment before all went silent again. The water swiveled above him like a glass case. Above a blurry outline of someone or something appeared. It placed its hands upon the wet aura above Kenny and pushed itself down toward him. He watched carefully, seeing the body grow and form.

His eyes widened in shock, seeing Robert above him. He reached up for him and gasped heavily in fear. Water rushed into his lungs and the black that once surrounded him dissolved into small pieces, revealing the underwater tunnel he had previously been in. Like small grains of sand, they blew off into the vortex that was dragging him toward his death.

Kenny tried to swim toward the figure that resembled Robert, but the power and suction of the waves dragged him further and further from where he had started. He was tossed around a bit before he wound up getting caught in a patch of vines. His leg tangled with the thick rope like material, and the more the waves pulled the more Kenny could feel his leg being torn out of socket.

Shoot! he thought angrily, trying to unknot the weeds. His hand (which was almost ready to rip apart from his body due to the unbearable suction) maneuvered its way down toward his pocket. He prayed he could find his pocket knife in time, before he would drown and that it was still even with him from being tossed around and thrown into as much as he had recently.

It seemed useless to continue. He wasn't strong enough to

save himself. But just when all seemed lost, he felt heavy pressure grip onto his wrist. The water rushed around the form of what had gotten him. It was a hand, blue in pigment and strong with a large dragonfly tattooed on the inside of his lower arm. It slowly pushed his hand down toward his pocket, gripping onto his cold skin tightly. Kenny winced in pain multiple times, feeling shock in his shoulder from falling earlier, but the person refused to let him quit, just like the one who had saved him from his fears before in the odd field. The one called Fireflood.

Before he realized, Kenny had his pocketknife in his hand. He flipped it open and reached for his tangled foot. The person continued to help, slowly pushing his hand down toward his ankle.

Kenny felt his body go limp right before he could untie himself. The knife slipped from his hand into the water, the person floated next to him grabbed it, and swam up toward Kenny's head. He leaned in close, until his mouth was right next to Kenny's ear. His defined face almost disappeared when Kenny looked at him. His eyes were gently open, but he couldn't see this figure in great detail.

"Don't give up, what would *he* say if he knew you were tempted to quit?" it said.

Kenny listened to him. The blue enigma waved the pocket knife in front of Kenny's face. With determination, Kenny grabbed the pocketknife and slowly, with the odd enigma's help, reached down toward the rope. In one quick motion the ropes were undone. Kenny's body grew deathly limp again. He broke under the pressure. He no longer had the will to continue. The stranger just grabbed him and began to swim away into the pitch black cavern ahead. Kenny's body was like a rag doll's, just floating around in the water, unable to help himself.

Resisting his body's need to fall into unconsciousness, Kenny's weak eyes looked up at the still blurry person who was saving him. This agile stranger was long and slender, his powder blue skin covered in tattoos. Kenny could barely tell if this odd person was even human, or if he could really trust him. But no matter what, he owed this person his life. He would be dead if he hadn't rescued him just then. And though he was grateful, he was somewhat scared as well. Kenny had a small smile on his face, he allowed this savior of his to take him wherever he pleased.

Once the speed of the water began to grow, Kenny saw the person clench onto his waist tightly. The two rushed down into a darker area. Kenny's eyes widened and he felt heavy pressure burst into his lungs. His air supply had vanished, and he wasn't going to last much longer. He began to feel his muscles become like putty, his vision blurred, and his brain shut down just as the water calmed. The last thing he felt was the slow water brushing across his cold skin.

It was a peaceful place now. The water was gently rolling inside a domed area where the two had emerged. The enigma let Kenny slip from his hands, thinking he was still conscious. With widened green eyes, the stranger began to swiftly swim up to the surface when realization struck. He turned his head and found Kenny dropping toward the floor.

In a few quick motions he was next to Kenny again. Grabbing his hand with a sturdy grip, he lifted him up so he was eye level. It wrapped its arms around him and floated up toward the surface.

Kenny felt like it was all going to end there, in that pool of crystal clear water, as he resurfaced and felt winds rush around his face. Where the moonlight basked every little drop of water in a crisp glow, and where he could almost hear soothing, gentle music high above. This wonderful place he had been taken to, where rain tapped down upon the surface of the riverbed and gently on his skin like a waterfall, and where crystals formed in the muddy floor surrounding a field of flowers gently swaying in the wind.

A holy, wonderful haven, he thought with a small smile. *It's a beautiful place to die.* It was quiet, and the unbearable nothing-ness surrounded everything. Not a sound was to be heard, nor a thing was to be felt. Just silence, utter silence unlike anything Kenny had ever experienced.

"Breathe!"

Heavy pressure blew down onto his chest. He felt water burst from his mouth in gallons. His face was instantly drenched again, but he couldn't catch a breath. Then, he felt icy water on his lips, like a hand. Arctic like coldness layering the top of soft skin belonging to thin, long fingers pressed harshly against his chapped lips, and he felt the water rush out of his lungs in a snake like motion. The hand had pulled the water from his lungs just by shear willpower. That shivering coldness that had touched his face was the only thing that kept him awake. And with sudden realization, Kenny knew that someone was there to protect him. He felt all the water being pulled from his body and in an instant, he could breathe. He coughed up the remaining water gasped heavily, and rolled onto his side, finally able to breathe again. He curled up a small bit, shaking from the cold breezes that blew around him and the light rain storm that was showering everything in the room.

It was deathly cold and then suddenly warm. Kenny turned his head and looked at this enigma. He had long dark blue hair and a face as defined as an old English royal. He looked like a woman from some angles and his eyes were filled with concern. It was like looking at Robert through water.

"Weak child, you amuse me. Your determination is admirable," he whispered. His voice was pure and soft. It gave Kenny a feeling of waves rolling across the shore, yet the same feeling of staring into a heavy storm, the night sky filled with lightning.

"Kenny," he said. He placed his hand on Kenny's cheek and tucked his loose hair behind his ear. "Sleep, regain your strength and dream of reunion."

After silence filled everything again, Kenny could hear no sound. The rustling of the trees above, the rolling waves from the pool he had emerged from moments ago, and even the rain slowly vanished. Kenny curled up into a ball, shivering like a child in the middle of winter without warmth or comfort. He slept there, feeling useless and scared. He wanted to get up, but he was trembling. He knew he would just fall over or hurt himself. He was alone and feeling very scared and fragile.

But the image of that aqua-like stranger kept him calm and brave and allowed him to sleep peacefully until the morning.

Chapter Eighteen:

THE DARK DREAMS

"ROBERT!"

Robert's small eyes opened, rain poured down into them heavily, which made them burn a bit. He felt grass beneath him and something sharp. The grass was surprisingly warm even though the rain was ice cold. It felt nice. The two temperatures balanced each other out wonderfully.

The last thing he remembered was shivering in some old rundown barn outside of town, wishing for some sort of warmth. And now he was lying in grass, in the dark and the rain. His tired, bloodshot eyes looked down toward his hand. *Is this...glass?* He questioned, gently pushing himself up off of the ground. He gazed across the dark land warily, wondering how he had gotten here. And why he had been placed in an all too familiar area that seemed to be haunting his thoughts recently. He hadn't remembered moving through the night, something must have moved him.

A few feet away, in a ditch that was flooded now, laid a pickup truck that was totaled, sitting on its top with the wheels still spinning. Glass was everywhere, and two bodies were lying on the ground next to it. Closer to him than the truck, but still far enough away that the image was blurry, stood a small car that was smashed on the left side. Two adults were slowly pushing their way out of the wreckage. The only other thing he could see was right in front of him. There, sprawled out on the ground, were two young boys. One was very young, he was awake unlike the other, darker haired boy, and he was trying to reach for the raven haired child next to him. But as far as Robert could see, he was hurt and hurt badly. His arm was bleeding nonstop, but he continued to reach for the other boy, as if he wanted to be comforted in this scary moment. The other one was in a bad state, half dead almost. He looked familiar, not as familiar as the lighter haired boy, but still very recognizable and sweet.

"Don't leave me," the young boy whispered, still trying to reach for the other. Robert watched as the two adults that were still breathing slowly made their way toward the other wreckage, most likely to see if the other two were still alive.

After, he slowly stood and walked over to the two almost dead children. The little blonde boy looked up at Robert weakly, breathing heavily in pain and trying to call out for help through his tears. Robert could hear his breaths slowly dying out. He sat down next to him, placed his finger against his lips with a comforting smile, and lifted the unknown child into his arms. As he stood, the little boy smiled, he grabbed onto his shirt as Robert gently hushed him as he tried to speak.

"Don't talk. You don't need to look at this...you should go to sleep and dream of something happy. Forget this," he whispered, trying to forget a similar nightmare himself.

Robert held onto this little one for dear life, even though he didn't know this child or even why he was here, he prayed that he would be all right. The two adults came close to him, and he looked at them in shock as they walked passed him, almost seeming to see right through him, like he wasn't even there. The woman was his mother, identical in every way. And the man heavily resembled pictures of his father that he had seen when he was young.

Mom and...dad...how is that possible? Robert asked himself, staring at the younger versions of his parents. He looked down quickly at the dying child lying at his feet, realizing that was him, and the child in his arms was Kenny. His eyes gazed down to the tiny, precious and kind boy, seeing the face of his best friend slowly go pale and his expression fade into a sad, longing one. *This is the night Kenny came tumbling into my life; the car accident.*

Robert gently knelt down and laid the young Kenny near the younger version of himself at his feet. The little Kenny grabbed the scared Robert's hand and smiled a bit as tears ran down his cheeks. He grasped his hand in his own and breathed out heavily.

And the matured, braver Robert thought back, reliving the memory as it replayed, in perfect timing with the events unfolding before him. Most of his life he hadn't remembered this moment, until he was actually looking into the eyes of his young counter-part.

"I'm scared," he whispered in perfect unison with his young doppelganger. "I don't want to die."

"You can't!"

Robert looked behind him, seeing a soaking wet Kenny standing in the rain. Tears poured from his eyes as he too relived this horrid moment, speaking at the same speed as the young one lying on the ground. He joined Robert, not questioning why he was here nor rejoicing that he had found what he had been searching for. Kenny grabbed Robert's hand. He grasped it back, feeling his body tremble. Both watched, feeling stings of pain in their sides from returning to this dark place.

"It's so faint, your voice," Robert continued. "And the pavement, it's so cold."

"Please don't leave me by myself," he whispered, "Please!"

Kenny slammed into Robert. His face was buried in his sweatshirt. And he trembled in the arms of his best friend. Robert embraced him and held Kenny's head against his chest. His shaking, weak hand rubbed the back of Kenny's head to comfort him. He watched carefully, seeing as the young Kenny's body slowly went limp. Robert gasped, realizing that the young Kenny was dying.

"Keep your eyes closed," he whispered, trying to keep Kenny's eyes away from this horrible nightmare. Kenny was terrified, but he listened. He kept his eyes closed and waited for this dark memory to end. The younger version of himself was asleep on the ground, the little Robert's hand gently sliding from his grasp.

Robert closed his eyes for a moment, looking away from the boys on the ground, holding onto Kenny for dear life as his warm tears slid from his pale flesh onto Kenny's drenched hair. He breathed in heavily, his lip trembling in fear, his teeth grinding together. The rest of this memory was distant, neither boy had been awake after this moment and both suffered from amnesia, so most all of it had vanished when they awoke.

Through his squinted eyelids, Robert saw a bright light. His eyes slowly re-opened, only to be forced shut again by the bright entities. Warmth stroked his cheek, wiping away the tears. Kenny looked up at him, wondering why his friend had become so calm. He let a small gasp escape his lips. "Fireflies!" he said in shock. Robert's eyes burst open. He gazed around the area that was now illuminated by dozens of fireflies.

Every blade of grass, still wet with water, was glowing with fiery light. Robert let go of Kenny and kneeled down next to his doppelganger. Some fireflies danced around the area until they reached the young boy on the ground. With one gentle stroke across any of his bloody skin, whatever was ailing the pain stricken young boy was gone. All of his wounds had vanished. Robert gazed over to the young Kenny. His arm began to heal and, instinctually, he grabbed onto the younger Robert's hand again.

Kenny laughed from behind. "That's how we made it through the accident," he said smiling. Robert nodded and turned his upper body around to look at him before he stood up to reply. Slowly, he confronted Kenny, who housed eyes full of confusion. The blonde stared into Robert's calmed irises.

"Rob, you okay?" Kenny asked as he went to place a hand on Robert's shoulder.

Nodding quickly, he smiled in reply. Robert's eyes closed a bit as he began to fall. Kenny screamed out his name as the ground shattered beneath him, revealing a blanket of pure black like the memory he had just relived. He still heard Kenny screaming as he fell, drifting down into the darkness.

Realizing what was happening, Robert let out a scream of terror, feeling sick to his stomach and frail, like he was about to shatter into a million pieces the moment he hit the bottom. As he drifted down, he could almost feel Kenny reaching out to him from somewhere deep in his memories. Maybe from that time he had just relived, when he was so small and fragile and needed comfort like he did now. Somehow Robert knew that Kenny needed him, not the one that was just next to him, that was merely a fragment of his mind. The real one that was scared and alone, the one that was calling him, just like he had all those years ago, was the one who needed him.

He opened his eyes, tears slipping down his cheeks heavily. A blur of white high above showered everything around it. Quickly he saw Kenny reach for him, floating down into the darkness toward him. He reached up to him, trying to grab onto his hand, but he felt so weak that it seemed pointless.

"Don't leave me, not again!" he heard Kenny scream. Robert's head tilted back a bit, his body hovering in the black abyss. He let his hand fall, and before he knew it, the ground was beneath him. The white light swallowed Kenny whole and Robert heard his name called once more, right before his head collided with the ground.

"Kenny!" Robert screamed, eyes snapping open. With a deep breath, he observed where he was. *Oh, I'm...I'm still in the barn.* He was all right, sitting up in the patch of hay he had fallen asleep in. With a small sigh and a shiver, he curled up. The rain was still tumbling onto him, a light fog appeared on the horizon, and a small wisp of light began to grow from the rising sun far off in the distance.

"Sorry," he whispered, slipping his hand into his pocket. He slowly pulled out his spare cell phone. Trembling, fingers shaking in weakness, he carefully dialed the number to Kenny's phone.

He pressed the phone against his ear and prayed Kenny would answer. He was drifting into a deep sleep which he feared he may never wake from. It rang a few times before he heard a click, and then a voice. Sadly, it was his. The recording for voice-mail played, signaling Kenny hadn't heard the phone ringing.

Man, why do you have to sleep now? he thought, grinding his teeth angrily together. He waited for a moment before he began to speak, hoping he would pick up during his message.

"Kenny! Kenny, please answer. I know you can hear me!" he said softly yet sternly, knowing Kenny was probably too afraid to pick up if he sounded angry. He could read him like an open book, and this page read fear. Kenny probably assumed Robert was calling to let him know he wasn't going to last very long and this was his farewell message.

"Please, Kenny, answer. I need to hear your voice," he whispered, "If you can hear this, please, please just answer."

Tears rolled down his cheeks, he breathed out heavily, his chest pounded harshly, and before he realized, the phone slipped from his hand onto the floor. His body slid down onto the muddy ground until he was covered in a thick brown layer of earth. With one last, heavy yet calming breath, he closed his eyes for a final time, a sad expression on his longing face. Like his wish, in that moment, was to be comforted. *I can't believe this is how I die, it's not fair*, he thought, grinding his teeth angrily. *What have I done to deserve this?*

Chapter Nineteen:

THE UNFORTUNATE

"WHY'S IT SO hot?" Kenny moaned, wiping more sweat from his head. He huffed angrily and continued down into the forest. For the last few hours he had trekked down into the deeper parts of the forest, trying to find a way out of the confusing maze he had gotten into.

The temperature, much like it had been the first few days he had lived in Heather Field, kept changing. When he had awoken, it was incredibly cold and slowly it became so hot he had stripped down to almost nothing. The knees of his jeans were ripped open, he had gathered all of his belongings into his baggy pockets and tossed away his leather jacket, and his shirt was now sleeveless.

I'm going to regret doing that to my clothes, he thought. *Knowing my luck.* He stopped and looked up, feeling cold rain pour onto his face. *That'll happen.*

Again he continued to walk deeper into the forest, drenched with sweat, rain, and mud. He rubbed his head gently and yawned. Luckily his head had stopped throbbing, and he had been able to use his sleeves to bandage the cut on his head, but he felt surprisingly chipper. For some reason, most of his wounds seemed to have slightly recovered and he had quite a bit of energy.

He was awoken earlier than he would have liked due to a loud explosion-like noise off in the distance somewhere. In fear he ran and ended up lost. Now, large trees towered over him, their monstrous roots unearthed themselves and tangled with one another like something from his favorite book. *Too cool*, he thought, smiling.

A screech sounded and made him lose focus. He came to a halt and tripped over a large, hollow-sounding root. He scraped open his knees and palms as he rolled across the floor. Whatever it was had spooked him, and just as Robert had always told him to do, he rolled for cover. Quickly, his numb body stopped under an incredibly wide, very old root, his back pressed against a smooth yet very cold stone. As he breathed, he felt what seemed to be writing rub against his skin.

His pupils grew large as he watched everything move, scanning every little detail of every tiny stone and every line that ran through the bark of the trees. He waited for the noises' host to walk by, or slither by, whichever one this *thing* did. And he wasn't hoping it would by any means.

It's nothing, idiot, just the wind echoing off of the rocks, he thought, taking a deep breath. His body shook, his eyes started to water and sting from withholding tears of agony. He had never favored being alone, especially when he heard things that terrified him or put unwanted thoughts into his head.

"Everything's all right," he whispered. His voice became shrill, which made him uncomfortable to the fact that he may have given his hiding spot away. His eyes struggled to gain a good focus on the movements above him through his tears. A rustling sound was heard in the distance. He swallowed hard and pushed himself up.

"Walking, walking away is a good idea," he whispered as he stood. He walked away, deep into the forest. The lights from the rising sun above danced through the trees, illuminating everything in a heavenly glow. He ducked under large vines that stood in his way, jumped over the others, and most of the time had to change his course because he became trapped. Nothing but a thick forest of vine and leaf stood on every side of him.

Kenny heard voices, and his body slowly wobbled a bit before he fell to his knees. His hands were pressed against his ears, and the voices kept growing louder and louder until they turned into screeching sounds; like nails brushing against a chalkboard. He shook his head. *Go away*, he thought, grinding his teeth together.

Across the fronts of the trees, small pictures, like the ones on the wall at the beginning of this adventure, began to grow and reach out to him. Ones depicting destruction brought on by the one eyed spiders, fleeing fairies and words in languages long gone. The spider-like monsters howled and screamed. Kenny was on the ground, using his elbows to support him somewhat as the noises kept growing louder and louder.

"Go away, please go away!" he shouted, shaking his head harshly. The pictures crawled across the floor over to him, the small fairies reaching their tiny hands out to him, needing salvation from the large spiders. Every second the noises grew louder, his body felt as if it was being consumed by the strange entities. He stood and darted off into the distance, hobbling around, slamming into trees, but the noise continued to follow him. He shoved vines out of the way, cutting his arms on the thorns they housed, but his body refused to stop.

In exhaustion, in a small area that was treeless, he collapsed, panting and sweating heavily. The noise seemed to stop for a moment. Sunlight was consuming the entire area, showering Kenny's body in light. He was instantly drenched in sweat, and his thick hair was sticking to his neck and face. He smiled a bit as he sat up, brushing back his bangs. His vision was clouded by the heavy droplets of sweat, and they stung the still open wound on his head as well.

"They're gone; all the noises are gone," Kenny said happily. "That was so weird. But I'm so tired now. I need to find somewhere to catch my breath."

Behind a large batch of trees, Kenny saw something which

made his body loosen in joy; he watched it for a second, staring mindlessly out into the thicket until he was able to fixate his gaze solidly on the object. A little house was perched deep in the thicket.

Kenny stood and ran off into the wooded area toward the shack, praying somebody was inside. He needed help, he was still weak, and his wounds were causing him great pain, his feet were aching, and his body was trembling. All in all, he was exhausted and really only wished for a bed to lie down in for a few moments. He had a small smile on his face as he walked inside the pitch black area.

"Hello?" he asked, staring off into the distance. It looked and smelled as if it had been uninhabited for a long time. There was a thick layer of dust and grime on everything, and you could hear water running from the faucet in the small kitchen across from where he stood. Giant logs were hanging from the ceiling for no apparent reason. The sound of clicking cogs filled the air along with a smell of burnt wood. Kenny slowly walked inside, the floor creaking and cracking under his feet.

"Who?" a gruff voice boomed.

Kenny stopped dead in his tracks, swallowed hard, and took one more step. In the floor, now that he paid more attention, stood a large hole with mud that sprayed outward like a fountain. A large dirt clod smacked his head; he let out a yelp and fell backward into the table.

"Who?" the voice shouted again. A man stuck his head from inside the hole. Upon his head an object which appeared to be a hardhat with huge glasses that had lenses like telescopes sitting on his dirty face. The lenses seemed to retract and expand like those in a telescope. He was a plump man that looked like a giant mole. He was dusty and smelled horrid and looked like he had spent most of his days in the mud.

"Sorry," Kenny said, rubbing his head. The man pulled himself from the hole and crawled over to Kenny. His eye twitched slightly in disgust at how the mole-man acted. He stopped near Kenny and looked at him with wonder. The lenses in his glasses expanded all the way up to Kenny's face, which was pretty far if you compared how tall Kenny was to the strange creature. They moved in and out and left to right, examining every little detail of his trembling body.

"Sir, I," Kenny began.

"Human!" the creature shouted.

Kenny fell onto the floor, and he watched in fear as the man crawled over to a large rope that was hanging from the ceiling. He grabbed it and pulled hard, a loud, ear-shattering siren rang. Kenny slammed his hands over his ears and fell completely to the floor. *Oh, come on! I just got away from the horrible screaming noises!* The hermit like man ran back over to Kenny, completely unaffected by the horrible noise. He looked at him, watching him writhing in pain.

"Please stop!" Kenny begged. "Please!"

"Human, dirty human!" he shouted again, pointing at him tauntingly.

A few odd-looking humans burst into the house, as though they had been summoned like police officers when there's an emergency call. They grabbed Kenny and stopped his attempts to run by slamming him into the ground. They bound him with thick ropes and kept him pinned to the muddy floor. His anger-filled eyes looked up at the green humans. But soon, wonder filled his eyes as he looked at the faces of these weird creatures.

Are those nymphs? Kenny thought. The alarm sounded again, which brought Kenny away from his thoughts into a state of agony. Screaming and hollering, his body tensing and trembling at the same time, which made the pain even worse. It was unbearable, his head was pounding and sweat poured down his face onto the floor. He could almost feel hands reaching for him, dragging him down further and further into the floor. Whatever this strange call was, it was made specifically for shutting down human's nervous systems to keep them pinned to the floor.

Wood chips scraped across his cheeks. Tears burst from his eyes again. The pain was just too much for his body in this condition.

"Seize him, cannot let him escape!" a tall, slender female shouted. The others listened and began to tie him up. Kenny looked at her. A dark wood, African style mask was placed upon her face. She grabbed the rim of his shirt and turned him around to make sure his attention wasn't elsewhere. She hissed, "Pathetic human."

The woman went to jam the pointed tip of her spear into his chest, his eyes widened in fear and his breathing came to a halt. He was desperate, wondering if she could understand fully what he planned to say to her. Though thinking it was hopeless, he tried to communicate anyway.

"Please stop!" Kenny shouted, hacking a bit from the tight rope that had just been tied around his neck. His eyes closed a bit, praying that she would listen. It fell somewhat silent. The siren that had been wailing suddenly died down. One eye slowly opened. The girl had stopped. She dropped him on the ground and pinned him there, the spear mere inches away from his Adam's apple.

"Why?" she asked.

"I'm innocent!" he replied. "This is all a misunderstanding!"

She looked at him closely and dropped the spear. With one hand, she kept him pinned to the ground, the other she used to remove her mask. Kenny's cheeks turned a deep crimson, realizing this woman resembled the same he had seen in Robert's grandfather's photographs in his hidden black room, only taller and more mature.

"Innocent?" she asked.

Kenny's eyes widened in shock. "Yeah, innocent! I didn't do anything!"

She scowled and removed her hands from his chest. He sat up a bit, the other women went to attack, but the one standing on Kenny only had to give them a look before they stopped.

This one was their leader, it appeared to Kenny. Without another word, she extended her hand for him as she stood. Kenny hesitated to take it for a moment, wondering if she would just jump him and end him the moment he trusted her. But even if he wasn't sure, he felt some sort of trust in the shimmers glistening across her irises. Kenny took her hand, eventually, and went to stand when he saw the small hermit man grab the rope.

"Stop him!" Kenny shouted. The leader snapped her head toward the creature, but she didn't have time to halt his motions.

The horrid screeching started again. Kenny slammed his head on the small table as he fell back down toward the ground, pulling the nymph with him. He let out screams and yelps of terror, realizing this noise would eventually shut down his nervous system.

Sorry, Robert, I tried, he thought, the noise started over. He heard the man continuing to yell, "Human, human!" as he had been before, continuously pulling the alarm rope. The noise just kept going and going until Kenny eventually broke down. Streams of tears rushing down his cheeks, a small stream of blood running from the open wounds he had received upon impact of the many items he had slammed into. He lay on the floor in agony, unable to move. The leader pushed her body off of Kenny, and placed her hand on his head.

"Robert!" he shouted. The noise reigned for a moment before all fell silent, Kenny letting out a last heavy moan before his breathing sped. He watched his captor stand up and grab her spear. She hissed and pointed her weapon at the hermit. Letting out a yelp of terror, he immediately stopped and fell to his knees in fear.

"Get help!" she commanded her team with anger. The others ran, going to get help like she had ordered. The leader placed her hand on Kenny's forehead and gently ran her hand down his face. She was infatuated with Kenny's strange facial features, his brown-hued eyes, and his pale yellow pigmented skin. His straw-like hair was strange compared to her soft silky green locks. It somewhat reminded her of touching wheat in the fields when she touched his head.

The woman looked at him. "Hang on," she whispered, brushing back his hair.

"I'll be okay," Kenny said, pushing himself upward. "Thank you for helping me."

"Lie down!" she demanded.

He didn't listen; he just continued to stand up. He felt as

though he needed to get away. The girl went to pull him down again when she felt pressure on her hand. Her eyes gazed up behind her, trying to see who had stopped her, as Kenny's vision followed.

"Fireflood ..." was all he could mutter. He was stunned to see the familiar man's outline, only catching a quick glimpse of the figure before he toppled over. The woman looked up at this enigma, crawled away from both Kenny and who he believed to be Fireflood, and bowed down. She was on all fours, shaking in fear at the site of the sprite, but it was not Fireflood. This new man looked a lot like the woman who was kneeling at the sight of his sudden appearance, his brittle green hair was entwined with vines and thorns and his skin was a deep green though parts looked peeled, like a mighty tree that was losing old bark. Kenny was lying still on the ground, unable to stand any longer. His eyes were closed lightly.

"Bloodwite," the girl whispered. This man she had called Bloodwite, walked over to Kenny and placed his hand on his forehead.

"You just don't know when to give up," he said.

Kenny's eyes widened in shock, and he looked up at the green man who resembled the other two people who helped him earlier. The blue man in the water, who had failed to speak his name, and Fireflood, but he appeared older and wiser. Kenny pushed himself off of the ground, hissing and screaming loudly in pain. The man stood and extended his hand for Kenny.

"But I admire your courage," Bloodwite said with pride.

"Human!" the woman shouted.

Bloodwite looked at her. "Child, are you certain? Look closer," he replied. "He may...or may not be what you think he is. But I'll let you decide on which your mind agrees with."

The woman's eyes were fixed upon Kenny's, and the rage and fear she saw showed powers hidden beneath his gentle-looking exterior. He was angry that he was unable to do anything further. Tears rolled down his cheeks in heavy numbers, an aura of hatred and confusion emitted from his body.

Kenny stood; he clenched his fist tightly in anger and turned to face Bloodwite. He started to walk over to the green man until he stumbled a bit. With strong arms, Bloodwite caught him and gripped his shoulders tightly to keep him upright. The elder man felt the human struggle to stay awake and felt how his body trembled and moved in shear anger. He placed his hand on the back of Kenny's head.

"Kenny, you don't need to struggle like this. You can endure this pain, this is nothing," he said calmly.

Kenny's eyes slowly closed and his body fell limp. He felt the warmth on his body as he buried his face into the man's shoulder, looking for any sort of comfort he could find. The woman looked at him; his only response was a smile.

"Allow him rest and shelter," Bloodwite demanded. Slowly, he laid Kenny on the ground and waved the nymph over to his side. She stood and headed to where her superior was standing ever so calmly. He pointed down to Kenny's sleeping face.

"He is special, so please take care of him," Bloodwite stated in a whisper.

She moved her eyes toward him in question. He waved his thorn-covered hand over Kenny's face and then ran his branch-like hand down his entire form, and all his wounds vanished. Kenny took a deep breath of relief. He felt brand new, like he was reborn, he almost felt as though he could take on the world.

Bloodwite placed a finger to his lips and he smiled. "Welcome to my world, my little firefly. Enjoy your stay."

Chapter Twenty:

THE TEMPTED

"GIVE IT UP, boy!" O'Reilly shouted as he slapped Robert with his cane.

"Ugh!" Robert screamed as the cane's top collided with his face. His head collided with the soft mud once he was knocked back down. He pushed himself up and wiped some blood from his lips. O'Reilly loomed over him, one of his brutish lackeys stood on either side of him, and the wall of the barn was brushing against his back. He was trapped and weaker than ever. It was puzzling how he hadn't died yet. It seemed as though every time he was breathing his last breath, somehow his body found the strength to go on. And then O'Reilly found him, and then the horrible cycle started all over again.

"Give me the key!" O'Reilly snapped.

"Yeah right, over my dead body!" Robert shouted.

"That can be arranged!" O'Reilly shouted, smacking him again. He fell to the ground and trembled but kept his guard up, knowing this battle was far from over. O'Reilly's two men grabbed his arms and slammed him against the wall.

"Why keep going when you know I'm going to win?" O'Reilly asked.

"I made a promise, I'm going to keep it no matter what!" he replied.

O'Reilly raised an eyebrow in question. "To whom, may I ask, dear child?"

"You actually think I'd tell you?" Robert spat.

The two men slammed him against the wall again. He felt his body snap as the brick and wood surface came in contact with his back. The men let him drop to the ground, and he gasped heavily. *I'm not going to last much longer!* he thought, grinding his teeth together. His cold eyes looked up at O'Reilly, even if he was angry, a tiny bit of kindness was to be found. He could never be angry with anyone truly. And even though he wanted to knock O'Reilly senseless right now, something deep inside restrained him.

"Let me make a deal with you," O'Reilly said, twisting his moustache. "Give me the key, and I'll give you your little friend back."

Kenny! Robert's eyes widened in shock. He stared up at O'Reilly with question. *He's lying, he has to be lying! There is no way he found Kenny!*

"Don't touch him!" Robert shouted. He became unaware that he was speaking out loud. He bit his lip and stared coldly at the elder man looking down upon him. O'Reilly lifted Robert's head up with his cane. He looked at him thoroughly and smirked deviously with a cold chuckle bursting from his lips. Robert knew that he had him right where he wanted him. He was too weak to fight or even protect himself. Chuckling, O'Reilly grew nearer. As Robert sighed and went to close his eyes, he stared down at his battered body. He was amazed at how long he had lasted in the condition he was in, and he felt proud in ways. Doctors had constantly told him he would never last to see thirty, and that his lungs would collapse if he ran too much and that even the slightest injury would mean death. And to look down and see his bloody body, and how he was still alive now, made him feel accomplished.

O'Reilly kneeled down next to him and placed his hand on Robert's pounding head. Robert let out a small yelp of pain as O'Reilly rubbed his cracked skull harshly, like he was a dog.

"With all the times I heard you were in the hospital, it amazes me that you're still breathing. I wonder what gives you the strength to keep going," he said, truly puzzled by Robert's strength. Robert looked up at him and blinked a few times, trying to gain a good focus on his surroundings. *How do I?* he asked. *I don't know, how do I keep going? I'm so tired but I keep getting back up. It can't be normal, no ordinary body could survive this much of a beating, especially mine.* His eyes closed and his head hung down a bit. O'Reilly stood and looked at his men.

"Carry him to the limo, gently," he demanded. He turned around and walked off toward the limo parked outside the old barn.

The two large brutes looked at each other in confusion, but eventually they picked him up and carried him toward O'Reilly's limo. The evil man watched as they brought him closer and closer until he was staring down at Robert's battered face. He opened the door and urged them to place him inside on the closest seat.

"Boss, why we helping this kid?" one man asked.

"Because, my good man, I think that the hiding place of the key has been closer than I had thought," O'Reilly said quietly, almost in a whisper. "But, we must make haste, time is of the essence! Now, come, to the house."

O'Reilly slid inside and shut the door, watching Robert every step of the way. His weak eyes opened, and he was shocked to see where he had been placed. Robert sat up and watched O'Reilly like a hawk, backing up as far as he could to get away, but he was almost blinded due to the intensity of the bright lights inside which made it hard to see. He sat up and rubbed his head, moaning loudly.

"Oh, so now you're playing the good guy?" Robert asked.

"A drink, my dear boy, you must be parched." O'Reilly replied, completely ignoring the question as he handed him a glass of imported red wine. Robert looked at him with sharpness in his eyes and a heavy huff of anger and pain coming from his lips.

"I promise it's not poisoned. We are both wealthy men, boy, we come from luxurious heritages, and we bathe in the purity of our riches and our titles and, dare I say it aloud, we are tempted by the same things," O'Reilly stated questionably.

"Cut the crap, O'Reilly! Where is this going?" Robert shouted as the limo began to move. O'Reilly laughed and took a drink of wine. Robert watched as he extended the cup to him once again. He took it and swirled it around, watching his reflection dance sorrowfully on the surface, but he dare not take a drink.

"You *obviously* want the gold as much as I do, Robert. Why else would you leave your beautiful home to come out here? You had it all! A good school, millions of 'friends' that worshiped the ground you walked on, ones that would die to breathe the same air as you. You had a wonderful career going with your talent for the violin. A mother, even as crazy as she is, adored you and loved you more than life itself. And your dear little friend that wants nothing more than to see you happy. Face it. You're a saint to those imbeciles. And you crave that attention," O'Reilly said cockily.

Robert gripped the wine glass tighter, painfully realizing he was right. He was a spoiled brat, and he did love the attention. O'Reilly pulled a wad of bills from his pocket and shook it in the air slowly, getting a good whiff of its rich scent as he continued to talk.

"And I bet you *all* of this that the first thing you mentioned about this town to the little blonde-haired bug was the legend, am I correct?" he asked.

Robert nodded slowly, now trembling in fear. He looked up. "That doesn't mean—"

"So face it," O'Reilly cut in. "You want it just as bad as I do. I'll make a deal with you. Open the door and help me find that treasure, and I'll make sure you and your little friend are set for life. A lovely cabin in the woods, money to spend freely, and all your medical problems taken care of. What more could you want? What do you say?"

He pulled out a cell phone, drenched in blood and water. Robert's eyes widened in shock and fear as he watched O'Reilly open the phone, he recognized it instantly.

"I got this from a co-worker of mine who found a few of your friend's things lying in a puddle. I also found a nice little pocket watch I believe belongs to your late father." O'Reilly stated as he hit a few buttons on the cell phone. He smirked, and waited before a record of Kenny's screaming started to play. Robert was in shock, sheer panic was all that was to be seen, and O'Reilly loved every minute of it. He shut the phone and slid it across the leather seat over to Robert.

A tear slipped from his eye unexpectedly and rolled down into the drink in his hands. Swirls and swivels formed inside and suddenly, just barely, you could see a fine line of shimmers dancing on it. Robert watched as a scene appeared inside, showing a large door standing in the middle of a blank area. It was covered in chains and weeds and looked old yet elegant. Around the bottom was a pond and fireflies dancing around it majestically.

No way, he thought. *It does exist*!?

"Robert!" O'Reilly shouted. He looked up in shock. O'Reilly was growing impatient and didn't intend to wait any longer. He crossed his legs and shook the glass of wine around.

"No," Robert replied in a whisper.

"What?" O'Reilly questioned.

"No! No, no, no!" he shouted, slamming the glass of wine on the floor. It shattered, wine was spilled everywhere, and glass shards were tossed into the air. O'Reilly backed away, feeling scared at the sudden action. His cold, bloodthirsty eyes looked at him.

"I'm not giving into your temptation! There is no way you're going to get that key, and there is no way I'm going to let you find that door!" Robert spat.

O'Reilly grabbed the rim of his shirt and snarled. "You little rat! Oh, so you do know where they are," he stated.

Robert gazed up at him before O'Reilly slammed him down into the chair. He slid onto the floor and watched as O'Reilly fished through the mini-fridge for something. He pulled out a new bottle of wine and gazed coldly over in Robert's direction. Robert watched as he loomed over him, having nowhere to run this time.

O'Reilly raised the bottle of wine above his head and prepared for an attack. Robert was completely defenseless and unable to protect himself. *Oh, I did it now!* he thought, clenching his fist angrily.

"Save your prayers," O'Reilly spat. "Because not even God in heaven is going to stop me from ending you!"

O'Reilly shot the glass bottle down onto his head. It shattered instantly, drenching Robert in a heavy red bath of alcohol and blood. Glass flew around his body as he headed toward the floor of the limo. O'Reilly shook some wine from his hands and looked down at Robert.

"That should keep you quiet for a while." O'Reilly turned his attention back to Robert. With a snicker, he pulled his limp body up by the rim of Robert's black sweatshirt. His body was completely useless, bathed in a shower of rain made from his own blood. He was whining a little in pain, breathing heavily from the pressure on his lungs. The only thing on his mind was the screams he had heard of Kenny moments ago as the limo came to a stop.

O'Reilly was tossed onto the seat from the sudden impact. He growled and snapped his hand to the side as he stood up.

"Jaster, you moron, watch where you're driving!" he shouted. But everything was silent. Now he was growing angry, he kicked Robert to the side and slammed the limo door open. He groaned. "I swear, I have to do everything myself."

The outside air smelled crisp and fresh, except for the faint smell of smoke. O'Reilly's eyes narrowed toward the front of the limo. Both of his henchmen were outside, staring at the burning wreckage that was once his prized limo.

"You imbeciles, what did you do to my limo?" he shouted, waving his hat in front of his face to clear the smoke.

"We didn't do anything, boss! Some big creature just came out of nowhere and smashed the front of your car!" Jaster replied. The other one just nodded, agreeing with his terrified friend.

Letting out a sigh of stress, O'Reilly rolled his eyes and crossed his arms. The two looked at each other in question, wondering what their boss was pondering.

"You really expect me to believe that some 'big creature' just jumped in front of the car and smashed it to smithereens, for no apparent reason?" he asked. "You two are...*morons!*"

O'Reilly angrily swung his cane at the two large men. They only cowered in fear and ran from his sharp swings. He went to smack Jaster across the head when he heard a sharp snap, like something large just crushed his car. He halted his moves, cane hovering in mid-air, as his eyes turned back toward his limo. His hands came slowly back down and his mouth was agape in terror.

With a slight "wow" escaping his lips, he stared at a strange, large shadow-like creature that had Robert, and the back half of his limo, in its mouth. Bright green eyes stared in his direction, the only illuminated part on the large black abyss hovering where he was standing only moments ago.

"Hey, boss! That thing's stealing the kid!" Jaster called, pointing out the obvious.

"I know," he replied quietly. "Let it go. We don't want him harmed. He's easy to track down. So, we'll let him get a head start for a couple of hours."

The three men watched as this strange monster carried their hostage away into the darkness. O'Reilly smirked and slapped his cane in his hand.

"Let the chase begin!" he shouted.

Chapter Twenty-one:

THE RESTLESS

MOONLIGHT SHOWERED THROUGH the high trees that towered above everything. It was late in the night, past midnight, and Kenny was growing bored just wandering through the forest. He was feeling ecstatic for having all of his energy back, and he was praying he would have the opportunity soon to thank Bloodwite for helping him. But at the moment, he had a bigger problem.

The green woman who was staring at him coldly, she had a smug look on her face and she was constantly studying his face. Her eyes met his, he tried to smile, but she just snarled angrily at him, like he had done something offensive. He looked off into the distance, watching some large elfin-like creatures wander around in front of what appeared to be a large gate. He was hiding in the shadows of an archway, where the green woman had told him to stay.

"Come," the woman snapped. She grabbed his hand and pulled him off toward a thicket outside of the small settlement. It looked like an ancient Indian building, made of clay with a wood roof, and it was covered in hieroglyphic like drawings. Kenny just followed, not feeling like arguing with her one bit. He was tired and just wanted to get to wherever she was taking him.

Kenny had regrets for a while after venturing off into the strange new area he now called home. He enjoyed the fresh air and the excitement, but most importantly the quality time he got to spend with Robert, like real brothers do during the summers on vacations. Everything, somehow, just seemed too magical when you were with a sibling, running around in a new area or fishing in the lake. Now, he just missed everything. He felt guilty for leaving it all behind.

"Where are we going?" Kenny finally asked. He kept his tone as low as a whisper to keep from being seen. She didn't respond. He sighed and continued walking. For a while, it seemed she was just taking him in circles. Everything started looking the same.

She's so pretty, he thought, smiling. He swallowed hard and tried to find some courage to ask her for a name, wanting to know all about this strange, mysterious woman. Unbeknownst to him, she wanted to ask him the same questions, but she was too conservative and unsure to speak.

"I'm Kenny," he said. *Smooth, idiot, real smooth.* He thought, rolling his eyes.

"Tooka," she snapped.

Kenny's eyes widened in shock. "Tooka, how pretty," he said, smiling. She chuckled and stopped. Kenny watched as she turned to face him, she grabbed the rims of his shirt, and tackled him into a large wall of ivy. Both fell through, leaving a large hole in the bush. The two began rolling down the hills below toward a stream, flattening everything in sight.

She's trying to kill me! Kenny thought, watching her smiling face rush around in his vision. After a moment they stopped. He let out a moan as he sat up. She got off of Kenny quickly and laughed. He stood and dusted himself off, watching as she followed and stretched.

"What was tha—" he began, but she stopped him by pressing her lips against his.

She pulled away quickly and pressed her finger against his mouth and gently uttered the word "quiet."

Kenny watched as she swung herself up onto a stone and pulled her leather boots off. She set them aside and patted the surface of the rock next to her. He nodded and sat down. He too removed his combat boots and socks and threw them onto the ground below. Every time he tried to speak she would hush him soothingly as he slid his feet into the pond. The water from the pond rushed against his tired feet. It was cold but refreshing and comforting in most ways.

"You should leave, go home," she said.

"I can't," he replied, staring at his reflection.

"You should continue your journey home, yes?" she asked, smiling.

Kenny listened to the swaying of the trees and the rushing of the water for a moment, letting the beauty of this place sink in. Tooka looked at him. She placed her hand on top of Kenny's and entwined her fingers with his. He blushed and looked at her kindly yet sadly, as if he wanted her to go on and continue comforting him.

"What's the point of traveling home through all the torture and heartache if, once you did finally get there, no one is standing on the porch to welcome you with open arms. To give you the comfort your heart has ached for so long to receive? Why should I go home, if it isn't even a home anymore?" he asked.

Tooka shrugged her shoulders and laid her head on his shoulder. *That was probably too in-depth for her to understand, she doesn't seem to speak English very well,* he thought.

"Stay with me then, yes?" she asked.

Kenny shook his head. "I can't do that either," he replied.

"Why?" she asked, looking up at him.

"I'm not like you. I'll probably get pummeled because I'm different."

Tooka sighed heavily and swung her legs up onto the platform. She backed away and turned around so her back was facing Kenny. He was in question.

Wait did she actually want me to stay? he asked himself, cocking his head gently to one side. He placed his hand on Tooka's shoulder and leaned in toward her, to make sure she was okay.

Tooka quickly spun around and kissed him. He went to recoil in fear but made himself stay put, realizing that this was all right, that it wasn't killing him to feel a little lustful about being with someone for the first time. He hadn't ever found someone who could tolerate his adventurous side, and it was nice to finally find a girl who was as crazy as he was.

Tooka pulled away and gently placed her hand on his cheek. He grasped her green pigmented hand in his own and smiled. Tears of joy slide down his dusty cheeks. He looked happy for a long time in some while. He embraced her in a gentle hug, wanting to feel comfort. She returned the hug, gently burying her face into his shoulder.

"I will protect you, yes?" she asked.

"You will? Yeah, you will," Kenny replied in a stutter.

Chapter Twenty-two:

THE PROPHECY

THE NEXT MORNING the sun was harshly blazing down onto everything, and the crisp smell of autumn showered the area in a heavy aura. Kenny buried his face into the warm, drool-soaked pillow under his pounding head. He curled up, shivering from a rush of cold air entering the room. His eye opened a bit to scan the surroundings. Tooka stood in the entry way, pulling back the brown-colored curtain that hid him from the outside.

"Five more minutes," he moaned, rolling over.

Tooka laughed and walked inside, her hands behind her back and a large smile on her face. She trekked over to him and pulled the blanket from his body. He rolled over and tried to snatch it from her, but she just pulled away. He rubbed his eyes.

"Come on, it's early!" he whined, reaching for it again.

"Come, we must hurry," she said smiling.

"Hurry, where?" Kenny asked, rubbing his eyes.

"She is waiting, yes?" Tooka replied.

She turned around and headed for the doorway, scanning everything outside. She turned back toward him and waved him out of the small house before she vanished. Kenny gasped and scrambled to his feet. *Dang, she's fast!* he thought, grinning as he skidded outside. He caught a mere glimpse of her before she darted off toward another area on the other side of the little wooden town.

Kenny hurried, hoping that he wouldn't be seen by anyone, and that he wouldn't lose track of Tooka in the huge city. The dirt was soft beneath him and the air was so fresh and wonderful, everything was at peace and not a thing was out of place. For once in quite a long time, he had a genuine smile on his face, and he felt like everything was all right. He ran behind a few buildings before he found Tooka again, hiding in the shadows of the archway he stood under last night. She waved him over to her side. Kenny sidled over to her and looked at her in question.

"Where are we going?" he asked.

Tooka hushed him and looked around the side of the building. Two guards were standing in front of an iron gate that sealed off a large temple-like building which was covered in red banners and flags.

"We're going...in there?" he asked, scanning the large temple.

Tooka nodded. "Yes," she replied before she darted off toward the guards.

Kenny watched as she sent them off in another direction. He guessed she had faked an accident somewhere else to get them to leave for a few moments. They listened to her, looking panicked, and hurriedly disappeared from the scene. She looked around carefully then waved Kenny into the light. He rushed to her side as fast as his feet would take him.

Tooka stuck the tip of her spear into the large lock and fiddled it around for a while, leaning in close to hear if it opened or not. She had obviously done this before as it opened almost instantly. She pushed it open a little bit and then grabbed Kenny's hand. Both entered and made their way toward the large staircase that stood before them. It was quiet inside and there were no people. Kenny became uncomfortable quickly, but Tooka provided reassurance and comfort with only her smile.

They headed up the stairs which seemed so large to Kenny. He was never one to like walking too much, and it bored him and tired him quickly, which usually resulted in whining or unnecessary sarcasm, which got him into many messes he rarely got out of without Robert's help. And Robert wasn't here right now. He needed to keep trouble to a minimum right now.

At the top of the stairs stood a large entryway which led into a dark hallway that housed very few lamps, all of them were currently un-lit. Both entered, and the moment they set foot inside, the doors behind closed and the flames burst on. Kenny jumped and grabbed onto Tooka's arm harshly, feeling quite scared. He could feel Tooka's body tense too, which came as a surprise to him. He never would have thought that she would be frightened so easily.

"Don't scare me!" Tooka giggled.

Kenny chuckled. "Sorry it won't happen again."

"Come," she whispered as she pulled him down the hallway.

Kenny heard music echoing from every angle. People were talking, and it sounded so vague and scratchy. Water bounced from the walls onto the floor, and his footsteps even made him jump. The voices grew louder and louder for a moment, until it sounded like screaming.

Kenny slammed his hands over his ears and wobbled around for a moment. Tooka looked back at him in wonder. She couldn't hear the voices calling out to him, and she wondered why he was panicking.

"Kenny, Kenny!" she shouted, reaching out to him. He fell to the ground, the noises growing louder and louder until Kenny's ears started ringing. He couldn't hear anything but a horrid buzzing sound from every direction. He screamed in pain, eyes wide in fear. *Dragging me down, crushing my thoughts. It hurts, it hurts so badly!*

Kenny screamed loudly, body trembling. Tooka kneeled down next to him and placed her hand on his head. He looked up, breathing heavily. She held him close and waited for him to calm himself a bit before she helped him stand.

"Tooka, they're gone now, I'm okay," Kenny said quietly.

The voices had stopped once again and everything was as it had been. He laughed a bit and rubbed the back of his head.

"S-sorry, that just happens sometimes. I don't know why," he said smiling. Tooka kissed his cheek and embraced him, rubbing his back gently. He held her and breathed in slowly, his hot breath dancing across her head.

"Come," she said again, grabbing his hand. She pulled him down the hallway, slowly, as he still couldn't stand without falling over.

They walked for a long time until they came to a series of doors. The one standing at the end of the room was large and painted like the one in his house. The two entered, blinded by the light from inside. Kenny shielded his tender eyes from the blinding aura and wandered into the round room. His eyes reopened, only to be paralyzed that way from the majestic beauty on the inside.

The room was lush with large bushes. It was covered with a damp fog and snow. Above, the ceiling was painted like a cloudy winter's dawn, stars slowly flickering like they would outside. In the far end of the room stood a stained glass window, depicting a young boy with black hair. In the center of a circle of bushes sat a woman. She was draped in a fur coat, her face was a slight blue-gray tint and her skin was wrinkled. Her eyelashes were long and thick, covered with small chips of ice. In her hands was a large rod, carved with pictures of small bugs. Set in two rows, lighting the short pathway over to her, stood tall lanterns that blew mass furies of heat at Kenny.

"Grandmother, I brought him for you," Tooka said, stepping down into the area below.

Grandmother, that's her grandmother? Kenny questioned, watching as Tooka looked at him. *Why does she want to see me?*

She waved him down into the area, signaling it was okay. He followed slowly, still in awe of the mysterious beauty of the place.

"Why look so surprised, my boy?" her grandmother asked. Kenny looked at her, and she looked back.

"Child of the humans, please come and sit in front of me. I

am Rui," she said, waving him toward the area before her. He nodded and sat down, bowing slightly. She laughed and smiled. "Dear child, my granddaughter tells me you have journeyed far to reach this place. Why?" she asked.

Kenny swallowed. "I...I was looking for something. The Grave of the Fireflies, I wasn't trying to steal it, but something terrible was happening, and I needed the gold to help—"

"Your friend, the one you call Robert," Rui said, cutting him off.

Kenny's eyes widened. "How, but how did you know?"

"I know all about you, child. You and your incredible, heart-wrenching journey here."

Rui waved her wrinkled hand in front of her. The water began to swivel and change. Kenny jumped a bit, watching closely at how the water at his feet swarmed around the stone lining. In that very shallow pond the vision of O'Reilly appeared. Kenny watched as a scene of a large shadow creature holding Robert in its mouth. Tooka looked at him in worry, and she grabbed his hand. He clenched it tightly, watching in fear and question.

"What is that?" he asked.

"One of my guardians. I sent him to save your friend from the monster known as O'Reilly," She replied. "He is safe."

"But O'Reilly will just find him again! He just can't keep avoiding all these problems! You've got to keep him safe. If you did it before, why don't you just bring him here?" Kenny spat.

"We cannot escape a destiny that was foretold before even I came to walk this land. I only saved him due to the fact his time has not yet come," she replied. "But for me to keep altering the future, it would be changing the lives of innocents not even involved in your problem. And I don't expect you to repent for sins of people other than you."

"Those sins, I can't do anything to repay for the ones I've already committed, the ones that are hurting him, can I? I'm not allowed to help him? I'm not allowed to try and help clear up these problems I've caused?" Kenny asked, looking at her.

"I have never tried, but it is possible, child. That is all I can speak of on that matter. Now, you say you seek the Grave of the Fireflies, yet do you even know how to reach it?"

Kenny shook his head in response, wondering where this conversation was going, and at times wondering if she was just toying with his mind and not really helping him.

"There is a prophecy, one that tells of the heir to our throne. The one with the all seeing eyes. It was once said, many eons ago, that our eighteenth heir in the bloodline of the ancestor who destroyed the Gohma, the family known as Uty, great descendant of the warrior we called M'nep, would be lost at a young age, vanishing into a rain-tattered sky one night, never to return. This child, if his blood should be spilled across the door, then and only then, deep into the night, the Grave shall be revealed.

"But that is only what had been said before. It is true that the child was lost on one rainy night and never returned. The bodies of the king and queen were found, but the boy was gone. But I do not believe in such a childish tale, the heir could never have enough power to undo the locks that Lord M'nep had placed on the Grave's door," she explained.

"So, you're saying I should just give up?" Kenny asked.

Tooka looked at him. She didn't want him to give up everything he had journeyed for, but she was hopeful that he may stay with her now. Kenny was perspiring from anger. His body was drenched in sweat due to the heavy flames surrounding him. His eyes bounced back and forth as he tried to gain a good focus on everything through the tears. The voices began to return, and they were growing louder and louder. Kenny listened for a moment before he began to feel strain again.

"Ah, the ancients speak highly of you," she said smiling. "They must be tearing you apart with their words, right child? You should listen to them, they may help you."

Kenny nodded. He grabbed his head and closed his eyes. He felt lightheaded again, trying to concentrate as best he could on everything.

"How do I listen to them? They don't even speak clearly," Kenny replied.

"Or your ears are not accustomed to their words. You are

untrained in our language. Give them time," Rui replied. Tooka placed her hands on his shoulder and looked at her grandmother.

"Why do they hurt him?" she asked.

"Child, they are trying to tell him something, something of great importance, yet he cannot understand them. His mind is concentrating on trying to hear their words clearly, while his heart already knows. There is great conflict in his body which will, slowly break him unless he opens up to them," she explained. Tooka's eyes widened and she held onto Kenny tightly and rubbed his head, his sweat-soaked hair weaving in between her fingers.

Tooka kissed his sweaty head and held onto him.

"All right?" she asked.

Her grandmother nodded. "Yes, he will be all right, but he will need time to recover. Invasions of the body are always the worst for humans, especially when the invasion is of our kind. A good few weeks of—"

"I don't have time to mess around," Kenny snapped. He looked at her sternly yet groggily and breathed in heavily. She raised an eyebrow in question, smirking slightly at his ambition. *The Lord Bloodwite was right; he is determined.*

"I only have seven days left before it's all over! I don't want to just give up, not without a fight, no way!" he spat. He grabbed his head and moaned loudly. He stood up, shook the grogginess from his mind, and began to walk off. Tooka went to follow him when her grandmother cleared her throat. She looked back at her elderly grandmother and waited for an answer as to why she was halted, Kenny already halfway to the door.

"Why?" Tooka asked.

"If his mind was set on this, you could change that opinion, but I feel his heart is the reason for this. The heart cannot be moved from its choice. It can be reversed in ways to help and or destroy, but it can never be changed. Do not try and halt him," she replied, watching as Kenny vanished behind the door. Tooka waited for a moment before standing anyway. She clenched her fists angrily and sighed heavily.

"You say his heart cannot be changed. Then neither will mine," Tooka said. She smiled a bit and rushed off toward Kenny. Completely ignoring her grandmother's words of wisdom. Her heart was determined on staying with Kenny. And Rui said nothing to stop her, destiny foretold this, and she was ready to embrace the fact her granddaughter was growing into an independent woman.

She eventually caught up to Kenny and grabbed his arm. He looked back at her in shock, his mouth open as he readied to speak. Tooka placed her finger on his lips and smiled. That was all Kenny needed. He knew that she wasn't going to leave, and that she would see this journey through to the end with him.

It felt wonderful, confusing, and intriguing all at the same time. It sent chills up his spine. He smiled and wrapped his arm around Tooka. He lifted her off of the ground and spun around in circles, a smile on his face.

"I knew you wouldn't leave me!" he shouted with a laugh.

She looked down at him and giggled. "I will always stand beside you, because you can't make it alone," she replied.

"Thank you," he whispered kindly.

Kenny smiled as he set her back onto solid ground. She tilted her head to the side in wonder, as if to ask "what now". He grabbed her hand and began to run off toward the entrance. Tooka laughed and ran with him, a blissful feeling ran from his finger tips to hers. Both felt alive for the first time, and Kenny felt reassured, realizing that everything might turn out all right after all.

Chapter Twenty-three:

THE FOREST OF WOE

KENNY AND TOOKA rode upon the backs of two strange lizard creatures that Kenny had never seen before, like scaly horses. They stood on their hind legs and ran as fast as a cheetah would. Tooka rode proudly, as she was used to it, but Kenny was sliding off of it, and it, whatever it was, didn't seem to like him much. He held onto the rims of the harness for dear life and followed behind Tooka through a musty forest setting.

A thick storm had rolled in, and rain was tumbling down upon them again. The sky seemed so far, hiding above the large leaves and trunks of the trees. A thick layer of fog was as high as the thighs of the creature's long, inverted legs, and their chicken-like feet left large tracks behind them in the mud.

Kenny felt sick and tired, as if the energy had been drained from his body the moment the rain started to pour in. He felt sorrowful too. He wanted to just break down and cry for a few moments.

"All right, Kenny?" Tooka asked.

"Yeah, I'm all right. I just feel depressed," Kenny replied.

Tooka made a clicking noise with her tongue and the two lizards started to speed up. Kenny grabbed the harness tightly and leaned inward toward the lizard's neck, its furry mane brushing against his face.

"Hold on, rain is getting too heavy. We must find shelter," Tooka said over the loud crash of thunder.

The lizards jumped and began to speed up. A few times the lizards slipped and almost came crashing down onto the muddy canvass beneath. It appeared they weren't overly good at running atop layers of slick mud. Kenny watched as Tooka became engulfed in the fog and soon her voice became distant.

"Tooka, Tooka!" Kenny shouted. "You have to stay close to me!"

He looked around, the lizard still speeding off into the distance. It apparently and luckily seemed to know where it was going, unlike Kenny. The rain droplets became large and most hurt upon impact. Lighting struck down onto the ground next to him multiple times. Thunder rolled through the air and the sound of Kenny's screaming became suppressed by the nature's melody.

A bolt of lightning shot down onto the ground next to the lizard. It became startled and jumped. Kenny grabbed onto the harness tightly, trying hard to stay upright. It bucked and kicked and screeched as it tried to pry Kenny from its grip.

Please stop, please stop! Kenny thought, burying his face into the mane of the lizard. The wind blew the brown, brush-like fur awkwardly around his face. The setting brought him back to distant memories, nights like this were the nights Robert had quietly told stories of magical places when he couldn't sleep. But even with Robert's fables, the times that scared him the most were the ones he could never escape from. He never understood why his memory only consisted of dark thoughts and terrifying things when he was younger. The black velvet blanket that consumed his mind on those rainy nights was supposed to scare him, but just looking at the petrified face of Robert made him realize he had to be the brave one to be able to take care of his scared friend.

The rain sort of brought him toward the night of the car accident too, the setting of the lizard dashing off and his vision blinded by the rain, the fear of being knocked off or hurt. That was what pulled him toward the edge again. Kenny never questioned how his parents had died or why he was living with Robert and his mother for almost all of his life, mainly because he had amnesia, but it never came to him as weird either. He was just happy being with Robert. The big brother that would care for him was something he always wondered if he ever dreamed of before that night.

Another crash of lightning brought him back into reality. The heavy sound of stomping feet and roaring people caught Kenny's attention. A spear was shot in his direction. More and more appeared until he was almost surrounded on all sides by the wooden weapons.

The lizard finally lost it and sent Kenny flying off toward a shallow pond in the distance. He skidded across the muddy ground for a moment before coming to a halt near a pile of rocks. He looked up at the pack of riding lizards dashing off into the distance toward where Tooka had vanished.

Kenny's lizard dashed over to him and gently pressed its nose against his arm, trying to see if he was all right. His eyes remained closed though for quite a while before he grabbed the harness. The lizard didn't budge when he used its large body to pull himself up. He struggled to gain a good footing but kept slipping, realizing he had stunned his leg from landing wrong.

"Help me," Kenny whispered. He wrapped the leather harness around his hand and looked up at the odd creature. It began to pull him off toward a large willow that had a small hole in it, dragging him through the mud and rocks as it went. *Dang, this is not a good time for my leg to give out! Come on, you've run track and field with a busted up knee, this is nothing!* Kenny thought, swallowing. He was drenched in mud, water, and clusters of weeds by the time he and the creature reached the tree. It drug him inside, he unwrapped the harness, and let himself fall to the floor. His water-soaked eyes looked up at the creature.

"Find Tooka!" he shouted. The creature sniffed his hair, apparently not understanding what Kenny had ordered. He waved his hand in front of its face and grabbed its harness tightly, bringing it nose to nose with him. Its big eyes looked at him, scanning every detail on his body.

"Go find Tooka!" he shouted again, hissing loudly. It screeched and shook its head, trying to get free of his tight grip again. Kenny thought for a moment and tried to make the clicking sound with his tongue that Tooka had been doing, hoping he could communicate with it. Its eyes widened a bit and it screeched.

Did I say something? He asked himself, blinking a few times. He watched as it bit its large side bag until it came undone. It fell to the floor, revealing a pack of arrows and a finely crafted bow. *Not exactly what I was asking for, but it works!* he thought, petting the lizard's face.

Kenny smiled, he slid the sheath of arrows onto his back, the finely crafted weapons were surprisingly heavy and brought pressure to his spine but he refused to quit. He grabbed the bow and used his good leg to climb onto the riding lizard's back. Shaking his bad leg in attempt to wake it up, he clicked his tongue and kicked the lizard's side with his good leg, the creature darted off into the rain storm. Kenny brought an arrow from the pack and slid it into place, his eyes fixed on a looming shadow in the distance. *Come on, make those lessons pay off,* he thought, swallowing. He readied the bow, targeted the spear in the man's hands, and shot.

The arrow skimmed through the rain, and the sound of the wind rushing around it was steady and then there came a sound of a man letting out a yelp of terror. A spear went flying, and the man was knocked off his lizard. Kenny readied another arrow and turned around, making the lizard turn around with him. He and the creature were perfectly in sync now, and every movement Kenny made it could read and comprehend. He let the arrow fly. He heard another scream as he readied another arrow, nailing yet another victim precisely.

There sure are a lot of them. Where do they keep coming from? Kenny thought as his eyes shot up to the sky. A blurry shadow consumed his vision, and before he knew it, he was knocked to the ground and pinned there by someone's foot. The bow slid from his hand and the arrows were spilled around him. The man held a spear to his neck and readied an attack. He heard another screech and a blur of black knocked the man away. He scrambled to the bow and readied another arrow.

The water in his eyes made it hard to see who was who. He recognized Tooka's voice, so he knew one of them was her, but he wasn't sure which one he should fire at. His hand bounced, and he tried to concentrate on the man, but it was too hard to see.

"Tooka, move it!" Kenny shouted. A shadow bounced away, and Kenny fired and saw a shadow fall to the ground. And then no other attacks came toward him. *Did I get them all? I hope so. I'm running out of arrows.*

Another blurry outline appeared and Tooka became visible soon after. She extended her hand to him. He happily grabbed it and pulled himself up. The riding lizard trotted over to him and shook its harness in his direction. He used it to stand, with a smile he burst out into a fit of laughter and pulled himself onto the lizard again. He extended his hand for Tooka to help her back onto the high sitting saddle. She took it and jumped up onto its back.

"Brave warrior, you are," Tooka said smiling, wrapping her arms around Kenny's stomach.

Kenny laughed. "Nah, I was just shooting arrows," he replied, handing Tooka the bow and arrow set. He grabbed onto the harness again, kicked the side of the lizard, and headed out toward what he believed to be north.

"Where to?" he asked, watching as Tooka wrapped the sheath strap around herself. She grabbed onto him and pointed off toward a large tree in the distance. Kenny nodded and told the lizard to head off into the rainy atmosphere ahead.

Chapter Twenty-four:
THE DEATH TRAP

THE RAIN LET up a small bit, and the weather drastically changed from a rainy, foggy atmosphere to a hot, fiery-like one, in an area filled with streams of lava. *Man, this place just keeps getting weirder and weirder!* Kenny dismounted the lizard with very little grace. He was in awe over the odd, scary area and forgot he couldn't stand very well. He fell to the ground, landing in a puddle of steaming hot water. Tooka laughed and got off of the lizard. She patted its face and walked over to Kenny.

He burst from the pond and shook his face. He was drenched in sweat thoroughly and was overheating. Tooka, on the other hand, was perfectly fine and comfortable.

"How can you stand this heat? You're not normal!" Kenny spat, eyes wide in question.

"This is like typical summer for me. Nothing," she replied, staring off into the wasteland ahead. Her eyes gazed back down to him, and with a bit of discouragement she spoke, "You cannot walk?"

Kenny looked at her apologetically and shook his head. "No,

I can walk. It's just numb from landing on it wrong. I should be ok in a while."

Tooka immediately brought the lizard to him and made him ride. He went to argue, but she gave him a cold look and he stopped. He mounted the lizard and waited for the rest of the heated area to come at him head on. Tooka grabbed the reigns and began to lead them all into the barren land.

Kenny pulled his white t-shirt off, revealing a sweat-stained tank, and used it to wipe the sweat and grime from his forehead. He gazed around for a moment before he searched through his jean pockets. He didn't want to lug unnecessary items around anymore, so he decided to search for anything of use and then toss the rest into the fire.

"Watch, wallet, cell phone...cell phone? Wait, where'd it go?" Kenny shouted, searching through his pockets. Tooka looked at him in worry. *It's gone! Robert's cell phone is gone!* He swallowed heavily in worry. *He may have tried to call me, and I couldn't have answered, he's probably ticked.* He bundled up what he didn't need in his t-shirt and tossed it all into a pit of lava. Then, he rang the sweat from his tank-top and sighed heavily in exhaustion.

Tooka stopped, her worried eyes gazed at him, but he just smiled in reply, not sparing a glance to her.

"Everything's fine, let's go," Kenny said. Tooka nodded and continued to walk. The horizon waved furiously in front of them, nothing but pits of lava and rocks were to be seen. A few large, elephant-like skulls were placed around the dirt paths along with some large rib cages and spines, but they were so ancient and were on the verge of falling apart he couldn't make out what they were exactly. Kenny gazed across the land warily, feeling a deep sense of insecurity running through his body. He sighed heavily and yawned after, feeling very bored from riding for what seemed like a long time.

"Tooka, if...if I do find the Grave and somehow I can't go home will...will you stay with me?" Kenny asked. Tooka stopped. Her eyes widened a bit and slowly gazed over to him. *I blew it, figures.* Kenny thought. *The first girl that actually thinks I'm not a loser and I blow it sky high! You should've just kept your big mouth shut, you idiot, you pathetic ...*

"Could I?" she asked.

His eyes widened in shock, tears almost swelled in his eyes. He cleared his throat. "I mean if you want to, I mean I barely know you, but I'd like to, you know, get to know you better," he said, looking away, mumbling his words a bit.

Tooka nodded in reply and quickly walked in front of the lizard to shield herself from Kenny's view. He gazed around the long neck of the lizard, trying to see her, but she jumped away onto the other side. He looked around the right side, and she moved away again. Kenny suddenly let his shoulders sag and let his head hang down.

"And this, Robert, is he not the one you are wanting?" she spat.

"Huh? N-no way, it's nothing like that!" Kenny shouted, almost falling off of the lizard. "No, he's my brother! I'm just worried he's in trouble, we're like family, and I couldn't live with myself if something happened to him. You're crazy to think of our relationship as *that* type!"

Tooka gave him a cocky look. He snarled and turned his head away angrily. *She probably doesn't get the whole brotherly relationship thing. She doesn't seem to have a big family or anybody around all the time like I have Robby.*

The streams of fire were growing larger and the land became scarce. Tooka wandered carefully around the area, making sure to choose pathways that would be wide enough for the large lizard. Kenny was still angry that he couldn't get Tooka to understand, but he couldn't do anything to make her understand at the moment. He probably needed to actually show her to Robert for her to understand.

"I'm sorry! Say something, will you?" Kenny spat.

Tooka raised her hand to silence him and pulled the lizard off behind a large rock to hide them from view.

Kenny looked at her. "What's going on?" he asked. Tooka pressed her finger against his lips and looked over a large rock. She showed him a blurry outline of something running through the heat waves. It looked like a giant mammoth that appeared to be hovering across the land. Kenny stepped down off of the lizard.

"We must run," Tooka said warily.

"What about this thing?" Kenny asked, pointing to the lizard. It shook its head in confusion and licked Kenny's cheek. He patted its head and continued to look at Tooka.

"It can find its way back home, but we cannot stand the chance of being seen by it. That creature could kill us," Tooka replied. She stood and darted off toward the shadows of a bigger pillar that formed a large curve, pointing off into the distance.

Kenny patted the lizard's head. "Be safe, okay?" he said kindly.

And with that, he darted off, following Tooka into the heat waves. He stumbled around some large pillars, trying to keep up with Tooka's catlike reflexes. He kept losing his footing because of his injured leg. It was better, but every now and again he stepped down wrong and lost his footing. Tooka kept urging him toward her, but every time he caught up to her, she ran off in a new direction.

Tooka led him in circles it seemed. Lost in the heat waves and the fog, Kenny was standing oblivious to his surroundings, searching for Tooka with hazy vision. *I lost her,* he thought. *This isn't good.*

A shadow soon towered above him, changing shape and position in the rolling heat waves.

"Not good!" he whispered, moving scared eyes up above him. The large mammoth now towered over Kenny; its eyes were ablaze in a red mass of fury. He stared up at it, and he was drenched immediately in sweat from fear and his body was locking up on him. It was an out-matched version of David and Goliath, and he didn't have a slingshot. Tooka stared at him. She had left all her weaponry in the side saddles of the riding lizard, and she couldn't help Kenny in any way against the huge monster.

It reared back on its hind legs and roared loudly. Kenny watched in fear as it came barreling down onto him. The large shadow loomed over him until he was blinded by darkness. He felt his body shoot through the air then across the rocky canvass of earth. He felt heat grow on his finger tip for a moment before something tugged on his body.

His weak eyes opened only to see his hand almost in a stream of lava, his eyes then wandered over to Tooka, who was pulling him away, trying to get him away from the large mammoth. He landed hard on the rocks, and it was taking a while for him to recover his balance.

"Tooka, go on," Kenny said, looking at her.

She shook her head and continued to pull on him, his body was too heavy for her, even with as strong as she was. His body drug across the ground as Tooka pulled him along the rocky floor. The mammoth loomed over them again, and both of their eyes gazed up in its direction.

"I'll catch up, go, now!" Kenny shouted. Tooka's eyes filled with worry as she stared off behind Kenny toward the river of flowing lava. His eyes too began to wander in that direction. Not too far away from them, wisps of lava grew from the rivers beneath, creating a massive heat wave. The dragon-like flame bursts rapidly shot down onto the ground near the mammoth's feet, one by one pushing him back further and further until it was standing feet away, unable to catch up to the two.

Kenny and Tooka took this chance to try and escape. Kenny was far behind her as he wasn't as fast in these conditions as she was, and he was afraid of losing her in the fog. The lava streams grew out of control and started shooting off in multiple directions around the area.

Tooka led Kenny to the deeper crevasses that weaved in and out of the canyon, lava streams shooting down onto everything, completely out of control. A rain of fire showered from the sky, leaving large craters in the ground upon the heavy impact. Tooka weaved in and out of them rapidly, Kenny fumbling behind, constantly losing his balance.

One, large and swift stream of fire shot down onto the ground near Kenny. As it hit the floor, bubbles of lava spewed in every direction around him. He barely dodged them. Tooka was too far ahead to realize he was in danger.

Another blast shot down next to him. It scorched his pant leg, setting it ablaze. He let out a cry of terror and tumbled to the ground, trying to put himself out. He rolled down a few hills into a large crater that housed many levels. The ones beneath were slowly filling with lava, and he couldn't stop himself.

Why me? Kenny questioned, trying to stop his body from rolling to its doom.

"Tooka help!" Kenny shouted. He gazed around above him, trying to see where he was. The lava was growing higher, and Kenny grabbed onto a large stone that was towering above his head and began to try and pull his weak body up onto higher ground, or at least onto its surface to keep from burning. He groaned a bit as his foot slipped from the wall, rocks pouring down into the rising lava, and they instantly went ablaze.

"T-Tooka...Help me!" Kenny shouted. His hand slipped from the wall, and he felt his body slowly fall down toward the lava. He closed his eyes and prayed for a miracle as he awaited the heavy flames to surround his body. Then they didn't. Kenny's eyes opened and he looked up, seeing Tooka holding onto his hand. She smiled and pulled him up onto the ledge slowly. Kenny groaned as he felt his arm slip from her grasp.

Tooka grabbed him tighter and tried again to get him to safety. Kenny helped as best he could, and with each other's strength aiding them, they somehow made it. Tooka grabbed onto Kenny and held him tightly, not wanting to ever let go again. Kenny held her for a moment before another blast of fire struck the ground next to them. Kenny jumped and rolled out of the way.

"Congratulations later, now we need to move!" Kenny screamed. Tooka nodded as both stood up. More blasts of fire were sent flying toward the two of them. Kenny pulled her along, downhill at a rate faster than he could actually go without falling over. The two tripped and rolled down a large hill toward a small cavern.

They tumbled down, feeling the lava waves surround them in heavy numbers. But then it all stopped. The two had made it into the cavern, and for the moment, both were safe. Kenny ended up on top of Tooka, breathing heavily in utter fear and relief that he actually made it. He giggled in joy. *I'm alive!* he thought.

Tooka shoved Kenny's heavy body off of her, beings he wasn't moving any time soon. She smacked him gently in the back of the head.

"You were crushing me!" she snapped.

He laughed and looked at her apologetically. "Sorry" he replied.

She stood up and waved him down into the darkness. He moaned. He wanted to finish basking in his dumb luck, but apparently Tooka wasn't going to let him stop. So he stood, stretched, dusted himself off, and followed her. The light from the outside slowly disintegrated the further down they went. The sounds of lava smashing down onto the roof filled the catacombs with heavy noise and fear.

"Hey, Tooka, I...Ugh!" Kenny suddenly felt a sharp pain on his temples. He grabbed his head and dropped to his knees. *Oh, shoot! That hurts...what the heck?* Tooka ran over to him, she rubbed his head gently for a few moments, and then she gasped. He let out a yelp and grabbed the back of his head, hissing in pain.

"Big bump, it's bruised," Tooka said. "Feel dizzy?"

Kenny nodded and rubbed the bump on the back of his head. He felt a scab he hadn't ever noticed before. *Oh, that's from the bookshelf incident. No wonder it hurts. I got smacked hard there.*

Tooka let Kenny lie down on a patch of leaves she found and carefully looked at his head. His eyes were closed lightly and his fingers kept pressing against the bump on his head to try and lighten the pressure. He had a migraine to end all migraines, and he was beginning to feel light headed.

"Kenny," Tooka whispered, gently rocking his body. He didn't respond, he could but he spent most of his energy trying to resist screaming from the pain. He just grabbed her arm and held onto it tightly, not letting go for any reason. Tooka placed her hand on his and brushed back his bangs a small bit, watching as his eyelids slowly loosened up and opened. He gazed at the blurry outline of Tooka then closed them again, feeling tired.

"My head really hurts!" he moaned.

"Rest, we will go on in a—" Tooka began, but Kenny raised his hand to silence her.

"Now, we go now, I just need to block it out. I'll be okay!" he said, even though he was lying. Tooka could clearly see he wasn't feeling the greatest right now.

"No, we mustn't!" she replied. Her eyes began to fill with tears, and she pulled a few purple leaves from the plant Kenny was lying on and placed them on his head, knowing that this special plant could help them heal a bit quicker. Kenny smiled and grabbed her hand to stop her. He smiled and rolled onto his back, raising an eyebrow in question as if to ask how long she will ignore him. He pulled her close and kissed her for a moment until he sat up fully. She ran her fingers across his chest and looked at his cuts and bruises as he smiled a bit.

"You amaze me," Tooka said quietly. "You must really be close to go through all this for him."

"He means a lot to me, sure...but so do you," Kenny finished in a whisper, so quiet she could barely hear him.

Tooka kissed him again. His eyes closed a bit as she wrapped one arm around his back, the other around his head. He winced in pain and she pulled away, watching as Kenny screamed. And then he laughed.

"Oh man that hurts!" he cried out. His vision became blurry for a moment and there was a ringing in his ears.

"We have to go on," Kenny moaned.

"Not yet, we can wait, at least sleep for a few hours," Tooka replied.

Kenny laughed a small bit and nodded, not wanting to agree, but he knew he had no other choice but to listen to her. He waited for the stinging to stop, staring blankly off into the distance where red shimmers caught his eye. It was like a blanket of rubies basking in the shallow sunlight that was seeping through some cracks in the ceiling. It reminded him of the rubies in the house, and then his mind crept back to that distant vision of Robert lying unconscious somewhere. He prayed somehow he managed to be all right, but then where, after that creature Rui had sent after him, could he have gone in that state? It was almost hopeless to think that he may still be alive.

"Hey, Tooka, can I ask you something?" Kenny started.

"Yes, Kenny?" she replied.

"Where do I go after this?" he asked.

"What do you mean?"

"When I find the Grave...if I find it, where do I go after that? I don't have a home to go to, and no one is going to be waiting for me, and even if he is, he won't be the same. This probably had damaged him emotionally, and I'm not sure he'll be Robert anymore."

Tooka laughed a bit and lied down next to him. His eyes met hers and a smile crept across his face. She grabbed his hand and laughed some more.

"Stay with me?" she asked. Kenny smiled and nodded, burying his face into the leaves.

"I'll stay," he replied, closing his eyes. Tooka placed her hand on his head and moved over a bit onto another large patch of leaves. She watched him doze off for a moment before he started snoring, rubbing his eyes unexpectedly for no reason as if he had something in them. She continued to watch him for a while, amazed at every detail on his face that differed from her own.

"I'm glad," Tooka said, "so very glad I found you."

Chapter Twenty-five:

THE LABYRINTH

USING TOOKA'S HAND as his only guide in the dark cavern, Kenny wandered with her down the musty old cave's main hallway. It was a tight fit; both of them felt the walls on either side of them. Their hands clenching together tightly was their only sense of security and sight. Somewhere far in the distance you could hear water bouncing from one rock to the next, and you could hear a roar from a mighty beast high above. Beneath him, Kenny could hear the heels of his combat boots clunking against the steel like surface of the floor, and sweat from his forehead slowly dripping off of his body onto the ground.

Echoes of different things could be heard all around. Kenny felt so enlightened for a while, and everything was slowly becoming clear with every second he spent in this odd area, almost like this place was his window to the truth.

He wondered if it was his flesh against Tooka's that did it. She seemed to be so free willed, and it looked as if she could sense things he couldn't. She knew the things he didn't understand. He liked the freedom of knowing what was around him all the time, and he didn't feel as scared.

"Oh man I'm so hungry!" Kenny moaned, realizing he hadn't eaten for quite a while. Tooka laughed a bit and pointed for him to sit down on a rock. He looked at her in wonder for a moment as she began to look through her many pockets for something as he made his way to the rock. Eventually she pulled out a packet and opened it.

"Hungry?" she asked. Kenny nodded, his face ablaze in joy from the thought of eating something. He was famished.

Tooka began to pull something from the packet, and Kenny was growing more anxious with every passing moment. *Oh, sweet food*, Kenny thought, staring at Tooka. *Wonderful, glorious foo—*

His thoughts were cut short as Tooka handed him some sort of small beetle as if she were offering food to him. And his face morphed to one of disgust. He jumped back in fear and fell to the ground; he stuck his tongue out in disgust.

"Food, eat," Tooka said, extending her hand to him again.

Kenny shook his head. "N-no way! That's so gross, are you crazy?" he spat.

Tooka laughed a bit and smile at him before she swallowed the thing whole. Kenny watched in fear, turning paler and paler every second. After, she slapped her hands together and smiled.

I think I'm going to be sick, Kenny thought, pressing his hand against his mouth.

"Eat head first, know which way to go, swallow easier," Tooka said.

Kenny wriggled in fear, shaking his head violently in disagreement. Tooka handed him the bag again, and he went to protest when she leaned in toward him. Her eyes locked with his, chills were sent up his spine the moment she gave him that look.

"Okay, okay," Kenny said quietly. He grabbed the bag and went to eat one of the slimy silver bugs when an explosion was triggered. Kenny's head shot up toward the ceiling. Tooka swiftly pulled him to his feet, pulled him down the corridor, and began to make their way deeper into the cavern.

Man, this place is dangerous, Kenny thought, gazing around the area slowly. He stared at the ceiling, wondering what exactly was going on up there. It seemed odd to have so many explosions for no apparent reason. It almost appeared as though the lava had a mind of its own, and in rage it burst into the air like fireworks.

"Swim," Tooka said.

Kenny snapped out of his thoughts and looked at Tooka. "Huh?" he asked. Kenny blinked a few times and leaned to his right, staring around Tooka's side into the distance. He now saw a large pond sitting ahead of his feet. His eyes wandered back to Tooka, and she smirked a bit. He laughed and shrugged his shoulders, wondering what she was planning on doing now.

"Can you?" she asked.

"Can I what?" he replied.

"Swim," she stated, pointing to the bubbling water in front of him.

"You don't think I can do it!" he spat, smiling widely.

Tooka shrugged her shoulders and smirked. Kenny looked at her as she took her boots off, and in a split second she dived into the water. Kenny stumbled a bit in shock. She hadn't even warned him that she was heading out. He tumbled face first into the pond, ungracefully. Water gushed up his nostrils as he floated back to the surface. The red tinted liquid was warm and murky like a hot spring. He floated around a bit and searched for Tooka. The intensity of the heat almost took his breath away.

Kenny felt something tap on his shoulder, and he saw Tooka behind him, but she quickly swam away. He rushed after her, not knowing how long he could hold his breath down there, but he had to hurry or he'd lose her in the shimmering heat waves.

She's fast! Man for once I'd like to lead! Kenny thought as he swam under a large rock that had sprung from the wall, and over time had become jagged. Her body was vanishing with the heat waves ahead, so he tried to gain some speed, feeling like he was losing his breath. The water pulled him down fast, like a whirlpool was forming beneath him. He felt the water swarm around his body as he was dragged down into the heat.

All of his breath burst from his lips, he gasped heavily, only to have his lungs become filled with water. He closed his eyes, trying to get some of the water out of them. His body flipped and tumbled around until he felt something grab onto him. He let it pull him deeper into the darkness until the rushing of the waves halted. He knew that Tooka had come back for him. He opened his eyes, catching a blurry glimpse of her in front of him, and followed her to the surface.

Kenny burst from the water, and Tooka followed. Both grabbed onto the nearby, newly discovered floor, which was nothing but soft sand, to keep their tired bodies above water. Kenny let his body float in the pond, using two larges weeds to keep himself upright.

"Nice job," Tooka said cockily.

"You didn't say the water was boiling," Kenny replied in the same smug tone. He hacked up some water and opened his eyes. They widened in shock once he saw where they had emerged. In front of him, made of manila-colored stone, was a large maze. The door was sealed by chains that, over time, had rusted and become frail, but they still stood proudly. All around him stood trees, and growing from the sand was a field of white and yellow flowers. They bloomed fully, and the smell of spring filled the air.

"Holy crap, look at this place!" Kenny shouted, pulling himself up.

"How beautiful! So this is what it is like," Tooka said, smiling as she stood. Her wet legs became covered in sand as they brushed against the ground. She helped Kenny up and walked out toward the large maze ahead.

It towered forty feet above her. It looked quite confusing, and it seemed to draw her in toward it. Kenny walked behind her, looking in awe at the large monument. It was unlike anything he had ever seen before. Even with how old and decrepit it was, it was beautiful and mysterious.

"This is the tomb of the three kings, still standing proudly," Tooka said. Kenny looked at her.

"What?" he asked.

"This is the tomb of the three kings," She repeated. "Here is where it was said that our ancestors, the ones that followed the ancient warrior, the one named M'nep, were buried when they died. Fireflood, Bloodwite, and Blueweed, the entities of the fire, earth, and water of our land. They kept our world full of beauty and power. They were so powerful and graceful. They used to be the protectors of this forest when the Gohma began to attack us many years ago.

"This was built to honor those warriors who died to save our kind from the wickedness of the humans who tried to take the belongings of the Grave away," Tooka said. Kenny's eyes widened; he bit his lip and hung his head in sorrow. He hadn't realized that the treasure he had been looking for was so precious to Tooka's world. Tooka looked at him with compassion. She placed her hand on his shoulder and kissed his cheek in reassurance.

"That was years ago, you are not like them, you wish to use it for good," she said. He looked at her and then looked off into the distance, not believing her one bit. *I am like them. I only wanted the treasure. I didn't care about what happened to these creatures, the people whose lives actually hung in the balance.*

"Open it?" Tooka asked. Kenny looked at her in question and then looked at his hand, wondering what he could do to open such a large door.

"How can I?" he asked.

"Touch it, it'll open. M'nep, our first king, foretold of one with pure heart who would be able to open the door to reach his goal," she replied.

Kenny nodded and walked over to it. He saw a small hand embossed into the front of the green colored door. He pressed his hand against it and waited. He was expecting the door to automatically open on contact, but nothing happened. With confusion, he looked at his hand and thought for a moment before trying again, this time leaving his hand on the door. But once again, to his great surprise, nothing happened.

"You still haven't learned," Kenny heard, the voiced boomed in his head for a moment. Suddenly, the chains shattered and sent pieces flying across the floor. The door slid open, crushing dozens of flowers as it skidded across the ground. Kenny backed away, peering inside it with wonder. The contents of this old building revealed itself to be one very large labyrinth filled with old cobwebs and large spiders the size of a sports car.

"I told you. You can open it," Tooka said, and she grabbed his hand and pulled him inside. He stumbled a bit as they entered. The large doors slowly closed behind them, and it concealed the light from entering inside and left them surrounded by a blanket of pitch black. Noises started to fill Kenny's head again, and on top of it all, they were trapped inside and he could feel the air slowly escaping somehow.

He wasn't worried, though. His mind was on one thing. Fireflood's voice and those words he had heard. *I still haven't learned?* Kenny questioned. Tooka looked at him and waved her hand in front of his face.

"Kenny, the air is escaping quickly in this room. We must go," she whispered.

He nodded and followed her into the pitch black veil that was lying ahead of them. Still questioning everything he had ever known due to this strange adventure he was placed in. He wondered if his life would ever be the same once this was all over with. If he'd look at things the same, if he'd ever think the same. This was changing his entire way of thinking.

Darkness was all Kenny saw. His eyes were filled with nothing but black and despair. He felt Tooka's warm hand in his own, and that was the only thing that kept him from collapsing from stress due to the heavy fear.

"Tooka, can we turn around?" Kenny moaned.

"No, we must continue. There are many things in here we cannot be found by," she replied.

He let his shoulders sag and continued to follow behind her. Her stamina level was unreal! She seemed to know where she was going, but he couldn't tell nor did he want to question. He trusted her.

Again that lust he felt for being back at that old house, in that warm bed, consumed him. Those pangs in his side for needing to know someone was there added more pressure. Kenny stopped, pulled Tooka close, and embraced her. He held her there for a moment, not letting her move a single inch.

"Kenny, let go!" Tooka shouted.

Kenny shook his head, tears rolled down his cheeks onto Tooka's head as she pounded her fist into his chest. He was frightened. She stopped and looked up at him, feeling his skin become deathly cold and his body limp. She held onto him tightly as he collapsed onto the ground. She caught him and held him in the shadows, running her fingers through his hair.

"I am sorry, I didn't realize ..." she whispered.

Kenny tried to look up at her, feeling a deep sense of confusion, anger, sorrow, pain, and agony rush through his body. It crept up his spine to his head and quickly he let out a cry of pain. He had no idea what had just happened, or why he was on the ground. But he couldn't take this stress anymore. It was going to drive him mad, and he couldn't stop it.

Tooka held onto him with all her might, trying to find hope for him, the hope he had lost somewhere.

"Kenny, why cry?" she asked.

He didn't reply, he just shook and cried in her arms, feeling very fragile and tender. His skin was so cold, and he felt so weak, as if he had just been hit with an incurable sickness. His breathing sped and his hands slowly grabbed onto her as he tried to stand. She pulled him back down, trying to keep him from moving.

"I believe it is time," a voice, familiar and welcoming, bellowed from somewhere behind Kenny. His eyes opened, and he recognized who this stranger was. A rush of warmth burst into Kenny's body like a fire that was just ignited. Then he felt a soothing feeling brush against his skin like a slow breeze rolling over the hills and finally a crisp, wonderful feeling of water consumed him. His eyes closed and his body stopped shaking from the odd combination of feelings he had just endured. Tooka let go, thinking he was all right, only to see him fall to the ground. The tall grass almost hid him. She too began to feeling very lightheaded, and she rubbed her temples in wonder and amazement. She hadn't ever felt like this before; it was so new and bizarre. She let out a heavy sigh and slowly fell to the ground near Kenny.

Kenny felt the grass beneath him and something very soft, like lying on a cloud. And a large smell of something sweet filled his nostrils. His weak eyes opened, Tooka's hair was covering his face, and he felt like he was inside of a dream. Tooka was lying next to him, her breathing gentle. Flowers like the ones outside of the maze all stood around him. He smiled and watched as three shadows stood around him.

One was Fireflood, his back was turned to Kenny, and from what he could tell he was holding someone. Another was a man who looked as though the water had chosen him itself to bear its likeness. His eyes shimmering and intimidating, but a wide, kind smile was on his face as he kneeled down next to them. He placed his hand on Kenny's head and instantly knew who he was, the ice cold feeling entering his head was refreshing, as though everything Kenny had feared was frozen and locked away forever.

The man who saved me from drowning, in the tunnel, Tooka called him...Blueweed...he thought smiling.

"You got it, chief," Blueweed said. "Good memory"

The last was Bloodwite, standing in his mysterious glory. Bloodwite and Blueweed began to walk off, Fireflood slowly following behind. Kenny went to sit up but stopped when Fireflood shook his head, he slowly turned around with wide eyes.

"Sleep, you deserve it," he said.

"But, Robert—" Kenny began.

"Is safe," he cut in.

He turned to face Kenny fully as the other two vanished in the horizon of white. Kenny's eyes widened in shock, and tears burst from his eyes when he saw Robert sleeping in Fireflood's arms. He was battered and exhausted but safe and looked at peace.

"You should be peaceful now. He is," Fireflood stated. He turned and continued to walk away, Robert still asleep in his arms. Kenny's eyes closed after he watched Fireflood become engulfed in the bright white horizon. They all slowly disappeared into what looked like a glorious sunset, leaving Kenny asleep in the field of flowers, Tooka resting at his side. He placed his arm on her shoulder, closed his eyes, and buried his face into a pure, snow white lily.

Thank you, Kenny thought, smiling a small bit in relief. *Thank you so much*.

Chapter Twenty-six:
THE PAINFUL TRUTHS

KENNY'S EYES OPENED again. He rubbed his face against the ground, trying to wake himself up fully. He gazed at Tooka who was still lying next to him and grasped her shoulder firmly, to make sure she was all right. She twitched and giggled a bit. *Yeah, she's okay, still asleep.* As he pushed himself up, sitting uncomfortably on his knees, he watched her for a moment, and then gazed around the room in wonder. He watched everything carefully, feeling weak still. He went to take a deep breath only to grasp his throat in his hands, feeling sweat roll down his body.

The air, I forgot about the air! Kenny thought, swallowing. He shook Tooka, trying to get her to awaken. She moaned a bit and rolled over, and Kenny shook her again. He wanted to call her name, but he would risk losing precious air due to it. He slapped her face and placed his hands above his head, closing his eyes tightly, wanting to protect himself if she retaliated.

But nothing happened. He opened one curious eye felt, only to feel some sort of pressure on his shoulder. Both of his eyes closed again quickly. The pressure began to grow heavy. He reopened both eyes and gazed at what was soaking through the strap of his tank top. He cringed, seeing some sort of green, sticky substance all over him. He placed his hand on his shoulder and pulled away, seeing the green slime attach to his flesh like a spider web.

"What the heck?" Kenny asked, looking up to the ceiling.

He saw a dozen orange eyes staring down at him, and green slime dripped from various areas onto the ground. Warmth grew on his shoulder, and before he knew it, he felt pain. He grabbed his burning flesh and slouched over, groaning loudly in agony. The slime was melting away a few layers of flesh. *What is this stuff?* He watched as more waterfalls of slime suddenly went tumbling down.

The ground, in the areas where the slime had come in contact with, began to dissolve and slowly vanish, leaving only a large hole. Kenny watched the creature above move through the air without any difficulties. He heard a small scratching sound and hissing followed. His worrisome eyes were caught inside the gaze of the creature's huge reflective, mirror-like eye. He watched it move across the ceiling over to the wall. It trekked down the stone barrier until it was standing face to face with him.

Kenny saw himself dancing in the creature's eyes as he shook, and he watched as his hand kept twitching as he held onto his shoulder. The monster crept into the light, revealing a thick coat of spiky hairs and snapping jaws. It looked just like a smaller version of the creature that had pried itself from the wall to attack Kenny when he first arrived in this strange area, when Fireflood first revealed himself.

Kenny quickly grabbed Tooka and darted off into another direction, and the spider bounced from wall to wall, chasing after him. Kenny's shoulder was pulsating with pain from the acid-like drool he had come in contact with. Tooka's body was dragging across the muddy ground below, getting scraped and bruised. He had her upper back slung over his non-injured shoulder, her feet dangling below onto the ground.

Eventually her eyes opened, and she looked up at Kenny in question then back at the monster chasing them.

"Kenny!" she shouted, trying to push her body from Kenny's grip.

"Quiet!" Kenny snapped, turning a sharp corner.

He let Tooka slide off of his shoulder and continued to run, her hand in his. Kenny could feel his shoulder lock up, his hand slipped from hers, but she grabbed it back, making sure not to lose him in the darkness. Kenny looked back; he saw more eyes appearing and heard more snapping of their ferocious jaws. Tooka picked up her pace, running ahead of Kenny now.

Kenny's foot kept getting caught in the mud, and his body was feeling so weak due to the lack of air. Tooka was going too fast for him right now, and with the pain in his arm, he was having trouble concentrating and continuing onward. His hand slipped from hers, and he stumbled over a rock, falling flat on the ground near a large, rot iron gate that lay wide open with nothing but dried leaves to accompany it in the dark, lonely maze.

Tooka skidded across the ground and went to go get Kenny when the gate slammed shut. She pounded on it and screamed his name, coughing horribly from lack of air just like Kenny was. He stumbled over to her and grasped the cold, rusting bars in his hands. He looked at her, and she looked back.

"I'll find another way out, don't wait for me," Kenny said, grabbing her hand again.

Tooka brushed her trembling hand against his face and shook her head in disagreement. Tears flew from her eyes as she continued to shake her head. Whispering "don't go" over and over again.

"I promise, I'll meet you at the end of this, if you'll be light and guide me," Kenny said kindly. Tooka sighed and looked at him, and her eyes widened in shock. Kenny grew worried and pale.

"Kenny!" she shouted.

He turned around only to see one of the spiders lunge at him. He jumped out of the way. The creature ran into the gate, knocking Tooka to the ground from the shock waves it sent.

Kenny pushed himself up and looked at Tooka who was unconscious on the other side; the spider looked hungrily at him with slime running from his mouth. He was deeply worried about Tooka, she was out cold but at least she was locked inside somewhere she couldn't be reached. He just prayed she would be able to find him somewhere in this huge maze again. He stumbled to his feet and headed for another hallway not too far from where he had just been. The creatures came at him from every direction, snarling angrily and hissing loudly.

He skidded around multiple corners, ran into hedges and dead bushes, and fell over many fallen pillars. Without a source of light he was blind, nothing was visible to him, even his own hand in front of his face. He could hear the monsters racing behind him, the whole area shaking as they chased him in hot pursuit. He felt their breath bursting down onto his body from above, and he was completely lost.

"Kenny!" Tooka shouted, Kenny came to an uneasy halt and quickly looked around for her. He saw her face, hidden behind a thick wall of vines.

"Tooka, run!" Kenny shouted. He sharply turned around to see more of the creatures growing closer. He looked back at Tooka with a complete look of confusion on his face.

"That tunnel over there! Go Kenny, run!" Tooka was pointing toward a small hole in the ground. It was apparent she knew what she was talking about so Kenny just had to trust her. He nodded and began to run again. He felt his way down the next corridor, hearing thunderous noises of the monsters running above him. He must've lost them as he went downward, but Tooka was still up there alone. He wanted to turn around and go find her but he knew she lead him into safety, and they would most likely meet up again on the other side. Kenny began to realize he was heading downward. He hoped he could lose them above and maybe find a way toward Tooka, praying he wasn't heading away from her.

"Man. It is *really* dark in here," Kenny whispered.

He knelt down and felt for some flint-like rocks, brushing his fingers multiple times on any rough surfaces he could find. He felt something soft and wet. He ran his fingers through it and sniffed it, letting out a moan of disgust. He pulled his fingers apart only to find them stick together due to the substance. It was like a non-toxic version of what had consumed his shoulder.

Kenny stood again and fished through his pant pocket, hoping to find his lighter. He prayed that, through all the water he had been tossed into, it still worked somewhat.

Got it, he thought, pulling it from his pocket. He flipped it open and instantly everything was clear. Though he wished it wasn't.

Hiding in sacks of green slime were bodies of fairies, nymphs, and elves. They were just sitting there, consumed by the sticky substance, in an almost comatose state, unmoving. All of them looked so sad and scared, lifeless almost, as he wandered through the small area. It was like a horrible nightmare or something he had read in a book long ago, though instead of stone it was webbing. It felt like walking into a gorgon's forest, filled with all its victims.

There was one that made him the saddest. It was a young elfin child; he appeared to have been crying. Kenny knelt down next to it and ran his fingers across the soft, slime-covered exterior.

"Oh, man. Poor thing," he whispered.

With his other hand he found his pocket knife. He hesitated to cut through; he wanted so dearly to feel relief on his aching heart, but then he would feel guilt for leaving the others. He raised his hand to cut through but stopped in the air, his eyes wide in fear with tears pouring from them. His lip trembled as his hand remained still, hovering with the point held toward the sky. The lighter fell from his hand onto the ground. He felt a heavy, cool feeling around his trembling hand and then a gentle squeeze.

"What did they ever do?" he asked, turning guilty eyes toward the blue enigma standing behind him.

"Nothing," Blueweed replied, appearing out of thin air. "This is what cruelty of human greed causes, horrible creatures that tear apart the very life force of this place."

Kenny dropped the pocket knife and buried his face in his hands, crying now with large streams of tears seeping through his fingers. Blueweed knelt down next to him and placed his hands on his shoulders, a small bit of light radiating from his body made him look angelic. Kenny, even though he was angry, couldn't help but think of Blueweed as an angel; one that was sent to help him through this confusing time.

Kenny continued to cry as Blueweed picked up the pocketknife. Kenny looked at his hands and the tears that had stained themselves into his flesh and then clenched them tightly together, looking at his trembling hands in question with no answer in sight.

Blueweed opened Kenny's hand and set the knife in his palm. Kenny looked at him with tearful eyes. He wiped a tear away and nodded, patting the old wood handle a few times. And then he smiled, with confidence and reassurance.

"This one but just him, since he's so adorable, but it'll probably disturb the Gohmas too much if we open too many sacks," he said smiling as he continuously wiped away Kenny's tears.

"What about all of them though?" Kenny asked.

Blueweed placed his finger in front of his own mouth and wagged another finger in front of Kenny's and giggled to keep him quiet. Both went back to staring at the young elf child. Kenny went to drive the knife into the shell when his hand stopped again; he couldn't do it. Something inside just racked him with pain from the thought of doing it.

"You've got a fear of knives, don't you? They hurt you once, didn't they?" Blueweed asked. Kenny lowered his head a bit and nodded, not really wanting to elaborate.

Blueweed grabbed his hand and, gently, moved it down toward the shell. He dug the knife a few centimeters inside and slowly helped Kenny cut, seeing that he was paralyzed and couldn't do it himself. Slowly the little child was freed; he fell out of the shell, into Kenny's arms.

"See, nothing to it. Now, let me lead you to an exit," Blueweed said.

Kenny looked at him, grasping the young child in his arms for dear life. Blueweed stood and watched as Kenny followed, his body trembling in fear. He went to start walking when Blueweed stopped him; Kenny looked up at him in wonder.

Blueweed brushed back a loose bang that was concealing his tear-stained eyes. In them he saw so many emotions that were bottled up for what seemed like an eternity. He took the child from Kenny's arms and stared him down for a moment, trying to read what had caused this deep fear. He was very interested in Kenny's fears. It appealed to him, it was mysterious. He gazed around the room for a moment, and Kenny's eyes followed. After a while Blueweed's eyes widened in realization, and he hung his head a bit and stared at the child then at Kenny.

"This is...not your fault," he said, honest truth coming from his smiling lips. Kenny looked away, not agreeing in the slightest bit. He cried some more, letting his tears stain the ground beneath.

For a moment all that remained was silence until Kenny heard a small crackling-like noise. He gasped in wonder.

"What is that?" He listened carefully as the noise grew louder, and soon his head shot to the area behind him. A large explosion started a chain reaction. Blueweed and Kenny darted off into the distance as the whole area went up in flames.

They passed dozens of pods; Kenny, feeling like his heart was failing more with each one. Everything behind was nothing but a big raging inferno, showering everything in a deep heat and energy. The two almost felt that they weren't going to make it. Blueweed was held back with the young child in his arms. They ran as fast as their feet would take them, but it seemed as though all hope was lost.

Soon they saw a light coming from the front, and the raging inferno from the back consumed their bodies. Both went flying outside into a lush green courtyard. Kenny landed in a shallow fountain, and Blueweed landed far away from the entrance, the young child still in his arms.

A large blast of fire shot from the area below, covering everything in a terrifying red light. Kenny watched as everything went up in flames. The land around became engulfed in a horrible rain of fire as well. Blueweed was lying still in the grass, not moving the slightest inch, with scorch marks all across his body.

Kenny quickly stood and stared up at the angel statue that

stood looking down at him. Much like the statue in the grave-yard, it nodded and smiled.

"Go on," it appeared to say as it moved its lips.

Kenny started to smash the angel. He bruised his palms and scratched himself up trying to crush it, but thankfully, it was old and rotted and eventually collapsed. Water flew out of the center where it once stood, dousing the heavy fire with a cleansing rain-fall. He climbed from the fountain and walked over to the hole he had emerged from, still being covered in the water.

Blueweed rolled over, the young child still asleep in his arms. The water was washing away the excess slime that was covering his small body. Blueweed let the child be, stood up, and walked over to Kenny. The moment he stood behind him, Kenny collapsed onto his hands and knees, crying in pain and agony.

"I killed them, the lighter...I killed all those people!" he shouted, slamming his fist onto the stone flooring beneath. It shattered under the impact of his rage; the blood that slipped from his trembling hand was taken away by the water. Like no matter how much he wanted to inflict pain upon himself to repay for those he had killed, he couldn't.

"It wasn't you're fault, none of this is," Blueweed stated. "So calm down, okay?"

Kenny refused to listen, racking himself with pain from the fear he had been inflicted with. He had seen the truth of what human greed had created here; he was scared and didn't know what to do but cry until he couldn't cry anymore.

Chapter Twenty-seven:

THE TIME LIMIT

KENNY HAD FALLEN into a deep sleep. After being racked with pain and fear, not knowing what to do, Kenny hid behind a pillar that had fallen near what seemed to be an entrance to a temple. Without even trying, he had fallen asleep.

He had a dream where he was in the front lawn of the Drake Estate. The sky was a bright auburn color, and you could see stars were appearing on the horizon. He opened his eyes, in this place he felt content and safe.

"Kenny, what are you doing?" a voice asked. Kenny turned. He was confronted by two feet. He traced them up to the head and laughed.

"Robby! You're okay!" Kenny shouted. Robert sat down next to him and stared out into the horizon.

"You shouldn't be sleeping," Robert started. "You should be up looking for Tooka."

Kenny cocked his head to the side in question. He grabbed his legs and stared out into a puddle of water at his feet, feeling like there was nothing he could do again. Robert patted him on the back and reclined. Both stayed there silently for a moment until Kenny had a realization.

"Robert!" Kenny embraced Robert and laughed. "Oh gosh, it's really you."

"Calm down, Kenny! Listen to me." Robert pushed Kenny off of him. "You're dreaming, I'm in trouble, and Tooka's probably lost! You've got to wake up! Got it, Kenny? You *need* to wake up!"

Kenny's eyes shot open in a panic. "Robert!" he shouted. He stared at the area and realized he was still in the courtyard he had fallen asleep in. Again the pain and regrets came flooding back. He unknowingly put his hands in his pockets as he sat up. *What's this?* He asked himself, pulling a note out of his pocket.

"The eviction notice...Rob, you do need me. You are in trouble, aren't you? You were telling me something, I wasn't sleeping, was I?" Kenny asked himself, "You were talking to me."

The white marble exterior surrounding Kenny made him feel he was in too holy of a place, a place he shouldn't be in. He sat staring up at the ceiling in wonder and confusion, hands over his stomach and eyes filled with so much sorrow.

Blueweed was near the child, cleaning the rest of the webbing from the little one's body. He had heard Kenny talking to himself but let him be. His eyes were filled with question, and he had a slightly smug look on his face.

"Come see him, won't you? He's so cute!" he said like a child.

Kenny did nothing but turn away, though he couldn't help but smile a bit after seeing Blueweed's expression of happiness. Something about his smile was contagious. Blueweed then sighed and looked at him; he didn't know what to do to aid him in this time of need. He could see in his eyes strain to withhold tears of rage. Kenny could almost feel his heart beating in his throat and his blood rushing in his ears like a violent storm. This was one situation he couldn't laugh at himself and feel like everything was ok.

The little child opened his eyes. They were bright orange, which accented well to his dark black hair. Blueweed looked at him and smiled. The little boy's pointed ears wiggled a bit as, for the first time in what Blueweed guessed was a long while, he heard things.

The little boy looked at him in fear but realized he was okay, because he was like him, a child of the forest. Blueweed helped him sit up, the little child entranced by how majestic he looked. Just like most children who find something new, he examined his superior. Touching is hair and his face, and though Blueweed was uncomfortable with these small hands feeling everything on his body, he let him be for a while.

Blueweed gazed back at Kenny and watched him shake for a moment until the little boy grabbed his blue hair. His head shot over to him, and a smile became planted on his face. The young child was so entrancing, if not somewhat annoying.

"Hello," he whispered, stroking the little boy's hair.

The little boy smiled and looked at him. "Hi," he replied, watching as he stood.

He patted the child's head and extended his hand for him. He took it with an ear to ear smile on his face. His hand was so small compared to Blueweed's, even though his were very feminine and small compared to most men.

"Do you have a name?" Blueweed asked, watching the little boy's eyes dance over to another target.

"Iis," he replied, looking in Kenny's direction.

Blueweed's eyes widened. *Could he be?* He thought with raised eyebrows. But he couldn't keep his eyes on the boy for long, so he turned over to Kenny. He watched him sit there, shaking and crying.

Orange eyes turned that direction as well, and the little boy saw Kenny for the first time. He hid, suddenly terrified, behind Blueweed, realizing he was human. With his quickness the boy almost knocked Blueweed to the ground while looking for shelter behind the tall, older man. Kenny's tear-stained eyes gazed in his direction. The boy saw so much fear and terror in them. He wasn't sure what to think. Should he be scared or should he be trying to figure out what was wrong with him?

"Why is he crying?" Iis asked, looking up at the blue stranger.

Blueweed kneeled down next to him and placed his hand on his head, gently weaving his fingers in and out of his hair.

"He is...very lonely right now," Blueweed replied. "And very sick, I'm afraid. He's not too careful here in our world. He's forgetful," he continued, lowering his tone.

He saw Kenny's pale face morph into an exhausted, almost lifeless state, his eyes still trying to gain focus on everything around him. He cried. A bundle of hair in his hand and tears flowing from his eyes, and as he coughed heavily he grasped his chest in his other hand. *Aw, Kenny, you're just exhausted,* Blueweed thought.

Blueweed looked at the little boy and watched as the strange elfin child rushed over to a small patch of flowers. For a moment Iis just watched the flowers, Blueweed watching him in wonder. The small child brushed the soft petals with his fingers and laughed. But soon he began to pick the biggest, brightest blooms. With a smile, Blueweed stood back up and watched as Iis darted past toward Kenny. He stayed still in the corner, his eyes locked onto the little elfin child, letting him try to cheer Kenny up any way he could.

The confused blonde looked down at him, the tears slowly seemed to stop as the little elf boy handed him the flowers. Kenny looked at him, seeing a familiar face in the small boy's. He sat up and looked deep into the orange eyes of the child he had saved.

"Stop crying, okay?" he asked.

Kenny wiped away the tears and looked at his drenched hand in shock as if he hadn't realized he had been crying for hours. He laughed a bit and continued to wipe the tears from his eyes as he took the flowers.

"Okay, I'll stop," he said, placing his hand on the boy's head.

The little boy smiled widely and grabbed Kenny's hand. He pulled him from the rock over to Blueweed.

Still silent and ever vigilant, Blueweed watched as the two approached. The little boy grabbed Blueweed's hand and placed

Kenny's in it, and both looked at their enclosed hands and then each other.

"See, happy is good," Iis said, giggling.

Kenny laughed a bit and nodded, and he looked at Blueweed, whose face slowly changed to a more relaxed state. The little boy watched as Kenny leaned in toward Blueweed, the older sprite concealed his petrified face with his head, trying to hide the panic in Kenny's face from Iis.

"What about the air?" he asked.

"Oh," he pointed up. "The ceiling isn't enclosed here, we'll be fine," he replied.

Kenny looked up, realizing he was right, noticing that the tree tops all spread out and away from each other, creating a gap, which allowed plenty of air. He sighed a bit, finally understanding that he was safe for now.

"I can't stand up right, I...I feel sick," he moaned.

Blueweed grabbed onto him to keep him upright. He held him tightly and tried to make sure he wouldn't fall over.

Blueweed looked at the little boy who was very confused. Iis grabbed Kenny's pant leg and looked up at him. Kenny was almost unconscious in Blueweed's arms, feeling terribly ill for a reason he couldn't understand. It seemed unfair, after traveling all this way only to grow this sick. He felt as though he was dying. And time was not on his side in this journey.

"He's all right, just a little tired," Blueweed said calmly, looking down at Iis.

Kenny's hot breath slowly faded into strained, hacking. His eyes struggled to stay open. He hadn't felt this bad in ages; it was horrible on his body, and it made his stomach churn.

Blueweed looked at his trembling body carefully, wondering what could have made him become so sick so quickly. The only thing he spotted was his wounded shoulder; the dead layers of skin were doused with a green liquid that seemed to slowly be eating it away.

He pushed Kenny off of him and looked him over, seeing how his body was still trembling. With the calming words "it's okay", he brushed back a few of Kenny's loose bangs and looked into his bouncing eyes, seeing they were slowly changing color to a deep purple.

Iis looked at Kenny and then Blueweed, wondering what was taking so long for them to say something. Kenny knelt down next to him and looked into his big, bright, confused eyes.

"Are you okay?" Iis asked, placing his tiny hand on Kenny's forehead.

Kenny nodded. "Yep, I'm okay," he replied.

Blueweed grabbed his hand and carefully pulled him back to his feet. He placed his hands on Kenny's shoulders. In fear, Kenny's eyes widened in question and shock, because Blueweed had concern in his eyes for the first time Kenny had noticed.

"What—" he began.

"You've got an infection," Blueweed cut in.

"What? What sort of infection?" Kenny questioned, turning his eyes toward Blueweed's terror-stricken ones.

"Don't talk, save your energy."

Kenny swallowed, and he felt Blueweed's grip tighten to restrain any movements he may try and attempt. Kenny stopped moving and let him do as he pleased, realizing he was right and everything might be resting on this strange man's shoulders.

"We have to find Tooka," Kenny spat.

Blueweed shook his head and let Kenny go. "Whoever that is can wait!"

Kenny stood up without Blueweed's help and rubbed the back of his head. He shrugged his shoulders and looked away, slight red marks dashed into his pale cheeks.

Blueweed bit his finger to restrain laughter, realizing this 'Tooka' was very important to the confused Kenny. *Aw, he's in love,* Blueweed thought. *How cute. I wonder if that's the green child with him.*

Kenny looked at him and pressed his pointer fingers together, a nervous look in his eyes and a sweet, pleading smile on his face. Blueweed could see it in his eyes. He was madly in love with that child of his world.

"Please," Kenny whispered, so calmly and quietly that Blueweed almost couldn't hear him.

"Are we going now?" Iis asked. His face was practically glowing with delight once he saw Kenny smile at him. His nervous brown and, now purple hued eyes gazed from the child back to Blueweed, and he waited for an answer, knowing he couldn't go anywhere without his approval. Something deep inside made his mind come rushing back to Robert, and his outline almost consumed Blueweed's.

"All right," he said finally.

Kenny raised his hands in the air, letting out a scream of joy. His eyes shot open and almost bulged out of his head for a moment. He grabbed his shoulder and fell to the ground, letting out a distraught cry of pain.

Iis placed his hands on Kenny's good shoulder, watching as a rainfall of sweat poured from his forehead. He gasped heavily, wheezing and hacking in pain. Blueweed knelt down beside him and placed his hand on Kenny's sweaty head.

Kenny grabbed Blueweed's hands; he jumped back a bit in fear, seeing the terror in the human's eyes change to a clear cry of help. His mouth was open as if he wanted to speak to him, ask him something, but nothing was coming out. With one loud scream, Kenny collapsed onto the ground again, crying in pain. Green, dyed blood was spilling from his shoulder; it was contaminating his palms with a horrid color as his fingers slowly unfurled around his shoulder.

Kenny lied there motionless on the ground, Iis was gently rocking his body in attempts to wake him up, and Blueweed was standing above, unable to move in the slightest. He just stood there, watching Kenny cry in pain and agony, screaming out Robert's name in attempts to gain comfort from his lost friend. He couldn't do anything to help him, not with the little time he had to work with. He especially didn't want the child to be there if he tried and failed.

Eventually he knelt down next to Kenny and placed his fingers on his temples, feeling his heart racing beneath his fingers. Kenny grabbed Blueweed's hand and looked into his eyes emotionlessly, breathing at a gasping, heavy pace.

"H-help," he moaned, a few streams of tears flowing from

his eyes, dampening his long eyelashes. Iis looked at him in fear. He too was crying as he slowly watched Kenny slip into unconsciousness.

"Help him! Please!" he shouted, crying into Kenny's good shoulder.

Blueweed looked at his hands and clenched them tightly together in anger; he shook in fear and watched Kenny slowly reach up to him. He stood and backed away, Kenny still reaching out to him with his injured arm, even though he was in so much pain he continued to try and reach out to him.

"I'm going to get help," Blueweed stated, grabbing Iis' small shoulder. "Stay here, don't leave."

With that he vanished, leaving Iis by himself, shaking Kenny harshly as he still fell into darkness. Kenny was praying under his breath, wishing he could see Tooka and Robert again one last time. He could almost see above him, hidden within a vision of white, Tooka and Robert standing there with extended hands. Kenny still held his hand out to them. Blood sliding from his torn arm started to grow from the pressure of him reaching up to them. Robert smiled and waved; he turned around and started to walk off into the distance. Tooka followed, nodding in agreement as she laughed a bit.

"Come on," she said.

They were calling to him, waiting for him somewhere so they could be together again for one last time. And he was answering.

Chapter Twenty-eight:
THE FINAL BREATH

"COME ON, COME on!"

Kenny's eyes burst open, hearing Tooka's voice ringing in his ears. He caught a small glimpse of Tooka as she brushed her hand against his forehead. Sweat poured down his face heavily, drenching his weak body. He reached up to her only to scream in pain as his arm fell to the ground again. He was still too weak to do anything, so he remained still on the ground.

"Tooka ..." Kenny whispered, stopping after he spoke her name only.

"All right?" she asked.

"No, not all right...nowhere near all right. I can barely see you," he replied.

Tooka gasped and embraced him, and out of the corner of his eye he saw the outline of Iis shaking, looking like he wanted to find some sort of comfort from him. From far behind he saw Blueweed in the corner, standing silently without moving. The blue enigma raised an eyebrow in question to him, wondering if he was going to be all right.

Kenny raised his sore arm into the air and extended his hand toward him. His eyes welded together in pain, he cringed and his muscles tightened to restrain movement. He hid it all from the child, though. Iis couldn't see him struggling.

Iis walked over to him and grabbed his hand; Tooka looked at the little boy and smiled. Kenny smiled at him and laughed a bit. Tooka helped him sit up some. She placed a large, smooth stone under his head and laid him on it, trying to support him somewhat and make him a bit more comfortable.

"Kenny, can't continue?" Tooka asked.

Kenny nodded. "I can still go," he replied, sitting up. He groaned and slowly laid his body back down onto the earth.

"I guess I can't," he said quietly. Tooka kissed his scruffy cheek and recoiled as she shook her head. Kenny brushed his cheeks and his chin. *Guess I need a shave*, he said to himself, laughing a little bit quietly at the way Tooka acted. Kenny took a deep breath and made his battered body more comfortable in the patch of thick grass. He laid there for a moment, almost drifting off again as Tooka wrapped his arm into a sling.

Iis lay down in the patch of grass next to Kenny. With a giggle, he looked at him and grabbed his other hand. With a small smile he dozed off, still grasping Kenny's hand in his own. *Sweet kid*, he thought, smiling.

"Sorry," Tooka said quietly.

"Why?" Kenny asked in a whisper, trying to keep Iis asleep.

"You won't have time to save Robert," she replied.

"He's okay; he's a grown man. I guess I shouldn't be too worried about him, man...I guess I was turning into him there for a while."

Kenny gazed off into the distance, staring at the white temple entrance ahead. He smiled guiltily and closed his eyes for a moment, letting the sudden realization sink in.

"What do you mean?" Tooka asked.

"Well, Robert has always been...sick. I was *really* overprotective of him when we were little, and I've been worried about him when I should've realized that it's okay now. He doesn't need me anymore," Kenny replied.

Tooka brushed back Kenny's bangs and smiled at him, with a small giggle she placed her finger on his lips to silence him before he could speak again.

"You stay with me then, yes? He could be ours?" Tooka asked.

Kenny's eyes widened in shock. "What, you mean that?" he asked.

"Stay with me, in my village. The boy," she stopped and pointed at Iis. "He could be ours?" she continued.

Kenny's eyes were wide with wonder and excitement. He could barely hold in a scream of joy. He shook his head in thought, realizing that his most precious dream had just come true. He wanted a family more than most anything.

"In a couple of years, yes," he replied. "But I'm not ready to be a man just yet."

Tooka nodded in agreement and extended her pinky finger to him; he slid his hand out of Iis' grip slowly and locked his finger with hers. Both smiled at each other and eventually broke out into a fit of laughter. Kenny could hear Blueweed laugh a bit and then he vanished, realizing his job was done.

Kenny looked over in Iis' direction and smiled after witnessing Blueweed bid him au due. Suddenly he felt a shock of realization shoot up his spine. He quickly looked up at Tooka and let out a joyful gasp.

"He's got to be the one!" he whispered.

"What?" Tooka asked, blinking a few times.

"The heir, Iis has to be the heir! I saw him in the stained glass window above where your grandmother sat, he looks the same! He has black hair!" Kenny spat.

"Lots of people have black hair."

Kenny scowled. "Come on, at least give it a thought or two!"

Tooka rolled her eyes and stood up. She wandered over to Iis and looked over his tiny body carefully, watching his every movement closely. She shook her head and looked back at Kenny in triumph.

"He is no heir," she spat.

Kenny moaned a bit and brushed back his sweaty bangs, his

vision bounced for a second as Tooka grew close to him. She placed her hand on his head and gasped heavily, pulling it away sharply. She pressed her trembling hand against her chest and looked at Kenny.

Kenny laughed a bit and watched her as she pulled a cloth from her side pack. She soaked the cloth with fresh water from a shallow puddle in the ground next to him.

"You have a fever," she said, placing the cloth on his head. He let out a sigh of sweet relief, feeling the fever release its grip on him a bit. He smiled to thank her, but she only continued to search her packs for something.

What's she looking for? he asked himself. He groaned in pain, feeling his body sting with sharp pricks in every area he could think of. Tooka gently pushed him down and placed his hand on his head.

"Try not to move," she said quietly.

Kenny listened, knowing she probably was speaking truthfully. He felt lightheaded for a moment, watching as she searched through her pack again, pulling out numerous items. Kenny closed his eyes and thought for a moment. Tooka looked at him in wonder, questioning why he had become so quiet lately. She saw tears stream down his cheeks in heavy numbers, his body trembling and his skin turning paler every moment. He had been injured and sick this entire journey, but now he looked and acted the weakest he had ever been.

Tooka pulled a vile of purple slime out of her pack. She opened the small cap and looked at it. Kenny's eyes slowly opened again, and he stared at her for a moment. He pointed to it with his good hand, asking what it was without speaking.

"Medicine, it will help," she said, handing the vile to him.

He breathed in heavily, catching a large whiff of the horrid-smelling antidote. He shook his head and handed it back to her.

"No, this is really nasty-smelling!" he shouted.

Tooka grabbed his arm and gave him a threatening look. *She's dead serious; she wants me to drink it. Whatever it is ...*

"Please, it is for the best," she said.

Kenny sat up and nodded; he was scared within every inch of his life of this bizarre thing, but he knew she was worried. He didn't want to stress her any more than she already was. He took a deep breath and drank the entire bottle. He felt like puking after engulfing the entire dose of the slime, but he did feel somewhat better.

Kenny closed his eyes again, feeling too weak to stay awake. He took one, deep, final breath. Realizing this last one would be the only one he would ever take again in the life he knew before. He looked toward the large tree-covered roof and blinked rapidly a few times as he let his battered limb recover. Everything was changing now, but for better or for worse?

Chapter Twenty-nine:

THE CONFUSION

KENNY LOOKED AT himself in a pond and slung the excess water and hair from the blade of his pocketknife. He rubbed his chin and nodded as he closed the knife and placed it back into his side pocket. He stood and turned to face Tooka and Iis, both looked at him with smiles on their faces. Tooka kissed his cheek and laughed.

"Better?" Kenny asked.

"Much," Tooka replied. Kenny turned around to face Iis and laughed a bit.

"I feel great!" Kenny shouted, jumping on top of a broken pillar. He posed like an army general and smiled proudly, feeling revived and wonderful. Tooka broke out into a fit of laughter and watched as Kenny spun around in a circle like a ballet dancer. Iis jumped up onto a pillar next to him and flexed his tiny muscles, trying to be just like Kenny.

"I'm ready to take on anything!" he boasted. He went to jump off of the pillar when he tripped and fell face first into a pile of mud. Iis sat down on the broken column and laughed at him as

Tooka helped Kenny stand again. He scraped the mud from his tongue and laughed a bit, not letting anything slow him down.

Robert always did say I wasn't coordinated, Kenny thought, smiling. He stood and rung the mud from his shirt then brushed back his hair. It stuck straight up due to the mud, and then quickly fell back down onto his face. It slung dirt into his eyes. He wiped it away. It was like nothing that happened could bring him down now. He was refreshed and ready to take on the world.

"Are you all right?" Tooka asked, wiping away some of the mud on his cheek.

"I feel like a million bucks!" Kenny shouted joyfully.

Tooka cocked her head to one side and blinked rapidly in question. "Why do you want to feel like deer?" she asked.

Kenny laughed. "No, see, a million bucks means that I'm happy," he replied, scratching the back of his head.

Tooka looked at him in question. *She doesn't get it,* Kenny thought with a sigh. Iis ran over to Kenny and grabbed his hand. With one harsh tug, he began to pull Kenny off toward another direction with a large smile on his face.

"Whoa, slow down, kid!" Kenny said, stumbling.

"Let's go, I'm bored!" Iis shouted, still tugging on Kenny's arm. He let the child pull him down toward a dark corridor, Tooka following behind slowly with a smile of relief on her face. She was glad to see Kenny feeling better and was finally happy again.

Kenny looked back at Tooka before he turned his head to face this new area ahead. With wide eyes, his mouth popped open, and he scanned every detail carved into the sides of two white pillars supporting a large archway. Everything was covered in thick ivy vines and beautiful azure blooms. Upon its surface were batches of moss that spread freely across the structure. Large spider webs strung from the walls up to the ceiling high above.

On the pillars stood pictures of more people running from giant spiders, terror showered their expressions, and it looked as though fire was spreading across the land. Kenny's eyes flashed to a deep orange color then green and back to brown. In his pupils you could see reflections of the pictures in motion. His hand slowly fell from Iis' and his body stopped moving. He watched the pictures move though no one else could see them. Tooka placed her hand on Kenny's shoulder and shook him gently, trying to get a response from him. Iis shook his hand and pulled him along, wanting to get out of the maze as soon as possible.

"They're moving again," he said quietly. Watching the pictures crawl from the wall he shook, he grabbed his companions' hands tightly as everything grew clearer and clearer. Iis looked at Kenny and then Tooka.

"Who's moving?" he asked. Tooka shook her head, not knowing just what to say.

Kenny moved away from them and walked into the darkness, Tooka and Iis following carefully behind. Every step Kenny took the sound bounced from one wall to the next, consuming everything in an uneven rhythm. The grass beneath seemed to reach up to him and every blade tried to grab onto his body. The moonlight quickly shimmered down through the trees as if the heavens were trying to reach down and touch his possessed face.

His hands tried to reach up toward the light, his fists clenched and would then loosen with every step. He was confused and needed guidance. From a far off place he saw a bright light and one shadow dancing ahead of him.

Kenny's eyes widened and his pace picked up. Tooka and Iis had to run to just keep him within their view. Both quickly found themselves mesmerized by the same thing Kenny was.

Tooka saw a person standing with an extended hand, his face was concealed beneath a thick blanket of black hair and a devious and kind smile was growing wider. He was tall and very handsome, like something from a far off dream she had long since forgotten. She stopped at Kenny's side and watched as he reached out for the man. The bright light soon surrounded all of them. Tooka huddled up with Iis, shielding herself and the child's eyes from the thick blanket of white.

Soon nothing remained but white and a quick burst of arctic winds. Tooka opened one eye a little to look at the surroundings. In shock she let out a gasp, staring wide-eyed at the field of snow she was now in. She was knee deep in the white flurries, yet surprisingly it wasn't cold. It felt almost like sitting in a rushing torrent of water.

With confusion, she looked down and saw Iis had vanished. With an open hand, Tooka caught a small ball of snow. It felt weird and new, nothing she had ever seen was as extraordinary as this.

In the distance she saw a bundle of black. Snow was brushing against it. This tall blur of black was hastily becoming consumed by the abyss of white. She walked through the thick blanket of white flurries toward it, realizing this strange object was a person. No, two people. Both were just looming there, staring at each other.

One was on his knees, clutching his shoulder in pain, staring up at the taller form. The other was showing him his hand. She quickly realized it was Kenny on his knees there, blood spilling from his open wound. He was entranced by the tall, mysterious black knight above him. Surrounding that man's body was a cloak of dark pigments. A hood covered his face, and in his hand was a necklace.

Kenny grabbed it firmly in his hand. He opened what looked like a locket, made of gold, attached to a thick chain the moment Tooka reached him. She leaned over his shoulder and watched as his eyes gazed across the picture inside.

It was of two young boys, both smiling. Tooka looked up at him in amazement. The man hovering above her smiled a bit and spoke, though no sound came from his mouth. Everything was quiet, no winds howling to fill the night sky, and no cries of people to give tension into the most fitting setting.

The man spoke again, looking as if he wanted an answer to what he was saying. "Protect him, protect him," it looked like, the two same words constantly spilling from his pale white lips. His skin was as light as the snow surrounding him. Tooka was caught in a mess of emotions, staring in awe and wonder at this beautiful angel.

"Will you?" he finally asked, snapping her from her trance.

"What?" she asked.

"Will you, protect him? He's lost, give him guidance," he replied. His voice was a pure chorus of the heavens, silent and majestic, absolutely oneiric and hazy. Tooka watched him in wonder, and Kenny reached out to him. He watched his own hand grow smaller in front of him as he tried to grab onto the man's cloak.

Soon his flesh touched the fabric. Its soft exterior weaving in and out of his fingers as the wind blew it around him. The man looked down at him, watching as he breathed heavily in fear and anticipation. Soon he grabbed the cloak. The moment he did winds burst from every area. It was cold and unbearable. The wind blew the hood from the man's head, revealing a familiar, welcoming face which resulted with Kenny in tears.

"R-Robert," he whispered, grabbing the cloak tighter. The winds blew again and Robert's form slowly melted away, blowing snowflakes in every direction around Kenny, and as he reached for him, his hand followed the dissolving form down until the cloak was all that remained on the ground. Kenny looked up at Tooka. Soon her body slowly blew away too. Kenny cried out in fear, trying to get her to stay. She reached for him, but her body was gone before her hand could connect with his.

Soon the snow was blown off into the distance, and everything was slowly vanishing like sand being washed away in the tide, nothing seemed to remain but cracked ground beneath and a fearsome young man, dark skies, and drops of rain. Kenny pushed himself up slowly, trying to get himself back onto his aching feet. His eyes gazed around slowly, from every direction he saw nothing but the grey dust beneath him and the darkest of skies above.

He hobbled off into the distance, watching how everything slowly changed from a dark exterior to an even darker one. He continued to find himself lost in the dark auras that had been trapping him for so long. He dropped to his knees, buried his face in his hands and trembled, wondering why this had to happen to him.

"Why? Why? Why, why, why!? Why me!? Why Robert? Tell me, please answer! Tell me why you're punishing me like this!

Please tell me what I did to make you so angry! Why do you hate me all of the sudden!? I tried to find you, I did. Honestly I did!" Kenny shouted. "Please, Robert, why? Tell me why!?"

He dropped to the ground and covered his head with his hands, screaming at the top of his lungs, praying for an answer to why this torture had suddenly begun. His hands clawed at his hair, and his body wouldn't cease its shaking. He was crying, gasping for a breath, prayers slipping from every drop of air that fell from his lips, his eyes losing all source of sight, his ears cutting the connection to sound. All in all, he was dying, his body being mentally torn apart slowly from this agony.

"Go away, go away!" he shouted. "Just go away!"

He felt a light touch on his shoulder. Through his teary eyes he saw someone standing high above him. Their outline was blurry, glowing with a small bit of light; the brightest orange colors surrounded his body. His hair was of ecru pigments, and his eyes were like two rubies. His anatomy was familiar.

A smile was on his face; it was gentle and calming. A memory shot into Kenny's head. It was brief but enough to make him remember who that man was. This man was the firefly that had led him into the cemetery at the beginning of his journey.

"Rise," he commanded, showing his hand to Kenny. This pose, this form, was like Robert's in the field mere moments ago. Kenny reached up to him, slowly placing his hand in the man's. Light surrounded them. Kenny was blinded by the heavy white auras bursting from around his body. Soon the man was consumed and Kenny followed, being pulled into another dark dream that he feared may alter the course of everything.

Chapter Thirty:

THE CONFUSED

THE SUN SHOWN down upon a very odd setting, and it looked as if it had been sketched by hand recently, moments before it had appeared. The light was vague and unmoving, and even though the wind was blowing around him, he heard no sound. Kenny felt as if his body was surrounded by nothing, even though grass was underneath him and chilled air was brushing against his body. Everything was hazy, the sky was pure white, and the only thing he could see was the tall blades of grass blowing in this bizarre wind that seemed to come from nowhere. Only one lonely tree shaded him from lights which had origins that were unable to be found.

Kenny's body was lying flat on the ground, on his side. He had no recollection of ever lying down. The last thing he remembered was staring into the eyes of a stranger through a thick blanket of darkness. And now, he awoke surrounded by tall, thin blades of grass.

A shadow loomed over him. The long sliver of black seemed surreal as it bounced slowly across his motionless form like a sundial. He rolled over and stared the man in the eyes, seeing someone who appeared to be no older than he was. The man knelt down next to him and cocked his head to the side a bit to look at Kenny from a different angle.

"Who are you?" Kenny asked.

The enigma placed his finger on his lips and hushed him quietly, in a fatherly like manner, with a wide smile on his face and compassion in his eyes. It was memorable; he could see it, hear it within many of his past emotions and memories, as if he knew him. The man looked so unreal to Kenny, so magical. But he wasn't like Tooka, his olive-tinted skin and brown eyes were far from normal according to these other creatures he kept running into. Even Iis, who did in fact appear human, had abnormal colored eyes, and his hair was tinted with sharp blue colors. But this man was almost as human as he was.

Kenny sat up, groaning a bit in agony. His body felt stiff, as if he had been asleep for the last few hours even though it seemed to be mere minutes since it all happened. The man sat there, using the balls of his feet to support him as he looked Kenny square in the eye, almost in a hypnotic state. It seemed as though he was trying to remember his face, like he would never see him again but wished he would, somewhere far in the future where he could never be, where he would never be able to go to.

"Who?" Kenny began but the man quickly shot his hand up in the air to cease his talking, and Kenny's eyes widened in shock. He pushed himself up and eventually stood to his aching feet once again. Standing as tall as his body would allow, he realized this man was about his height as well. It felt like he was looking into a mirror.

With his trembling fingers, he grabbed his bruised shoulder, gently pressing the tips of each finger lightly against the sore flesh that seemed to peel as he rubbed it. Beneath his finger stood a mark, one that was of a pure black circle with a small white dot, barely visible, almost like an ninja's throwing star, four points with a small hole in the center.

The man grabbed his hand and pulled it away from the marking. He looked at it, his mouth at Kenny's ear by the time he stopped easing his way toward the symbol. Kenny could feel his breath slipping into his ear. It was cold and sent chills down his spine. The temperature in his body slowly decreasing with every breath that escaped that man's lungs, Kenny felt like his soul was freezing inside of his body.

"Gohma," he whispered his voice cold and unwelcoming.

Kenny's eyes widened in shock. *Gohma*? he questioned, wondering where he had heard that name before.

The man pulled away and looked him in the eyes. Within them Kenny saw his own reflection dancing on the surface of the stranger's pupils, the worry in his face was all too clear. He panicked and pushed himself away, shoving the man with all his might, letting out a small yelp.

Moments passed as everything fell quiet. Kenny blinked a few times, seeing his hands going through the man. He saw straight through the creature, all the way into the abyss of white that surrounded where he stood. Gusts of wind blew around the both of them, the ground below gently being churned like sand with the graceful breezes.

Kenny quickly turned around to face the tree, feeling as if something was grasping onto his back. Nothing stood but the pure white background that was just in front of him moments ago. He looked behind him again, and the tree was now far off in the deep beyond, hidden behind rolling hills.

The white was slowly being painted with dark blue pigments, everything being overtaken with black. Hatred was creeping within the lines etched beneath Kenny's feet, engulfing everything in its path with deadly poison.

Only one spot remained with minimal color, the area where the man now stood, though he looked different. Long, thin, and brittle strands of hair blew around his body, those which were a color of the brightest crescent moons, dipped lightly in yellow. His skin was pale as snow. His eyes were gentle yet emotionless. His body looked cold, his aura was unwelcoming, yet the expression on his face was of longing. White surrounded everything in his eyes, and it consumed his pupil and iris. He looked like a corpse, standing there in the twilight, awaiting something or someone more likely.

Kenny's mind could only create more terror as he looked on at the haunting portrait. For a brisk moment he could almost see wings on his back, yet no angel's wings were that glorious, that incredible. No, those were fairy's wings, ones of many colors. But they vanished and left only the pale anatomy.

The entranced Kenny walked up the hilltop toward him, but the closer he grew, the further the man seemed to grow. Soon he collapsed onto the ground, staring up into the man's eyes. He was looking down upon him with bitterness and hatred in his expression.

"Why do you hate me?" Kenny asked.

The man looked at him. The moonlight illuminated every terrifying detail on his face. Lightning seemed to flash, and the outline of his body was replaced with another for a few moments. His eyes changed to that of what seemed like cat's then changed back to the calm state but rage still consumed everything.

Kenny looked at him, watching as he slowly drifted off into the distance. He reached for him but stopped, his expression changed to anger, and his body became tense in rage. He stood, breathing heavily in agony, and gazed across the land for a moment. He felt his shoulder begin to tense, like something was pulling on it, trying to make him change direction.

"You don't scare me," he mumbled. "I'm stronger than that!"

He sharply turned the upper half of his body around, ready to attack whatever was sneaking up behind him. His fist cutting through the air like a knife, he moved with great stiffness. His eyes narrowed but quickly widened. Tooka's head was mere inches away from his fist.

With a heavy gasp, Kenny scanned the area, finding himself in the identical spot he had been standing before the misfortunate meeting with Robert's doppelganger had occurred. Everything was calm, and it seemed as though nothing had ever happened. Had he possibly dreamed up the entire nightmare? He couldn't have been that tired.

"What?" he asked.

Tooka grabbed his hand and held it, rubbing his arm in worry. Iis was grabbing his pant leg, looking up into his eyes with fear, and slight boredom in his expression. Kenny looked around for a moment before he let his body relax and un-tense, and he continued to watch everything like a hawk, grabbing his head in confusion. He rubbed his temples and stood there in deep thought for a few moments.

"Kenny is all right?" Tooka asked.

Kenny nodded. "Yeah, I'm all right," he replied, moving his fist from in front of her face. He continued to rub his head and sighed, trying to register the last few moments in his boggled brain. His mind was spinning around in circles with so many questions entering and exiting with no answers to be found. *Was I...hallucinating?* he asked himself.

Kenny laughed a bit and crossed his arms. "I'll be darned, I must've been dreaming," he mumbled, looking at Tooka. She raised an eyebrow in question, but he just shrugged his shoulders a bit with a cocky yet reassuring grin on his dusty face. His eyes once again gazed over to the front of him.

A large gate once again stood in his path, concealed in complete and utter darkness, sounds of strange creatures consumed his ears, but a haunting melody dragged him off into the abyss of black. Kenny was almost tempted to just rush in there without the others. It was so incredibly magical he could barely stand there calmly. He went to move again but halted himself.

Kenny slowly slid his hand into Tooka's, making sure she was still beside him, and his other hand was taken by Iis' tiny little hand. He pulled it away and stuck his tongue out.

"You're sweaty," he mumbled in disgust.

Kenny laughed a bit and raised his hand into the air, not looking at anything else but the child.

"My bad," he said smiling, his eyes moving toward his sweaty palm. He blinked a bit, staring at this strange little object now in his hand. It was a small locket, drenched in sweat, the color was fading and the chain was rusted. He hadn't even felt it there, like it had just appeared out of thin air. Tooka looked at him in wonder, watching as he continued to gaze at the locket's surface.

You really were by my side, he thought, smiling, closing his hand around the gold chain. *Just like you always were...and just like you always had been.*

Chapter Thirty-one:

THE TRUTH REVEALED

WHILE KENNY WAS reuniting with the odd phantom, like Robert, in the strange, enigmatic snow-covered field, Heather Field was heavily basked in a storm. The window panes of the old Drake Estate knocked and shook, the floorboards creaking under the pressure, and the old wood was swollen with the heavy moisture.

In the windowless room across from Kenny's, Robert was sprawled on the floor, in a deep sleep which resulted in no rest. His eyes fluttered open a bit. He heard the noise outside, and turned his head toward the door. He began to wonder what was going on; the last he remembered was being attacked by O'Reilly. With a gasp, he grabbed the back of his head, wondering if he was injured, but to his great surprise and joy, he was completely unharmed.

Scrambling to his feet as soon as he realized where he was, he darted for the door. He heard the winds howling and the thunder booming off in the distance as he entered Kenny's room. Robert was a little confused as to how he had suddenly gotten back into his house, but he didn't question it. Much like every-thing that had happened lately, it didn't have an answer that was very reasonable or made much sense. He prayed Kenny would be sleeping in his own bed, that the past few days were nothing but a dream. But he knew, deep down, that it was too much to hope for.

The old door creaked as Robert slid it open, and he stared into the dark room, looking out to the window, watching as lightning bounced from one corner of his vision to the next. The windows were wide open, rain was drenching Kenny's bed in a heavy shower, and the piles of books were now ruined. Ink spilled from their many pages onto the ground.

Robert made his way over to the bed and sat down, trying to conserve some energy. He closed the windows, soon after finding himself a soaking wet mess and frighteningly cold. He turned the old oil lamp on and watched as the old room, the one that held so many of his precious childhood memories, was sud-denly engulfed in a mass glow of red and heat.

"I wonder," he whispered, opening the side table drawer. He fished through some old papers, books, and feather pens, feel-ing around for an old book he used to read when stormy nights rolled in. His fingers stopped on something rough, and out of curiosity he pulled it out. It revealed itself to be another diary, but this one was being used a lot it seemed, quite unlike most of the others which were lined with dust.

Every page was tattered and used up, some with dates going back as far as the nineteen fifties. All were signed with his grand-mother's name, in a rosy red ink, with a small stamp mark of a flower in the lower corner. Robert stopped on a page that had an all too familiar date on it. He began to slowly read the text aloud to himself, feeling as if he had to read it just to make it seem as real as he was imagining it to be.

"What an odd day," it began. "Olivia told me of something very catastrophic that had happened to her and poor Michael on their way over here tonight. It was raining just as hard as it was here, and the windshield wipers on their car stopped working suddenly, even though they had just been replaced.

"Out of the blue a very large van collided with them. Both adults in the car were killed, leaving only a small boy she claimed had hair as dark as raven's feathers, and for a brief moment, she said, he almost looked inhuman, and his eyes appeared almost fake. And then she had told me that the mother had said something strange.

"His mother had told me," she began, "that no one may ever know his true identity. And as she breathed her final breath, she slid a piece of paper into my hand. One which looked to be medical charts that belonged to the young boy, but they seemed almost brand new and fake in some spots. The young man's father was named Kenneth Mathis and his mother was Lily Mathis, the son seemed to be named after the father.

"And I wasn't going to listen, but she seemed as if it was her final wish, so we're keeping the boy's identity a secret.

"And so she now has some crazy idea of switching the boy's identities around. "They'll never know," she said. "Both have amnesia and can hardly even remember how to even speak. It was our fault those poor people were killed, and I believe it's our duty to respect her final wish.

"I don't like the idea, but I guess I should respect her wishes and how much she honors her word. But it will take time getting used to calling my poor grandbaby Kenny instead of Robby like I have since he was born."

Robert stopped and swallowed hard. *I'm...I'm Kenny?* he asked himself.

He set the book down and looked at his hands in confusion and fear, trying to register this newfound discovery in his boggled mind. How could he live with himself when he wasn't even the person he thought he was? He was living his best friend's, his brother's life, and now he may never get to tell him.

Robert sat there for a moment before he heard voices and what sounded like a heavy creaking of wood followed by another sound of glass snapping against a wall. *Was that the door? Oh man, he's back!* He quickly stood and rushed out the door, heading toward the end of the hallway.

O'Reilly's voice was screeching through the night, consuming everything in its path with a heavy, haunting howl. He darted toward the small hallway at the back of the house, the one that hid Kenny's secret green door. That was the only place he could go, if O'Reilly was below him, blocking the door, this was the only place for him to hide.

Dang it! I'm trapped like a rat! Robert was backed into a corner with nowhere to run, and he had a wall to his back, another to his left, one vicious snake and two giants in front of him, and a staircase that led to a locked door to his right. He was in hot water, with little hope in sight.

O'Reilly's shadow bounced across the top of the staircase and soon his horrid face appeared. He caught one glimpse of Robert and pulled out his gun, ready to end him at any second. The two brutes were mere inches behind him now, and if the bullet didn't kill him, they would the moment O'Reilly snapped his greedy little fingers.

"I have had just about enough of you!" he shouted, pressing the gun to Robert's forehead.

He sat there, trembled, tears in his eyes, and his breathing completely halted in fear. O'Reilly had his finger on the trigger. He was ready to shoot when something stopped him. The echoes of a crying animal's howl it seemed to be. Robert heard it, the sound rushing into his ears like something from a horror movie.

"Gohma, wonderful, just what I need right now. If this doesn't end you," O'Reilly whispered, shaking the gun, "my howling little friend there will."

He grabbed Robert's arm and pulled him up the stairs harshly, dragging him along like some rag doll. The two of them stepped foot onto the landing, and soon they were both face to face with the odd green door, the very one Kenny had kept a secret.

"Jasper, Rocco, go tell that half-wit of a mayor that the boy decided to give me the house!" O'Reilly snapped.

"You got it, boss," one replied.

Robert heard both of them run off as O'Reilly pulled him to his feet. He slammed him against the door with great strength. Robert gasped a bit as O'Reilly grabbed his chin, he sharply snapped Robert's head forward and stared straight into his trembling eyes, and tears gushed down his pale cheeks from the straight fear of O'Reilly.

"Leave me alone," Robert whispered. His breathing sped up, his eyes tried to stay closed but they wouldn't, no matter how hard he tried to force them shut. Robert turned his eyes toward the door, shook his head toward the door and gathered some courage. He coughed a bit. "You moron, the stupid thing is locked," he whispered.

O'Reilly scowled a bit, jamming the barrel of the gun into his hostage's throat. Robert grabbed the weapon in fear, trying to move it away, but his grip was too weak compared to his enemy's.

O'Reilly laughed, moving his hand down toward the trigger. "Well then, we'll just have to open it, won't we?"

Chapter Thirty-two:

THE LOST SOUL

"I'M SO HUNGRY!" Kenny groaned, grabbing his stomach. Tooka rolled her eyes and placed her hands on her hips. She stuck her tongue out. "Already ate," she replied.

"I know, but it was bugs!" Kenny spat.

Iis grabbed his stomach too and nodded in agreement, not satisfied in the least bit with the small, squirming meal. Kenny knew he probably hadn't eaten in a while, much like himself, but with the situation they were in it wasn't going to be easy finding a decent meal.

Kenny sat down on a rock and pondered the situation for a moment, staring blankly into the distance without much feeling in his expression. *Five days left, that's not a lot of time, especially since I have no idea where I am or how I'm going to get out of here.* He thought as he yawned, staring into space until he started hacking and wheezing.

Oh crap, the air! he thought, quickly gasping for a breath. His eyes shot up toward the ceiling. They must have wandered into an enclosed area without realizing it. Kenny began to feel light headed. He stood and hobbled around a bit, trying to make sure he wouldn't fall over. It wouldn't have been so bad if he wasn't already sick to his stomach from not eating in days, but it seemed the longer he lingered there, the worse his condition grew.

"Took—" Kenny began.

"The air!" she cut in, quickly turning to face Kenny. All across her face was a portrait of worry. She seemed to have had the same realization he had, grabbing her throat. The terror rocked the foundation just from the look she had given Kenny.

Kenny quickly grabbed Iis' hand and held onto him tightly as Tooka darted off into the distance, trying to find an exit before they all suffocated. Iis looked at Kenny, though he didn't make eye contact with the small boy like he had wished. He didn't want to worry the confused child, that would just make the situation worse.

"Kenny?" Iis asked.

"Not now, kiddo. This isn't a good time," he replied calmly, rushing off into the darkness where Tooka had vanished while the small boy was running behind him. Beneath him, Kenny felt mud, and the air smelled as though it had just rained. But there was no possible way for rain to enter through the thick vine ceiling.

Rushes of cold air swept around him, the fog rolling in made Kenny think of being underwater. Mist clung to everything heavily, like bloodsucking leaches on fresh prey. The noises Kenny had heard before roared in the night. Iis became frightened and grabbed onto Kenny's hand tightly. His tiny legs could barely allow him to keep up with the older people.

Spider hatchlings began to shoot from random nests in the walls, hissing loudly in pleasure from the rare thrill of the chase. Kenny's shoulder was racked with pain the moment one came within ten feet of his area, the marking seemed to dig deeper into his flesh, as though their presence tore into his body. Through all the pain it was hard to stay focused on where he was going, but the fearful cries and shrieks of Iis continued to help him stay strong.

Kenny turned a sharp corner, skidding across wet stone. He

slammed into a wall hard as Iis quickly stumbled to the ground. Tooka grabbed Kenny's hand and continued to pull him along. He had no time to react and grab Iis, forcing the young boy to run on his own. His boggled mind barely registered what had happened, though, so he had no idea of what was surrounding him or where he was going. The young boy just sat there, rubbing his head in wonder as Kenny vanished into the distance.

The forest behind them slowly seemed to become petrified, leaving only cold stone and frozen statues of the spiders, remnants of what had just been breathing. One by one each leaf became nothing but lifeless figures, time quickly running out for Kenny and his companions as everything was brushed away by the wicked spell.

We won't make it! Kenny thought, swallowing.

Iis stumbled behind Kenny, and he heard him scream a small bit, but everything was soon replaced by screeching noises and bloodthirsty howls of triumph. He came to a screeching halt, Tooka rushing off for a moment before she too was completely paralyzed where she stood. Iis was lying on the ground, unable to move. He looked up at Kenny, tears filling his eyes.

Kenny's mind flashed back to the car accident again, and he saw Robert's face in Iis' and the tears showed the same sorrowful plea for help that his friend's had all those years ago.

"Help," he gently cooed, reaching out for him. Kenny went to aid him when he was halted, unable to take another step. He was unable to do anything but stare at Iis' sad face with worry and compassion. Like a lifeless doll, one with broken legs that could never be replaced, one whose creator died and left him unfinished, a chapter in a book that was destined to never be finished, its secrets never to be revealed. That was how Iis seemed to Kenny.

Tooka pulled on Kenny's arm, trying to pry him away from the place he had been planted in, but the more she pulled the worse he became, still standing there without feeling in his numb body.

"This is not the way it shall end, not on my watch," Kenny heard.

This voice, not like the others that had been haunting him, this one was not Fireflood, nor Bloodwite, but it was identifiable, and the aura that emitted in the room was recognizable too. This was the one he had come to trust more than any, Blueweed.

Tooka quickly pulled on his arm, over-extending the muscles with one sharp tug. Kenny was brought back into reality and quickly let out a cry of pain, the sharpness running through his arm felt horrible. He turned to face Iis and went to grab him, but something seemed to halt his movements again. This time, it wasn't an unrecognizable force. It was truly something else, prying him away from the young boy.

A large shock wave sent Iis flying in Kenny's direction. He opened his arms up, ready to catch him and dart off the moment his body came in the slightest contact with the young boy's. As soon as he was close enough to grab, Kenny wrapped his arms around him. Though he felt nothing, he watched as the young child's body slid straight through his, like an elaborate illusion, he faded through his body and vanished.

Tooka, too, tried to catch the child, but to her surprise the same trickery happened. Iis was blown away, turned into dust like the phantom Robert, leaving only Kenny and Tooka. The gusts of wind picked up, as did the paralyzing spell over the forest.

"You must find the light," Kenny heard.

He watched as black wisps blew around him, like sand in the tide. Soon both he and Tooka were swept off their feet and blown deeper into the land, the darkness swallowing them whole.

Chapter Thirty-three:

THE SANCTUARY

The moment Kenny's body hit the ground, he shot up in fear. He dashed over to the entrance he had just been tossed out of, just as it became paralyzed and sealed shut. He slammed his hands against the sealed vines, screaming Iis' name in agony, trying to get a response from the lost child. His hands were scraped open and cut from the intensity of his fists slamming against the solid, unbreakable stone. Tooka rushed to his side and grabbed his waist, trying to pull him away and calm him a bit before he permanently damaged his hands.

"Kenny, quiet!" she shouted, trying to cease his screaming.

Kenny eventually calmed himself a bit and fell to his knees, hanging his head in sorrow and failure. Tooka looked at him, listening as his breathing quickly sped and tears began to form in his eyes from losing the child. Tooka pulled him away and held onto him, brushing her hands through his hair slowly to cease his crying.

"They all get hurt when they stay with me. They all trust me enough with their lives, and I end up halting it all, stopping their heartbeats in a second. I can't take it anymore! They all died because of me!" Kenny shouted.

Tooka shook her head a bit. Kenny just looked at her in question and in fear. She went to brush her hand against his face, but he just slammed it down, holding her back from her attempts to comfort him. He knew he needed it right now, he knew that he wanted her to hold him and make him feel like he wasn't useless, but he couldn't bear it, he couldn't take any more lies. And he couldn't stand the thought of her getting hurt because of him.

Kenny feared her safety now, he wanted her to leave, to turn back and never see him again. There would be nothing more he could ever want at any time, in any place than to see her leave and never look back. Though he knew she could only protest.

"Kenny...feel like lots of deer!" Tooka said, trying to cheer him up.

Kenny shook his head in reply. He held onto himself, feeling shots of pain rush all across his body. Tooka sighed a bit and cocked her head to one side gently, smiling the widest her face would allow her to. She looked at Kenny, hoping that she may be able to make him laugh a bit but he only looked away.

"Not your fault," she said. "Not useless, just tired."

"Tired? This isn't just tired, Tooka, this is failure. I promised them I'd be there, and all I did was let them down!" Kenny shouted, slamming his fist onto the floor.

Tooka almost heard the bones shatter in his hand upon impact. She grabbed his hand and gently held it, rubbing the palm tenderly, feeling the battered bones under her fingers. She pulled him close and held him, not letting him move the slightest inch. She wanted him to relax and stay there in her arms for a moment, so she could let everything sink in and try to find some sort of method to comfort her scared friend.

"Tooka," Kenny began, looking at her. "Why?"

"I love you," Tooka whispered.

"I love you too," Kenny replied. "I really do."

"You hide from me too much. I thought Kenny didn't like me anymore."

"Huh? No, I do like you!"

"I like Kenny too."

Kenny closed his eyes, smiling giddily. The words were so gentle and clear to him. The remnants of lost memories in his head, more visions of Robert's pale, bloody face rubbing against the concrete began to grow into memories of the happiest times he could think of, and he could barely even consider the thought of his friend in pain.

Time passed and yet Kenny spoke no other words, only the voice of Tooka singing the remaining lines of a lullaby were to be heard in the large, barren chamber. Stars showered the room in light through the leaves above them. Kenny looked at her and watched as she slowly began to find some comfort herself.

"You okay?" Tooka asked.

Kenny smiled and nodded, he loved those words. They rushed through his head like a migraine, so pulsating and fast, but it was only pain to his aching heart. But he smiled still for no reason. He guessed this was what love sometimes felt like.

"It hurts, Tooka, their words," Kenny said, tears rolling from his eyes. That gentle, harmless smile was still on his face as he spoke and cried.

"I still can't," he continued, "I still can't understand them like I want to. They hurt me, they want something, they want me to listen and I can't."

Kenny pushed himself from Tooka and looked at her, his body pale and limp. The sweat made his clothes hang off of his body and his hair stick to his greasy face. He wiped his eyes with his arm, brushing the tears away one by one. They hid themselves across his skin, much like Kenny they didn't want to be alone anymore.

Kenny listened to the voices talking to him, his eyes gazing from one end of the room to the next, catching a glimpse of every blade of grass and every leaf on the trees. All were wet with dew, much like everything was in the room before. But there were no clouds in the skies, and no rainfall was heard at all the past day. Kenny knew that Blueweed had been here, the guardian of the waves. It was the only explanation to it, plus Kenny could feel his presence rushing into his veins.

The words he could barely understand before were almost clear now, Kenny's heart was racing, and its beats were becoming uneven and harsh. His body was giving out on him now, not a thing was to be done. Winds were blowing around him, and he felt enlightened and peaceful, not scared and tormented like he had been. All was calm. *What do you want?* Kenny asked, unable to speak now. *How can I make you go away?*

"Escape is inevitable," the voice of a man replied, it was crisp and fresh like an early winter's morn, soft and vigorous. *Can anything, anything at all be done to make the pain stop?* Kenny continued. His eyes closed harshly to concentrate.

"This pain is not our fault," he continued.

Kenny opened his eyes and found nothing but white surrounding him. He turned his head a small bit and saw the man from before, the one who resembled a human more than those of the world Kenny had been thrown into. He was looming over him, his back was against Kenny's and his head was tilted toward the sky. He laughed a bit and Kenny's body tensed in fear, the haunting voice ringing in his ears.

"This pain, this torture you feel now, is your doing. You rack yourself with pain, trying to resist the voices," he said quietly.

"I'm not resisting," Kenny said, trembling a bit now.

"Not now, but you were," he snapped back. "What changed?"

Kenny sat for a moment, listening to a distant melody he heard from somewhere unseen by human eyes. The noises that surrounded him were peaceful yet like an angry torrent at the same time. At war with one another to gain control of the illusionary world Kenny had been suddenly taken to.

"I...I think I want to be forgiven for what I did, or for what I didn't do," Kenny said, nodding. "Yes, I want to be forgiven, forgiven for taking those people's lives. For betraying their trust..."

The man laughed. "Whose trust?"

Kenny snapped his head behind him to catch a glimpse of the man, hearing his voice go faint. The white had vanished, replaced by the chamber. Tooka was staring at him in question, wondering what had happened to make him suddenly go silent on her.

"Is Kenny still awake or asleep now?" Tooka asked, placing her hand on Kenny's.

He nodded and smiled as wide as he could. Sweat and tears still consuming his face.

"Awake and all right," he said smiling. "Now...I'm all right, thanks to him."

Chapter Thirty-four:

THE RUINS

"WE'VE GOT TO get out of here," Kenny whispered into Tooka's ear as the two ducked down behind a large bush. She nodded, staring off into the distance. In front of them was a nest, one which housed many large spiders, all of which looked like the monster from Kenny's visions. They were sleeping, peacefully, which was how Kenny wished to keep it at any length possible.

"What are those things?" Kenny asked, turning his eyes toward Tooka.

"Spawns," she replied.

"I know that!" Kenny stopped and slapped his hand over his mouth. He held his breath, praying he didn't just give their hiding place away with his short temper. There was rustling in the bushes, and the sounds of snapping jaws filled his ears, but it seemed as though they were safe.

Tooka glared at him coldly, and he let his shoulders tense a bit, and his upper body lean in toward the ground. He looked at her apologetically, but she didn't respond. She was too busy trying to find a way around the large hoard of monsters. Kenny continued to look at her longingly, and he felt much better now, reassured in some ways, but she grew angry that he hadn't returned her affections earlier. And when he said he was 'all right, thanks to him' she took it offensively, as though Robert had helped overcome his fears and Tooka had done nothing to help. And she wouldn't listen to reason.

"I'm sorry," Kenny whispered.

Tooka only turned her head and began to sidle her way over to a large ruin. The large cobwebs hanging from its surface gave Kenny chills and made him feel uncomfortable, but he had no choice but to follow Tooka. The exterior of the large gateway was almost identical to the one outside of the large maze, but the flowers were only rotting and the stones only molding and growing weak, most crumbling. There was no life in this dull place.

Kenny heard his footsteps beneath him growing louder as the ground changed from grass to stone. Tooka was already deep in the tunnel, hidden in the shadows. Kenny continued to run until his foot suddenly stopped moving. He looked down only to find himself caught in between the stones in the floor, unable to pry himself free from its grip. He pulled and tugged with all his might but couldn't move the slightest inch. Some loose stones rubbed against his worn boot cut the surface of his boot as he struggled with all his might to get himself free, before something found him.

The more he struggled, it seemed, the deeper it went. *Dang it!* Kenny thought, hissing. Out of the corner of his eye, he caught Tooka's outline in the shadows. She looked at him with worry and anger on her face, the worry for his safety but the anger from what had happened earlier. Tooka quickly rushed over to Kenny and tried to help him get free. She pulled as hard as she could on his leg, but it wouldn't seem to budge.

Tooka stopped struggling. Kenny watched as she was instantly consumed by a large entity of some sort standing in front of them. A shadow overpowered the area around them with a hazy blanket. Kenny's head quickly shot up above him to follow where Tooka's gaze had gone.

Another very large spider was above them, this one was

covered in markings unlike anything Kenny had ever seen. All of them were glowing with a deep yellow pigment. In a mere instant, Kenny's body grew pale, and he was shaking harshly in terror. Kenny quickly grabbed onto Tooka, making sure she was safe if it tried to attack. Drool was falling down onto him from the monster's large mouth, and it lowered its head to look at him, and soon Kenny could only see himself, his reflection dancing across the monster's eye. Tooka looked up at Kenny then buried her face in his chest, watching as the monster's eye changed from its bright yellow state to a crimson blanket.

It reared back on its hind leg and roared angrily. The others behind him began to howl in unison with him. The noise was ear-shattering, and at most times Kenny could barely keep himself upright it was so loud.

Soon the beast shot itself down onto them. Kenny quickly grabbed Tooka and tossed her aside. Her body went tumbling across the stone and grass until she stopped many feet away from him, under the entrance of the ruins. The shadow of the creature moved quickly like a sundial would as it grew closer to Kenny. Soon it was the only thing he saw.

His body was racked with heavy pressure as it came crushing down onto him. The ground beneath shattered, Kenny fell down into the darkness with the large spider falling with him. It all happened so fast, one moment Kenny was hovering in the air, stones and rocks colliding with his head, and darkness consuming everything around him, sending chills and horrifying thoughts into his head. The next, he was drowning in a large pool of water with the large spider on top of him, making him sink faster into the muck-filled lake.

Every now and then he would hit the wall, feeling mud brush against his body and his arms tangle with weeds, but he couldn't find the strength to grab onto any of it to try and stop the creature from pulling him down further.

All seemed lost again, no matter how hard he tried, no matter how much he prayed, or how much he tried to do the right thing he couldn't find good in anything anymore. His life seemed meaningless. The water was cold, like needles sticking into his body. No warmth found him there, and he just continued to sink further and further down, the air in his lungs gone the moment he had entered the lake.

Kenny heard something, like someone shouting his name. His eyes opened quickly, and he saw Blueweed above him, his aquatic form slowly becoming visible. He extended his hand to him, and Kenny tried to reach up to grab it, but he had no strength. He could barely even move anymore. He wanted to just fall into a deep sleep and never wake up. Maybe he would find happiness somewhere else. In a place that no one could get hurt because of him, his pain would stop, and everything would be somewhat normal. Did such a place really exist? That is what he wondered.

Blueweed refused to let him go any further, and he grabbed his hair and pulled him up through the water until his hand came in contact with his own. Kenny looked up at him a bit through the water, watching as his outline seemed to be brushed away with the current.

Light was showering onto the top of the river, Kenny could almost feel the sweet relief of air burst into his lungs the moment he saw it. Hope was returning to him but quickly shattered in an instant as he felt tugging on his leg. His head shot down, catching a quick glimpse of something very large swarm beneath him. His foot was tangled in some sort of webbing, one that was almost eating the flesh from his leg. He clenched his teeth tightly in anger, using all his strength to help Blueweed pull him up. Air continuously slipped from his lips with every passing second and soon it was all gone.

Blueweed's hand slipped from Kenny's. He was quickly pulled down into the water, into the darkness. Blueweed swam down after him as fast as he could, trying to find some way to stop the creature that was attacking them as he went. More webs shot through the water, Blueweed merely able to dodge them. Most grabbed onto Kenny's body, and soon he was entangled inside a mass of them.

He was lost in the trap, the webs squeezing harder on his body with every second. Choking the few moments of life he had left out of him. Blueweed quickly grabbed a loose log that was bursting from the muddy, rocky wall. He pressed down on it with all his might, feeling the earth from where it had been housed move and shake. Kenny was almost gone, hidden deep in the muck and filth he had been tossed into. The water poisoned Blueweed and weakened his strength, turning his own element against him.

Before he even realized, Blueweed had broken the wall into pieces. He was sent away from the wall during the sudden impact, tumbling around until he found himself upside down, on the other side of the bank. Rocks and dirt clods went pouring through the water, down onto the sinking spider. Loud screams were heard, howls from the monster entered Kenny's ears, and soon he could feel his body again as the tangled webs undid themselves and set him free.

Blueweed, once again, grabbed Kenny and began to swim to the surface. Kenny was unconscious, and his breathing had been stopped for well over ten minutes. Any longer and Blueweed would have given up all his hope on him. *He's lighter*, Blueweed thought warily. *He's lost so much weight, and he's getting sick.*

Soon both burst from the water's hold, the surface around them shattering like a glass plate. Blueweed shoved Kenny's body up onto the bank and pulled himself up along with him. He pressed his ear against his chest and listened closely, waiting to hear even the slightest heartbeat.

"Help...me," Kenny moaned, to him it seemed well over a minute between each word and no breath was entering his lungs. Blueweed placed his hand gently on Kenny's mouth and slowly pulled it away, water followed his hand in a trail, dancing through the air like a hurricane up into his hand, just as he had done before during their first meeting. Small specks of dark red coloring were to be seen in the water, but Blueweed paid no attention to the odd coloring.

Kenny coughed a bit, finally allowed to breathe. Though he took no breath, he almost couldn't. Blueweed heard no water rushing in his body, and he was allowed freedom to breathe, but he soon came to realize what Kenny had since the moment he had been freed from the water's grip. Blueweed lifted his head up with his hand and looked at his wet, peeling flesh. He pulled some of the excess, already dead skin from his face and watched Kenny for a moment before he let his head rest on the muddy ground again, his eyes were slightly open, tears forming from the stinging pain of the poisoned water and his breathing still stopped completely.

Blueweed looked at his hands for a moment in shock, shaking in fear. He gasped. "B-blood!"

Chapter Thirty-five:

THE LOSS

BLOOD WAS SEEPING through Blueweed's fingers down onto Kenny's battered body. His mangled form was already covered in thick layers of the red liquid. Blueweed looked around quickly, trying to find something to stop the bleeding and maybe save him from slipping back into unconsciousness. He went to place his hand on Kenny's shoulder to calm him some, give him reassurance, though Kenny only protested by grabbing his wrist tightly, his blue skin turning a deep white from lack of circulation.

He pulled himself up, using Blueweed to support him as he went, the elder man placed his free hand on Kenny's back and helped him straighten out a bit. He watched as Kenny became eye level, his body still weak and unable to do much on its own, but the moment their eyes met for the first time, Kenny felt a bit reassured and safe.

"B-blueweed...?" Kenny whispered his question gently, feeling a bit embarrassed that he may have misnamed him for another. He couldn't even see him clearly.

"Yes?" Blueweed asked, Kenny feeling a burst of cold, bitter chills rushing into his spine when he spoke, though his voice was very calm and gentle.

"Are we close to the Grave?" Kenny asked.

Blueweed nodded a bit in reply, Kenny only smiled, though you could hardly tell do it the size of his joyous expression being so small, the burnt flesh on his face pausing most facial actions he attempted.

"Please, go find Tooka. Let her know I'm okay, and take her home...This isn't her fight, it...is mine," he explained, speaking as if it were his final wish.

Blueweed watched him as he grasped his shoulder, and he could see the pain he was in all too clearly, and an all too familiar marking on his flesh, though he dared not speak its name. He wanted to listen, knowing it was what he truly wanted. But would he leave Kenny alone, in such a state?

"I will," he finally said.

Kenny smiled a bit, but it faded as he felt the ground shake beneath him harshly. He tried to keep himself upright but fell over on the ground, unable to sit up due to the immense level of gravity being turned against him. His body landing only a few centimeters away from Blueweed's legs. The frightened man quickly placed his hands on Kenny's shoulders and almost threw himself on top of him to protect him from whatever perils they were about to face.

"The wall...!" Blueweed shouted, realizing that he had just caused their demise by destroying the monster. He stood, trying to catch his footing again. He heard the ground shattering around him, and he saw Kenny panicking, trying to figure out what was going on. Blueweed heard rumbling and saw a large shadow looming over Kenny, his eyes traced the tall shadow back to the wall, seeing as a large pillar come tumbling down onto the paralyzed, bloody blonde.

Without second thoughts or another word, Blueweed dove and tackled Kenny away from the pillar. Kenny had no time to react. All he saw was Blueweed's form consuming his vision and nothing but an array of black after. He was sent flying away a few feet before he came to a stop as everything fell deathly silent.

With his weak arms he pushed himself to his feet again, hoping that he may find strength to see what had happened. He hobbled over to the pillar that had collapsed near him, looming over it as he scanned the area for any sign of Blueweed.

A form lay underneath, and Kenny kneeled down next to it and saw Blueweed's pale, already cold face buried under piles of mud and his battered body crushed beneath the ancient structure.

"Blueweed please...Open up your eyes!" Kenny asked, gently shaking him.

No response was given. Kenny pushed against the pillar with all his might, not moving it much, but he refused to give up and let Blueweed just lie there. He groaned as he used all his might in attempts to pry this heavy pillar from his savior's body.

Weakened, he somehow managed to move it enough to pull Blueweed away and let him lie without strain. His breathing was stopping and his wondrous, gentle blue-pigmented skin was turning pale grey.

"Kenny," Blueweed laughed. Kenny used his leg to support Blueweed's head in the air, the rest of his body limply lying on the ground.

"Blueweed, can you hear me? Are you all right?" Kenny asked, worry in his voice.

Blueweed tried to answer, but the deficits were all too clear, his mind was going and soon Kenny could feel him leaving, his body not struggling to wake anymore.

Kenny shook his head. "Don't leave me," he whispered.

Blueweed smiled a bit and closed his eyes, deep breaths continued to slip from his lips, more strain and continuous lack of air growing larger with every passing moment.

"It is...my time. I am sorry," he said, tears rolling down his cheeks. "I only wish...I could've known you...like Robert does."

With that said, his breathing stopped, his eyes shut, and Kenny felt him finally release his hold on life, now finally ready to rest in peace like he had wished, like Kenny knew he deserved.

Somehow, Kenny found enough strength to lift him into his arms and gently carry him down into the darkness of the corridors, the only exit he could see. He couldn't bear to leave him in that wretched area. Blueweed's head bobbled as Kenny walked into the darkness. Kenny's eyes not removing themselves from his face. He felt like Blueweed had given him his remaining strength. Sure he was weakened and a bloody mess but he found some sort of courage and power to keep going. Another life sacrificed for his cause, he knew he could *not* give up, he refused to.

Soon, Kenny found himself in front of a glorious room. There was a shallow pond, filled with light blue and white lilies. Behind was a large willow, growing from the stone wall, the long branches cascaded down onto the still, crystal clear liquid, the leaves all wet with the crystal clear water.

In the middle of it all stood what looked like a table made of stone, encrypted with blue writing and sapphires. Dried blood was on top of it, the way it was shaped and the way the blood had been spilled, Kenny could only guess someone had been stabbed there. Long, silky strands of blue hair covered the top of the block of stone. The room emitted with heavy, blazing energy that flowed from Blueweed's lifeless body, the last bits of strength he had finally leaving him, like the fog that was escaping the river's hold outside, gently soothing its way into an unwilling night.

Kenny laid Blueweed's body on the rock and let him lie there; thinking this place of rest, this small deed was the very least he could do for him. Pressure, light, and gentle, was placed on Kenny's shoulder. It was a hand, one that was of a green pigment. Leaves and vines with long thorns had been wrapped around this stranger's flesh. Kenny watched Blueweed for a moment before he turned to look at who had entered the room.

"I'm sorry," Kenny whispered.

"Nay, this was neither your fault nor his, my son. We were all chosen to die at one point. To finally rest in peace, is all he wished, his time just came sooner than we all had liked," Bloodwite said, coming into the shallow pond next to Kenny.

Kenny watched as Bloodwite gently brushed his hand against Blueweed's face, and held his hand calmly. Gently whispering words he couldn't understand. Kenny looked at the wording on the stone he had placed Blueweed on, questioning what the odd thing was doing in this place.

"You should feel honored, Blueweed, even the stars refuse to shine tonight. They are bowing their heads in your honor," he whispered.

"He was your brother," Kenny finally said, breaking the silence. Bloodwite lifted his head and looked at Kenny. He stood up straight and turned to face him. He placed his hands together and smiled a bit, sorrowfully.

"Yes, very observant," Bloodwite said. "He, myself, and Fireflood, we are all brethren. Before your time, most likely before your world even knew of our presence, the times when very few actually had seen us, we three followed the master, M'nep, to fight the Gohma. The Gohma, in the end, was vanquished! Our poor master was slain brutally, and we could not do anything to help him. Lonely and guilt-stricken, all of us perished with him.

Yet somehow, none of us could rest in peace. We heard voices in a tongue we could not understand one day, and we felt called back to the surface world only to find humans loitering on our land without purposes except a search for freedom. They taught us their language, and in exchange we allowed them to prosper in the area called Heather Field."

Bloodwite kept his eyes on Kenny the entire time, watching as he explained a question he had long wanted answered.

"Our lord told of one who would one day come searching for his treasure, and he told us to allow this child to take it if his heart was pure enough and to protect him with our lives. I believe Blueweed has fulfilled his duty to M'nep."

"But," Kenny began, "how do you actually defy death?"

"With this knowledge of someone to protect, we had no choice but to find a way to defy death. We waited in the dark for him, for this chosen child. Only with half of our powers, half of our strength though. Blueweed came back sickly, as did Fireflood, and myself...myself unable to do anything about it," Bloodwite said sadly.

"Why?" Kenny asked.

"We were unable to find our bodies. Without them, we might as well have stayed slain. But we had a duty, and we were bound by an undying devotion to withhold it," Bloodwite replied.

He let his hand run across the surface of the stone that Blueweed's body was on, feeling as if the life was draining out of him with every motion. He patted the top of the stone and looked at Kenny, watching as Bloodwite slid his thumb into a crack. His eyes gazed at Kenny, the deep colors almost hypnotizing him.

"In there?" Kenny asked, kneeling down in the water. Bloodwite removed his finger from the crack and let Kenny look inside. A pale, sleeping Blueweed was inside, his body very weak, and his breathing stopped. He looked up at Bloodwite in question as he stood.

"This was his final resting place, in our lives before, the ones that have past us. If only he had not left," Bloodwite said, placing his hand on Blueweed's. "His body was so close, If only...no! His sacrifice was not in vain! It ..."

Tears rolled down Bloodwite's cheeks in heavy numbers, and Kenny placed his hand on Bloodwite's shoulder. The elder man turned to look at him. He almost immediately found hope by looking into Kenny's eyes. He smiled and placed his hands on Kenny's shoulders. Kenny looked at his hand, wiggling his fingers in front of his face as he stood wondering what had changed so quickly.

"It, truly, was not in vain. I see what he saw, now...I see what he saw in you," Bloodwite said quietly. *What Blueweed saw in me?* Kenny questioned, grabbing his chest. Bloodwite nodded, almost reading his mind.

"Kenny, listen to me. I am very weak right now as there is a great disturbance in the tomb and my powers aren't at full strength. But I am going to try and help you, alright?" Bloodwite explained. Kenny raised an eyebrow in question, not really understanding what he meant. Bloodwite's hands began to glow a faint green tint, Kenny watched the wounds on his body heal somewhat, it never ceased to amaze him the powers of these creatures.

A few moments had passed and Kenny's body was in decent shape again, he was still a peeling, blood stained mess but he was better than he had been for a while. Kenny thanked Bloodwite, but without another word he began to fade out, Kenny saw through his body to the other side of the wall. He went to stop him, trying to halt his movements, but Bloodwite vanished too quickly.

Kenny stopped moving and let his body un-tense, the question still running through his mind. What did he see? Kenny looked down at Blueweed's face. He smiled a bit and turned around, walking off into the darkness. He was confused, and in question, but he felt confident knowing that somehow Blueweed had finally found peace.

Chapter Thirty-six:

THE STONE MAN

KENNY LIMPED DOWN into the dark corridors, trying to find some way outside, maybe to the surface to find Tooka again. He prayed she somehow had gotten away from the large insects and was able to find shelter. Above, Kenny heard thunder and the sound of a heavy storm. He knew that it was probably pouring above. The mud walls were leaking with large streams of water.

Kenny, lost in his thoughts and the dark, felt his foot slip from under him. He stumbled a bit, and soon he felt his body rolling downhill at and unstoppable speed. He hit rocks and was covered in mud, landing in large piles of dirt and stone almost every second. He tumbled downward before he found himself not only a shedding, bloody mess, but also covered in thick layers of grime and tangled in many plants that he knew, just due to his horrid luck, were probably poison ivy.

Soon he came to a halt, stopping in a large puddle of mud. He lifted his head up as best he could to look at his surroundings, finding himself in pure darkness with only strange, glowing red eyes watching him to give feeling to the night. They all blinked and vanished. He heard things which sounded like suction cups prying themselves from stone and the noises of snapping jaws as they disappeared. He guessed they were plotting his demise, waiting for him to be hypnotized by something before they would strike.

But, again he stood, and hobbled his way off into the darkness, not caring where he was going or where he would end up, as long as he could finally rest and be away from the fear and heartache.

The tunnel he was in had been encrusted with sapphires, ones that seemed to be leading him deeper and deeper into the cavern. His eyes wandered into a small room, one that seemed to be boarded off loosely. He knew this would be the only spot he could be safe in. The only holes he could enter or exit from would be too small for most anything, even him it seemed.

He slid his way into one of the cracks, slicing himself open as he went, the nails ripping his skin apart even more. His body barely fit through the small opening the boards made, but somehow, miraculously, he was able to get through in one piece. He fell to the ground, landing on a patch of leaves growing from the soft soil, though water splashed around him as well. He felt as though he had landed in a shallow pond.

Kenny closed his eyes for a moment before he let them wander, and it looked as though another large willow tree was growing from the little lake, and he gazed at some large root-like formations in the wall up to the very top. He let out a yelp of shock, seeing the form of a man pressed into the wall, leaving only his face hidden beneath the tree branches and arms, one sticking into the wall, looking as though he was ready to embrace someone, the other was sticking out of the rocky canvass, in his hand was a lamp that was dimly shinning.

Two eyes opened; they were calm yet full of shock. Kenny quickly pulled himself up and tried to get out through the hole he had entered through. He felt leaves brush against him and a voice of someone old; it sounded brittle and scratchy.

"After a hundred years," it said.

Kenny stopped and turned his head to look at him, in his

hand he was holding a lantern, and his eyes were almost filled with tears from the sight of Kenny.

"A hundred years?" Kenny questioned. "A hundred years since what?"

"Since I've seen another human being," he replied, longing in his tone

He looked down but quickly looked up at Kenny again, seeing blood running into his pond from the boy's feet. He let out a gasp and quickly pulled his other hand from the wall. It looked like a skeletal cage, like the other side was completely gone, decayed from the passage of time, leaving only a curved stone form like jagged teeth of a monster. He quickly pulled an old coat from a rock on the wall and handed it to Kenny.

The frightened youth realized he was struggling to give him the clothing so he walked down into the pond and took it, wrapping it around himself to keep warm. He then urged Kenny to sit down on the ground to rest some and regain as much strength as he could. Both remained silent for a moment, both wanting to speak to the other but unable to find the right words.

"What are you?" Kenny asked.

He only laughed. "Not what, my boy, who, I am only who. A who which lost his identity as well as his face many years ago, so long ago I can barely remember it. And you, my boy, are who too, one who still has his face and his life though, unlike this old, washed up traveler."

"Are you asking for my name?" Kenny asked. The man nodded, Kenny heard the rocks behind him creek and crack. This man was incredible. Kenny saw how he had become the rock wall itself, his skin was all jagged and grey like the stones, yet he still kept every little detail on his face. Kenny felt sorry for him, to be trapped down here and then boarded off so no one could ever find you. It must have been lonely.

"Kenny, Kenny Mathis," he replied. "And you?"

"I was once known as Alexander, my last name of no importance anymore. Though now I have no name, I am just a mere remnant of what once was something, something great," he replied.

Life story, here we come, Kenny thought, smiling. He was actually quite excited. Something to keep his mind from his current condition and situation was just what he needed to keep himself sane.

"But I won't bore you with details," he said kindly.

Kenny shook his head. "I don't have anything better to do," he replied.

The old man laughed a bit, the willow leaves bouncing up and down.

"What about you my boy? You must have had some reason to travel all this way down here," he said, question in his tone.

"When I was young there was an accident, I was orphaned and I ended up living with the family who was also part of the accident. I'm really close to their son, Robert, we're like brothers.

"But there's this guy, he wants the land Robert's family owns. He thinks there's some door that leads to the Grave of the Fireflies in there, and he's bound and determined to get that treasure. Come hell or water high he's going to get it, even if it means shooting every last person on this earth. If I could find it, everything would be okay," he explained.

"Would it really?" Alexander asked.

Kenny's head shot up to look at him. He began to question everything, thoughts and fears shot into his head so fast he almost collapsed into the pond. Would finding the treasure really be enough to stop O'Reilly? Would it make everything better? If he *was* dead, it still couldn't bring Robert back, and even if he was all right, it wouldn't be enough to heal his wounds. Tears started to form in Kenny's eyes, he bit his lip, trying to suppress the tears, but they continued to come. He hadn't ever considered what would actually happen if and when he found the famous lost gold.

"It won't," Kenny finally said, grabbing onto the coat tighter to keep his shivering body warm. He lowered his head in shame, feeling useless and unworthy of all the people who were sacrificing their safety and even their lives for him. He didn't deserve the kindness he was being given, or the shelter he was now in.

"I can't do anything now, can I?" he asked, looking up at the stone man's face. He almost looked ashamed that he had spoken to him and crushed all of his hopes. But the truth needed to, one way or another, be implanted into his head.

Alexander shook his head a bit and sighed, Kenny knowing he was through talking about the subject now. He was getting annoyed with the silence and somewhat paranoid as well. He looked up at him and smiled, trying to stop the tears with all his might.

"Why are you like this, what did you do to become paralyzed like that?" he asked, his voice shrill and high. The man raised a rocky eyebrow in question.

"Ah, this strange figure is finally getting the better of you, eh?" he asked, smirking slightly.

Kenny nodded, trying to find a kind way to say that he was getting disturbed by the strange stone exterior he had. It was a little unnerving seeing a man made of stone talking to him and giving him life-changing advice.

"You see here, on my neck, that marking? And the ones that slowly have been pressed into my flesh, now covered in stone along with it?" he asked. Kenny nodded in reply, quickly swallowing hard at the sight of the familiar mark. Kenny grabbed his shoulder, gently rubbing the small tattoo-like marking. The very same one Alexander had just pointed out.

"This is the mark of the Gohma, and most people aren't as lucky as me when they get this horrifying black spot. Most rot somewhere in the catacombs, leaving nothing but ink-covered skeletons, and the echoes of their screams from their final moments, it's a horrifying thought, isn't it?" He stopped and watched as Kenny grabbed his head and moaned loudly in agony, just the thought of that horror movie-like sentence made his stomach upset and his body tremble, and what was worst, he was going to suffer the same fate. Yet, Alexander continued, "It is unpredictable, this marking of greed, you may never know what will happen once you get marked with it. Luckily, my son, you have not received this curse. You won't become like us, the anathema of the Grave."

He couldn't take it anymore. Kenny collapsed onto the ground, his face buried under the water, the thought of all those things and the returning questions of what this journey's endeavor really would give him; reprieve or punishment?

Chapter Thirty-seven:
THE MURDER

"HOW COULD YOU?" Bloodwite asked, stepping into a puddle of water after Fireflood. Both men walked deep into the tunnels, their footsteps echoing throughout the night. Bloodwite's robe was soaked thoroughly due to the strange, odd humidity that had crept over them. He knew that something strange was happening yet, somehow, he couldn't place his finger on it. The more he continued to walk, the weirder this feeling was. And worst of all his energy was drained from reviving Kenny.

Fireflood's aura had changed; it seemed cold and unfeeling. He made no eye contact with his brother and spoke little words. His whole demeanor had changed in a mere few minutes.

"He is dead, dead! And yet you neither cry nor mourn this loss!" Bloodwite cried out.

"I have more important things to worry about," Fireflood snapped.

"I'm ashamed of you; I'm ashamed to be walking behind you right now!" he spat.

"Oh, cry me a river."

Bloodwite stopped dead in his tracks, his breathing halted, and his eyes wide in shock. Fireflood refused to look at him. He just continued to walk down into the darkness of the corridors, heading straight into the heart of M'nep's tomb. Bloodwite quickly ran to catch up with his brother, and soon he was standing at his side. He was almost tempted to just step in front of him and ask him what he was thinking.

Bloodwite shook his head. "Why?" Tears were swelling in his eyes again, and Fireflood watched him for a moment, almost tempted to wipe those tears away like he had always done when his brothers needed comforted but he stopped. He pushed his brother out of the way and stormed off. Bloodwite was paralyzed, in shock over this strange behavior of his brother. Fireflood raised his head and gazed at him coldly.

"He is dead. There is no possible way of allowing him another passage into this world!" Bloodwite shouted, watching as Fireflood continued to walk passed him. "We can only escape death once!"

Fireflood stopped dead in his tracks, he mumbled some words under his breath, ones which Bloodwite could not understand. Soon he broke out into fits of laughter, almost hyperventilating as he did, the sick noise continued to reign through the night. He turned his upper body to look at Bloodwite a bit then quickly turned around and continued walking.

Bloodwite followed him in utter silence, unable to question anything anymore. Obviously, questioning his brother would lead him nowhere. Both headed on into the darkness, Bloodwite not knowing where Fireflood was taking him. The sounds of his own footsteps made him jump. He hadn't ever remembered being this tense, this uneasy. Not since the night M'nep left their sides. It felt horrid.

Soon they approached a flight of old, mold-covered stairs, and light was shinning down onto the passage, and the sound of rain was consuming their ears. They ascended onward, heading up into the area above, straight into the heart of the labyrinth.

To Bloodwite's great surprise, this room, this forbidden area, was now covered in blood. It was a large, circular chamber. Trees lined the outside of a very large, crystal pond. Rocks with carvings floated inside, small boats with candles were hovering around in the water, lighting the dark area. Bloodwite and Fireflood stood at the top of another small flight of stairs that crept down into a solid bowl like surface. The clay platform floated in the far end of the room. From this area, on the other end of the platform where they stood, another flight of stairs lay at the bottom of a large, rounded surface that served as a walkway. The inside layer of this floating object was filled with moss and water.

At the very end of the oval chamber, where the wall finally connected to solid ground, was another large round disk. At its end, lying on the wall stood a rounded door, locked with ancient technology. Beyond it, hidden from the world, was the very thing Kenny had been searching for.

It had been ages since Bloodwite had seen this place. His eyes wandered across the setting in a bit of question and misunderstanding, feeling as though something had changed since his last visit. Wonder-filled eyes gazed down into the platform ahead, and he gasped, seeing a bloody form lying at the bottom of the stairs. He pushed himself away from Fireflood's side and rushed to the aid of the man lying on the ground. His raven black hair was dyed with blood, his body was in critical conditions, and his pulse was weak.

"Fireflood, if you knew he was here, why didn't—" Bloodwite halted his words before he continued. His eyebrows narrowed and his eyes flooded with rage. That was the final nail on Bloodwite's coffin. He laid the bloody body down onto the floor and confronted his elder brother.

"What has gotten into you?" he hissed.

"I believe humans call it...bribery," Fireflood replied, smirking as wide as his mouth would allow him.

Bloodwite shook his head. "You've spoken with humans?"

Fireflood laughed and walked down a small flight of stairs into the small area the bloody boy and Bloodwite were in. He felt the disk move in the water as his weight was shifted against him. He pressed his hand on his chest and shrugged his shoulders sadistically. Deriving every bit of pleasure he could from his brother's fear.

"And haven't you?" Fireflood asked. His deep voice was filled with smugness as he cocked his head to the side. He continued to walk onward until he was dead center in the platform.

"As the humans say, money makes the world go round. I couldn't help myself, the sweet seduction of being surrounded by the glorious riches was too much for this poor old battered soul," he said, shaking his head with fake sincerity. "I now understand why M'nep basked himself in riches untold, like a maniac. But that maniac was a brilliant man, and I was blinded for too long."

Bloodwite backed away as he grew closer. He went as far as he could until his movements were halted by the body at his feet.

"But, I couldn't get my hands on those riches until I was able to get the final piece into place," Fireflood said.

His face only mere inches from Bloodwite's, he snarled a bit and whispered the word "Grave". He pointed down to the boy, and Bloodwite's eyes followed.

"He couldn't be," Bloodwite whispered, letting a small gasp of realization escape his lips. He moved as quickly as he could to get away from this possessed form of Fireflood, almost throwing himself over to the other end of the platform. He headed up the stairs to the doorway he had previously come from. He needed to find Kenny and warn him of this foul play. Fireflood wasn't moving. He only smirked widely as Bloodwite turned to run. He was suddenly stopped by an old, greed-stricken man. Fireflood burst into laughter again.

"Sir," Fireflood said happily, "how wonderful of you to join us! I was just telling my brother here about our little agreement."

"Wonderful," O'Reilly said, stepping out into the light.

Bloodwite took a few steps backward, back down onto the platform's surface again. He was trapped with nowhere to go, his only exits blocked off, and he was unarmed, unable to protect himself. He heard the sound of a machine click in his ears. He turned to look at Fireflood, his eyes showed worry and strain as he gazed at the gun pointing to his head.

Fireflood's finger was on the trigger. His eyes showed no remorse whatsoever for the action he was preparing to do. Bloodwite's eyes filled with tears again. "You hideous monster," He whispered

Fireflood laughed. "Monster or not, I'm the one with the advantage. It seems, my brother, you will finally live up to your name. Adieu, my brother."

With those final words, he pulled the trigger. The bullet collided with Bloodwite's side. The only thought on his mind was Kenny's safety, and he was heading this way, and he stood no chance against these two. He felt the flesh be pierced by the invading object. His arms fell down to his sides and his body tumbled over onto the ground, landing on the cold stone without a final breath to whisper his last warning.

Chapter Thirty-eight:

THE FINAL PASSAGES

KENNY'S BODY WAS sticking to the cold stone beneath him, his eyes fluttered open, and with a loud groan he rolled onto his back. He caught very little of his surroundings with his blurred eyes, and he was unable see what was happening around him, but he heard rushing water and a gruff voice booming over him also caught his attention.

"Kenneth!" it shouted. He blinked a few times and opened his eyes, trying to concentrate better. He rubbed his head and rolled back over onto his side, seeing that the room was tilted wrongly from that angle. Everything cleared up finally and Alexander still stood high above him. His body was covered with the old brown duster he was given moments before, which was soaked thoroughly now.

"How long was I out?" he asked, mostly speaking to himself.

"Only a few minutes, by gum I swear if you hadn't woken I would've given up all hope on you!" he shouted.

Kenny rubbed his face, trying to get the liquids dripping into his eyes to leave. He looked at his hand, seeing blood was all over it. It didn't surprise him, though, he knew he was already a bloody mess anyway, and the loss of blood making him pass out wasn't a surprise either.

"Why?" he moaned, pushing himself back up.

"You cracked your skull open. The blood just kept coming," he replied.

Kenny laughed a bit, not shocked in the least bit by the response he had gotten. He stood, using the wall to help support him for a moment before he turned to face Alexander again.

"I have to leave now. I don't have much time left," he replied. This wasn't about the time limit he had been given by the government. This was the time limit he had to save Robert. He still had a good five days left before the debt needed to be paid, but Robert's body would only last a day, if he was lucky enough to be spared that much time. He may not be able to save the house, but he still could save his friend.

Alexander nodded. "I wish you the best, my boy."

"Thank you. I promise I'll find a way to break that curse. You won't have to spend any more time down here," Kenny replied, grabbing onto the coat's shoulder to keep it up.

Alexander smiled, he didn't agree with him in the slightest, but he felt hope, which was something he had never thought he would be given the chance to experience again. Kenny bolted for the boards again when Alexander coughed to draw his attention away from the exit.

He unlatched his skeletal hand from the wall and pressed a small emblem at his side. It began to glow deep red and soon the wall began to shake and move. It revealed itself to be a doorway, cobwebs hung in the entrance, and only one light stood in the distance.

"This passage leads straight into the heart of the Grave," Alexander said.

Kenny's eyes widened in shock as he turned to face him with a confused grin. "This? It goes straight there?" he stuttered.

"Yes, why do you think they kept me around, my boy? I was supposed to make sure no one ever found it...but I believe you deserve this. Head straight as much as you can, avoid the water, many deadly things lie in there, and keep your hands off of the walls. It's lined with coffins that may house traps, so I had been told. Be careful," Alexander said, handing his lantern to Kenny. Kenny took it, the look on his face was one of protest, but the elder man just shook his head in reply.

With a smile, Kenny headed off into the darkness, the room behind him becoming dark without the light, and soon the door closed, leaving Kenny to stand alone in the shadows of the remnants of something once great. He let the lantern hang high, his arm slowly falling asleep, but he knew he needed to keep light on as many objects as he could.

The reflections of the fire danced on the surface of the onyx coffins. They were lined with rubies, all looking as though they were following him, his form bouncing from the surface of one to the next. He jumped at every noise and felt as if he was going to puke, but he had no other choice than to suck it up and find courage. This was his reckoning night, his one chance to find himself and become the hero he had always dreamed of becoming.

His fantasies, his dreams—were now his reality, his story unfolding unlike anything he had ever wished for. This was his final battle, and he was going to need to destroy the man who was beating and abusing his best friend, his brother. He was going to find truths no one else would ever dare dream of finding. He was maybe, finally going to be able to go home. His only regret being Tooka, his inability to bid her farewell. He promised he'd stay and he didn't. Strict, utter remorse on his mind from that was tearing him apart.

The further into the darkness he went, the more lost he felt. The only sounds were composed of hissing noises and the rushing of water. Cobwebs were entangling with one another, making beautiful shapes that, when Kenny showered light onto them, were ablaze in a fury, in a dance that seemed too unreal.

Kenny stepped down and felt his boot get caught in some odd texture. He moved around, trying to get free, but soon he felt hot breath dance on his backside. He looked down, seeing he had stepping a large pile of green slime. His back was against the mouth of one of the large spider spawns. He felt it snarl, every hair on the back of his neck was on end, and he felt slime drip down his shirt.

He turned his head a bit to look at the creature, the fire from his lantern making it look like some sort of horrid devil that had just crawled from the flaming pits of Satan. Its eye was glowing in a mass fury of rage and, guessing by the noises it made, it was hungry.

"Hi," Kenny whispered.

The creature opened its mouth wide to snap at him, and he quickly ran, trying to get out of the way before he was eaten. He felt his body half in the waterways and half on the stone pathways, creatures of weird origins began to nip at his heel from the water, and the large spider was only mere feet away from him.

Kenny turned a sharp corner, almost slamming into the wall. He saw the spider slide across the floor past the doorway he had just entered. Then he heard it running like a large dog, the sound resonating back toward the entrance where he had run into it. Kenny felt room on his sides now, like the path had just grown incredibly wide.

Just great! he thought, hissing. *I went into an area he can actually fit into*!

The monster was once again only feet behind him, and Kenny looked back for a split moment. Panicking, he picked up his pace and turned to face what was in front of him. He came to a screeching halt, finding himself in front of a dead end. Above was nothing but spider webs stuck to a large brick wall. Dozens of skeletons were trapped beneath the spider's poison slime.

Kenny sharply turned around. The spider's large head was mere centimeters away from his trembling body. It pulled back a bit and let out a screeching howl; it was almost ear-shattering as it echoed in the night. Slime by the gallons shot from his mouth, and it all went flying toward the wall and Kenny. He stood there, twitching in a disturbed manner as he slung the excess slime from his body.

"If my life wasn't at stake," he moaned. "I would puke right now."

The spider grinned widely, showing all its rotting teeth. Kenny's nose scrunched up from the horrid smell escaping its lips. It licked him, wanting a good taste before he swallowed him whole.

Kenny backed up as far as he could until he hit the wall, finding himself stuck to it due to the webbing like slobber that both he and the wall were drenched in.

The creature knew it had him, and it wasn't planning on sparing another second. It opened its mouth to rip him from the wall then swallow him, finding pleasure in this game of cat and mouse. Kenny closed his eyes, waiting for it to all end, smelling the rancid breath escaping the creature's mouth. It reared on its hind leg, preparing itself to end the hunt. Kenny slammed his head back onto the wall, trying to get away.

Suddenly the floor moved. His eyes widened just as the creature came into view, but suddenly it vanished. Kenny felt his body being moved along with the wall. It was rotating at a quick speed, just fast enough to get him free. It was like a trap door in an old British manor, swinging in a large motion. He must have triggered it when he slammed his head onto the wall.

Kenny really didn't care how it happened; he was just extremely happy he had found a way to free himself from his predator. He breathed a sigh of relief for a moment before he felt the spider slam into the other side of the wall. The impact shook him off of the wall onto the ground. He landed with his face in another pile of slime. *At least I didn't land in a load of gunk inside of the creature*, he thought, quickly shoving himself up, trying to free his face so he could get a breath. He gasped and grabbed his chest, trying to calm his beating heart. He slowly looked up, the joyous smile he had on his face was replaced with a nervous grin.

Large suits of armor were standing in front of him, moving closer to him with weapons of any sort in their hands, swords, spears, axes and things of the like in their hands. He had once again found a lovely trap that he had no way of getting out of. Kenny let his shoulders sag. "Oh, come on!"

Chapter Thirty-nine:

THE CAPTURE

THE SUITS OF armor lunged at Kenny. He tossed himself out of the way, throwing his body into a pile of spider webbing. He quickly stood back up and began to run to what he prayed was the exit, the armors throwing large spears and swords at him, each barely missing him every time. His dumb luck was once again paying off, but he wasn't sure how long he could pull this off.

There was a path of weaponry along the wall behind him. More armored suits began to pull themselves from the wall and attack him. The ground was slick beneath him, making him slide across the brick flooring. He ran as fast as he could into the shadows, trying to avoid the iron beasts at all cost.

There were no lights in the passage. He was as blind as a bat as he ran off into the unknown, praying he was heading in the right direction. He heard his footsteps and the rusty noises of the bodies of metal in unison with his own. It sounded like there were well over a dozen of them. Even with how large they were, they were quick.

Beneath his fingers, Kenny felt sharp objects. He quickly pulled one out of the wall and turned around. He felt the impact of a large, thick weapon smack against his own. His knees buckled and his body almost collapsed under the pressure of the sudden shocking burst of energy that crushed his body like a twig. Luckily, the object he had grabbed was sturdy and didn't break upon impact, but it felt rough unlike metal. The air that emitted from the blast was almost breathtaking, and on top of it all, the armor's strength was tenfold of his. The armor continued to push his weapon down against him, an almost wicked laughter coming from the empty helmet.

Kenny felt wood begin to break in his hands. *Figures I had to grab a wooden spear.* He thought, worry in his eyes. He knew the moment he went to run they would attack him, but the longer he stayed where he was, in the position he was in, the spear would snap, and he would be done for. Either way he had no easy way of escaping and a very slim chance of survival.

He began to slide his feet back a bit, scooting across the slick floor slowly toward the exit. *I've got one chance to do this*, Kenny thought, swallowing. In one quick, sharp movement, he rolled onto the ground and jammed the spear into the nearby wall. The armor sliced through the spear as Kenny stood back up. He darted off into the exit, trying to get away in one piece.

The echoing sounds the armors made as they ran was in perfect unison, that ringing in Kenny's ears gave him a very risky, very dangerous idea. He ran as fast as his tired feet would allow him, trying to speed up enough to get a good eight feet in front of the armors.

Once he guessed he was far enough away, he sharply turned around and slid across the floor, in perfect alignment with the monsters. His foot collided with one of the armors, knocking it backward toward the one behind. Like dominos, they fell down onto the floor one by one. All of them were too heavy to be lifted from the floor. With nothing but wits and dumb luck, Kenny had executed his plan perfectly. He stood up again and went to run, just in case they somehow managed to get up again, but his ankle buckled beneath him and he fell to the floor.

Shoot! He thought. He used his hands to push himself up a bit until he was standing. He hobbled his way down the hall, trying to get out in one piece, moving against all warnings his body was giving him. The pain was almost too much at times, but he could feel how close he was to Robert so nothing was going to stop him. He turned another corner, away from the brick-lined corridor he had just escaped, into another tunnel formed from clay and mud. He pressed his body against a line of bricks sticking from the soft surface behind him for a moment as he rested, until he slid down the wall and breathed a sigh of relief, finally able to catch his breath.

His eyes gazed over to the other direction, catching a glimpse of something as it rushed by him. It was almost like a blur of light, a firefly, dashing into the next corridor. Kenny fumbled to his feet and followed it, down into the dark, musty tunnel. He stumbled into the mud and spider webs, following the light down into the passages. He couldn't place his finger on it, but this presence was familiar.

"The light is strong in the dark, follow the path to the ark," Kenny whispered. "He's going to take me where I need to be."

A small glimmer of hope was all it took for him to snap out of his tired state back into the reality or how close he was to where he needed to be. Like a sign from heaven it was so quick, but enough to make him rise to his feet and continue onward.

The further down he went, the harder it became to breathe. It was humid, and all of his clothes were sticking to his body heavily. He began to sweat heavily too, wondering just how deep this strange ball of light was going to take him.

He began to find himself going further and further underground, and he heard more howling winds and more strange noised which made his mind race in fear and wonder. *Where am I?* he asked himself, finding a flight of stairs now at his feet, he crept his way to the top, hearing voices as loud as fireworks, and as violent as well. He remained hidden in the shadows, finding himself coming above ground again. He heard rain, rushing water, the winds and thunder all at once. He smelled fresh salt water and lilacs and could almost feel a cool breeze rush around him. He found himself entranced at how easily the area could change from being only a few feet beneath the earth. But as he reached the stairs, he found himself more entranced with the sights around him and the one at his feet.

With a heavy gasp, almost cry for help from the pain of the sight, he ran down the stairs to the side of the unconscious Bloodwite. Carefully he looked at him, holding him in his arms to get a better view of him. His eyes were wide open, his body nothing but a mere rag doll, a cold, lifeless being with tears in its eyes.

"I shouldn't have stopped. I could've done something," he whispered, lowering his head in shame. As he laid the cold body of his friend on the ground, he heard a frightening noise. It was a loud, horrid scream. And the sound of heavy liquid, like water, bursting onto the ground then bitter laughter, all coming from the area above him. He stood and ran up the stairs, not even cringing at the pressures on all of his injuries.

At the top his eyes came across the site of his final battle, but it came colliding to the floor as he was pushed to the ground and grabbed onto harshly. His body was then brought back up and was forced to walk down into the center platform where Fireflood, O'Reilly, and one of the lackeys that followed him stood impatiently. Kenny looked up and saw the other goon above him, bringing him down the stairs to face the reason for all of his pain.

"Wonderful job, Rocco, now we can finally let this little ritual begin," O'Reilly said, moving to the side of the other large man. In his large hands was the bloody, bruised, and almost lifeless Robert. O'Reilly pressed the tip of his gun to the underside of Robert's chin to make him look up at Kenny. His eyes were a deep orange, almost blood red color, and he looked petrified.

"Shall we?" O'Reilly asked.

Chapter Forty:

THE GRAVE OF THE FIREFLIES

KENNY HISSED, "YOU better get your hands off of him, you sick son of a—" But he was halted by Rocco squeezing his neck. His eyes gazed coldly at O'Reilly, then at Fireflood who was standing impatiently next to Robert.

"Why'd we have to wait for him? I want my gold," he hissed, turning to face O'Reilly.

With a devilish grin he merely replied, "You'll see."

He pulled his gun from under Robert's head and walked over to Kenny, placing his hands behind his back as he looked down on him. No look Kenny could give, no noise he could make, no punch he could ever throw, no name he could call him would ever intimidate him now. He had won; he knew he had.

"It's locked, and you have no way of opening it! The heir is dead. I saw him die!" Kenny shouted. O'Reilly broke out into a fit of laughter, looking down at him one more time.

"Dead, dead you say?" he chuckled. "No, dear boy, he is, for now alive and well. And I must emphasize on *is*. For after the next few minutes, he'll be nothing but a mere memory."

Kenny looked at him in question, unable to figure it out. Fireflood laughed and walked over to him, and he looked him in the eyes and smiled coldly, seeing him tremble and shake in fear.

"You really don't get it," he whispered, pulling away.

He looked at O'Reilly who was heading back over to Robert. Fireflood tilted his head down toward Kenny and smiled. "That's why we waited, the thrill of seeing his face when he finds out! Oh sir, I am just having too much fun with this!" he laughed.

"As you should my good man, as you should," O'Reilly replied in the same way, laughing at the confusion filling the room. Fireflood spun around like a child in a fit of joy; he was ecstatic and could barely keep it withheld.

Kenny looked at them and finally spoke. "You're sick," he spat.

"No, my boy, I believe it's your mother who is sick," O'Reilly replied. "I mean to keep such a secret!"

Kenny felt his body just completely lock up, his face was flushed, and he just stood still. Fireflood continued to laugh, almost throwing himself on the floor from the utter excitement he was enduring.

O'Reilly pulled an old diary from his suit and walked back over in Kenny's direction. He opened up a page and held it in front of Kenny.

"Read it," he demanded, hissing loudly like the snake that he was.

Kenny recoiled in fear a bit and opened one eye slowly to look at it. He skimmed over it, finding himself reading a page from Robert's grandmother's diary, with all too familiar happenings in it.

"You've heard the story, that there is a prophecy, one that tells of the heir to one of the high thrones of the forests, the races of the fairies, and the Gohmas. Their all seeing *eyes* they called him, descendant of the one known as M'nep. It was once said, many eons ago, that the *eighteenth* heir in the bloodline of the ancestor who destroyed the Gohma, the Uty, would be lost at a young age. Vanishing into a rain-tattered sky one night, never to return. This child—"

"If his blood should be spilled across the door," Kenny continued, picking up where he had cut in. "Then and only then, deep into the night, the Grave shall be revealed."

"The all-seeing eyes, eighteenth, figured it out?" O'Reilly asked. Kenny remained silent, unable to put the pieces back together. O'Reilly turned again and grabbed his face, looking into his terrified eyes with anger.

"Foolish child, you don't get it, put two and two together!" he howled, slapping him across the face.

"When the car accident so *tragically* happened, your pathetic parents granted his mother's final wish," O'Reilly boomed, looking back at Robert.

"So the two of you were switched, just like his mother had asked with her dying breath, and with the both of you unable to remember anything, it was the perfect way to hide the precious heir."

"Leaving every one of us, the people who raised the brat since birth, the ones who worshiped the ground he walked on by force, to search for him frantically day in and day out, unable to rest, unable to sleep until we found him!" Fireflood screamed, anger bursting into the air from his body. He grabbed onto Kenny's head and snapped it up to him, making him look at the torture that consumed his being.

"We searched, and we waited, wondering when our precious little heir would come home to us and make us *happy* again. But that day never came, and still the pathetic creatures that ruled this forest, that contaminated the ground I helped create, the earth and soil I put my soul into, still waited for him, withering in the spot that they planted themselves in to pray for his safe return while I was stuck here to rot, unnoticed and unappreciated!" he continued, slamming his fist down onto Kenny.

Kenny fell to the ground, watching the blood trickle from his cheek onto the floor and off of the concealed knife that Fireflood was holding.

"Calm yourself, dear boy," O'Reilly said, grasping onto

Fireflood's shoulder. He pulled him back and looked at Kenny, and then he looked at Fireflood, who was calming himself, shaking in anger and then back down to Kenny. He couldn't decide who to watch, the confused Kenny or the angry Fireflood.

"Got it figured out yet?" he asked.

Kenny just sat there, his mind racing, trying to register everything, but the more he thought, the more confused he became. Could it have been the fear, or the pain in his body that was stopping him from registering everything, or maybe it was his wonder about Tooka's safety and where she was, if she was all right, maybe the same with Robert. His bloody form was enough to make Kenny's heart stop.

"Are you really that stupid, you moronic child?" O'Reilly asked, looking down upon him. "Robert is the heir; he's the one you've been searching for!" he screamed.

Kenny's eyes burst open, tears flowing from them in heavy numbers. He sat there on all fours shaking, whimpering, and whining like a dog.

"That's right. Kneel with your tail between your legs," O'Reilly shouted cockily.

"Eyes' wasn't referring to actual eyes, but Iis, the name of the heir. Eighteenth meant the eighteenth year of his life. The car accident, the night, the whole thing...Robert ..." he whispered, feeling the whole impact rush into his body, finally able to realize the truth, finally able to see it with his own eyes. Robert was still motionless, his eyes as bright orange as the sun, just like Iis' had been.

Fireflood crept up next to Kenny and looked at him for a moment before he kicked him in the gut, tossing him across the platform. He calmly walked over to him and grabbed his hair, making him stand back up again. Kenny looked up at Fireflood, his eyes filled with tears and anger, his teeth grinding together in anguish.

"How could you? How could you just betray them like that?" he asked, screaming at the top of his lungs. Fireflood only grinned and looked at O'Reilly.

"I'm getting bored," he groaned, turning back to O'Reilly.

"Let's get on with it; the sun's almost up. I do *not* want to wait until tomorrow. The less I get of these pathetic humans the better."

O'Reilly looked at him angrily. He stiffened in fear and lowered his head a bit in shame. "Except for you, sir," he said with a smirk; he was fully dedicated to O'Reilly.

O'Reilly nodded and ordered Rocco to grab Robert's other arm. Both men held him up against the door, O'Reilly followed them up the stairs as he pulled out his gun and loaded a bullet. Kenny tried to run to him, but Fireflood grabbed his arm and threw him onto the ground, holding him there as O'Reilly went to finish what he had started. Both Kenny and Fireflood looked on, Kenny in tears and Fireflood with a large, triumphant grin on his face.

"Dear boy, did you know that you can't spell slaughter without laughter?" O'Reilly asked, holding the gun in Robert's direction, laughing maniacally.

"Please, he's all I have left!" Kenny shouted.

"I'm sorry," O'Reilly said, turning to face him. "I missed the part where that was my problem."

Kenny's eyes stood wide in shock and anger, watching on with little else to do. O'Reilly turned to face Robert. He pointed the gun to his chest and pulled the trigger, Kenny, screaming out in agony, as he watched Robert be murdered. The bright orange eyes Robert now had burst open as he felt his body completely stop. Blood went flying all over the large gate behind him. He slowly slid down the wall onto the floor, leaving a large trail of blood across the door, just as O'Reilly had planned. He snapped his fingers, and the two men tossed the now useless body into the lower platform.

Robert's body rolled down the stairs onto the floor near Kenny. His head was mere inches away from his own. Fireflood burst out laughing, still holding onto Kenny, his grip continuing to get tighter. Kenny looked into Robert's bright, wide orange eyes. Tears were running down both of their cheeks as they sat there, one still breathing, the other breathing his final breath. Kenny pulled his hand free of Fireflood's grip and placed it on

Robert's bloody cheek to let him know, if he was somehow still with him, for maybe a mere moment so he would know, that he was still beside him and hadn't left.

There was a large clicking sound in the background. O'Reilly turned his attention away from Kenny and looked at the gate. The blood began to run up the small streams carved into its surface, and soon the entire exterior was covered in a large design of the same symbol that represented the Gohma, the tiny four point star in dead center of the giant black sphere.

It began to glow brightly; Kenny turned his eyes up toward it and watched in awe as it began to move and soon open. Like a very detailed old Grandfather clock, the mechanics of it were just fascinating to watch. Fireflood was grinning widely. He could almost taste the sweet money that was awaiting him inside.

O'Reilly turned to face Fireflood and waved his hand in the air, signaling him the ok to finally move inside and claim the victory prize. At long last, after all the years of planning this day, he finally had his gold lying just ahead of him.

"Bring the boy!" he shouted. Fireflood stood and brought Kenny with him. No matter how much he struggled to get away, Fireflood refused to let him go. He pulled on him and eventually had him up the stairs, both staring face to face with the door.

"This is what you wanted, the treasure, happy now?" Fireflood asked with fake sincerity. Kenny hissed and looked away. Fireflood snarled a bit and continued to follow O'Reilly. Soon Kenny was once again face to face with O'Reilly.

"Don't feel bad, my boy, you played such a big role in this little game, so we won't let you go without a little consolation prize," he said, grinning cockily.

"I don't want your stupid treasure! It means nothing to me, unlike you, you self-centered, egotistical megalomaniac!" Kenny spat.

O'Reilly growled angrily and smacked him, leaving his face beat red. His expression was still full of rage. He stood as hard as a stone, not letting anything faze him now.

O'Reilly turned and entered with Fireflood, Kenny, and the two large brutes following behind. They set foot in the old, musty area, and once inside the gate re-closed and darkness showering everything inside Kenny's vision, leaving nothing but black. Leaving Robert on the ground, and the outside world hidden once again.

Chapter Forty-one:

THE GOHMA

O'REILLY LOOKED AROUND the dark area for a moment before turning to Fireflood. He just shrugged his shoulders in reply, not really getting what the horrid expression on his face was asking. With an angry scowl, O'Reilly took another step into the pitch black room. The moment his foot met the floor, lights all around were set ablaze, illuminating the entire room. The flames from the torches stood proudly as if they hadn't ever been put out. It was a large, circular chamber that had deep red and orange pillars all around it. Another emblem of the Gohma was pressed into the floor in the center and above was nothing but pure darkness.

O'Reilly walked inside a bit; Fireflood and Kenny following. Nothing was inside, no shinning gold, no swords with jewels pressed into their blades, no chests made of pure silver. Nothing, nothing was there but dust.

O'Reilly stood still for a moment before turning to face Fireflood. He quickly headed in his direction and grabbed his light red tunic, pulling him in closer. His hot, horrid breath danced across Fireflood's face, both of their angry eyes met and became locked in combat for a moment.

"Where is the treasure? I see nothing but ashes and stupid odd-shaped balls!" he spat. "Where are the stones, the crowns, the riches, all the so called wonders of the Grave?"

"How the heck am I supposed to know?" Fireflood snapped back. "I'm not allowed in this chamber!" Fireflood stared at the odd shaped balls he had mentioned. He hadn't ever seen anything like them before. They were almost like a puzzle ball with many indents and curves in them. Red and black, colors he had seen all too often many years ago. They were the colors of the Gohmas.

O'Reilly hissed, released his grip on Fireflood and grabbed Kenny's shirt; he made the terrified youth turn his attention to him and him alone and scowled.

"Where is the treasure? I'm sure you, of all people, should know," he said coldly.

Kenny said nothing. He only turned away smugly with eyes closed in anger. Everyone stood still for a moment, listening to the utter silence that surrounded them, until Kenny let out a heavy scream of agony. He slid from Fireflood's grip onto the floor, grasping onto his shoulder so tightly it almost pierced his skin. O'Reilly backed away for a moment then looked over at Fireflood again.

"What's wrong with that imbecile?" he shouted, trying to hear himself over Kenny's screaming.

"How should I know? He's a stupid human!" Fireflood said, slamming his hands over his ears. Another loud, hissing noise was heard and then a rush of wind was felt. A torrent of unknown properties had entered the room. Kenny stopped screaming once it halted. Everyone's eyes headed to the area where the wind had come from. Rocco and Jasper were gone, vanished into thin air. Whatever *it* was had completely erased the two large men.

All of the hairs on Kenny's neck stood up quickly in fear and wonder; his body was still trying to recover from the sudden attack. He took a deep breath and sat up straight, rubbing the flesh on his shoulder gently.

"What was that?" Fireflood asked, backing away in fear a small bit. Kenny quickly stood back up and looked back at O'Reilly, a small smirk on his face and pure evil in his eyes. He licked his lips a bit, his eyes almost pure black like the Gohma emblem. He laughed a bit. "Gohma," he whispered. His breathing sped to a heavy gasping pace, and his eyes showed little emotion.

In one sharp movement he dove over to the doorway. His body felt so light and free, and before he could even register it, he was standing next to the large locked gate. His eyes flashed back to normal, and his body collapsed again due to it being so weak and the sudden motions drained so much energy. *Ah, man, what's happening to me?* Kenny asked himself, rubbing his temples.

Both O'Reilly and Fireflood watched him for a moment before feeling a shadow befall them. Both turned to look at what was looming over them. The Gohma, the mother of the spider creatures that had possessed Kenny, was standing above. Drool by the gallons flowing from her mouth. Fireflood stumbled back a bit in fear; he tripped over a rock and fell to the ground, landing hard on the jagged surface. *It's a lot bigger than I remember*, he thought. Eyes wide in fear, he crawled away from the monster that had defeated so many of his kind many years ago. O'Reilly kneeled down next to him and placed his hand on Fireflood's shoulder. Fireflood looked at him, wondering why he had such a sadistic look on his face. He had complete confusion on his normally serious face, his worried eyebrows rising in question.

"I think she's hungry," he said, grinning evilly.

Fireflood's eyes widened in shock; he had fallen for O'Reilly's trickery like a fool.

He snarled. "Filthy human!" he screamed, reaching up to attack.

O'Reilly shoved Fireflood over to the Gohma. He rolled across the floor for a moment before stopping at the Gohma's feet. He let out a scream as it dove for him.

Kenny regained some consciousness just as Fireflood was almost ripped in two by the monster. He saw the shadow of his body dance on the wall next to him, the fiery sprite being tossed into the air then swallowed whole. And just like that, Fireflood was just another memory.

Oh, dang it! Kenny thought as his eyes widened in shock. His gaze shifted to the shadow of O'Reilly dancing on the wall across from him. The wicked man extended his arms out wide to the Gohma. Kenny snuck over to a large pillar next to him, to watch on in secrecy.

"Oh Gohma, mighty lord of the forest and all you survey, I have come seeking the treasure within the Grave!" he shouted.

Kenny watched as the Gohma turned to face him. Its face was soon only mere inches away from O'Reilly's, and soon it stood back up straight and looked down upon him.

It appeared as though the creature and nodded a bit as it turned to face him. The impact of its head turning almost blew Kenny off of his feet. O'Reilly smiled widely and nodded, ready to finally be able to claim the prize he had so eagerly been awaiting.

The strange, round balls O'Reilly had mentioned when they first arrived, hidden in the ashes, began to crack and break and soon very small versions of the Gohma burst from inside, slinging ooze across the lair as they went. *Wonderful! Little bitty baby spiders! That's just great,* Kenny thought with a snarl. They howled a bit and walked over to O'Reilly. He watched, not afraid of them at all as they grew closer and closer until nothing was in his sight but the creatures.

They sniffed him and let out an almost painful howl. The Gohma's eye turned red. She leaned in next to him and hissed. Almost trying to tell him that he was not worthy of being in this area. O'Reilly's eyes narrowed a bit, his arms went down to his side, and he shook his head.

"My dear, I believe we can come to some sort of agreement here," he said sharply.

The Gohma reared back on her hind leg. She towered high above O'Reilly, showering everything with a heavy atmosphere of terror. All of the smaller spider's eyes turned bright red as their mother became angry. O'Reilly went to back away but found nowhere to go, no way to escape this mess he had gotten himself into. The Gohma slammed her self down onto the floor.

Large cracks formed, the impact shook Kenny off of his feet, back onto the floor. He watched, almost puking from the pain that he was being racked with from being so close to the spider creature. The miniature Gohmas jumped O'Reilly. He let out a scream of sheer terror as they dove onto him; Kenny guessing he was being ripped apart without struggle. The Gohma howled loudly, the noise echoing everywhere inside the Grave. Kenny let out another cry for help as she walked around the small pile of spiders toward where he had been hiding. He let his head rest on the wall, grabbing his shoulder in agony. The Gohma looked at him and he stared back with wide eyes. It seemed to almost understand his terror.

O'Reilly's screaming stopped for a moment. The spiders moved away from him one by one, almost bowing their heads for their mother as she paced around the room, waiting to see the result. Kenny watched too, waiting to see what had happened to O'Reilly.

Where he once stood, was now a stone replica, much like Alexander had been turned into. His stone exterior was covered in green, oozing slime, and his face showed nothing but fear.

Kenny hobbled his way into the light, looking to see if O'Reilly was really gone now. The spiders didn't attack him, and the Gohma only watched above, looking on as Kenny came face to face with the stone form of his enemy. He stood there for a moment, watching, examining every detail on it, and soon fell to his knees, breathing the sigh of complete and utter relief he had been longing for. It was all over now, nothing else could be done. Nothing could change what had happened, but now there was no more O'Reilly to terrorize the world, and if there really was treasure somewhere, it was safe and out of greed's way.

"It's over," he whispered, smiling.

The Gohma made a grunting noise and continued to walk around the room. Kenny looked up at the large monster as she loomed over him. He stood a bit and bowed politely, not really realizing what he was doing. It almost seemed as though she chuckled a bit in amusement to Kenny's behaviors.

"I'm sorry I bothered you," Kenny said quietly, looking up at the spider.

He went to back away and head for the exit when he was halted by a horrid sound. His head quickly shot above him as he was knocked to the ground by O'Reilly.

This strange new stone form of his enemy had eyes that glowed like two rubies, and his body as heavy as ten tons. The stone statue had sprung to life and began to attack. He scratched Kenny's body with his jagged stone hands, cutting his body severely. Kenny let out a howl of fear as he watched O'Reilly's hand come toward his head. He turned himself away with only a mere second to spare as the man's fist collided with the ground.

The impact continued to break the ground from the previous battering the Gohma inflicted on it, almost shattering it in two. Kenny grabbed O'Reilly's hands as he tried to continue his attacks, blocking him momentarily as the Gohma went on the offensive. She once again threw herself onto the ground, this time shattering the floor completely.

Fire began to spew from the cracks. The small spiders fell through the floor into the fire, all going at once. Kenny was still rolling on the floor, trying to get the more powerful version of his foe off of him for a moment's rest. Both were still fighting as the cracks continued to grow larger and larger. The Gohma had very little area to go. It was backed into a corner, jumping around from one area to the next, barely avoiding Kenny and O'Reilly every time.

"If I'm going down, you're coming with me!" O'Reilly shouted.

"Not a chance!" Kenny spat, thrusting himself on top of O'Reilly.

He spun over onto his back; Kenny jumped on him and kept him pinned to the ground as the Gohma jumped over to their area. Kenny's eyes widened in shock and fear, watching as it came crushing down on him.

He threw his arms over his head and fell to the ground, trying to keep himself somewhat protected, but he had no chance of surviving this. O'Reilly jumped towards him, knocking him to the ground again just before the Gohma fell onto the floor. It tumbled down into the fire, letting out one loud cry of fear before it met its doom.

Fire blew from the river, rolling across the rocky canvass where O'Reilly and Kenny were. Kenny swung his legs up in the air, his foot colliding with the man's abdomen. He flew across the floor away from Kenny, into a pile of lava. Yet it didn't even scratch his immortal exterior.

Kenny grabbed a large, dagger-like rock and prepared himself for one final battle, the battle that would determine life or death.

Chapter Forty-two:

THE REASSURANCE

KENNY LOOKED AT the glowing red rock in his hand, seeing that the way it shined was the same way O'Reilly's body did now. As the stone man lunged at him, Kenny drove the dagger into his leg. He let out a cry of pain, watching as the rocks began to take over his body. He cursed himself under his breath for what he had just done, but he knew he needed to do it. He had to fight fire with fire, and this was the only way. He felt himself almost collapse under the pressure, letting his body fall to the ground. As soon as he found himself on the floor, the area was wiped away, leaving nothing but a pure white canvass under him. His fingers felt water rush around them, as if the strange area he had been placed in was under water.

"Be strong, young one," a voice bellowed.

Kenny saw feet in front of him; he watched as the man now standing in front of him kneeled down. A hand was placed on his forehead calmly. He felt freed of the pain for a moment, but it was very brief.

"Bloodwite...?" Kenny asked.

"It is all right," he replied.

"But I thought ..." he stammered.

"Yes, I have now left, but I can finally rest in peace."

Kenny felt a few tears slide from his eyes onto the ground and then a hand on his shoulder. It gently helped him roll onto his back. He felt weak, like it was no use to go on any longer, but these remnants, these little memories were helping him, made it seem worth it once again.

"We have very little strength left," Blueweed said sadly. He was standing next to Bloodwite, both looming over Kenny gently with an apologetic look on their faces.

"But just enough to help you continue, our heir is dead because of that maniac, and you are the only one who can stop him!" Bloodwite interrupted. "Do *not* let him get away with what he has done!"

"It's no use. I don't have the strength to continue. I have no reason to go on," Kenny cried out, feeling horrible and useless again. His eyes closed tightly, feeling like nothing was worth it, that they should just stay closed. He wanted to go to sleep. He wanted to be with Robert again and with Tooka. Laughter caught his attention. Kenny opened his eyes and saw Tooka above him, her face mere inches away from his.

"I'm sorry," he said quietly.

"Why?" she asked.

"I said I would stay with you, and I didn't, I left and—" he was stopped as Tooka kissed him to halt his apology.

Blueweed was laughing a bit, finding the sight somewhat interesting and new. She pulled away and continued to look at him, trying to help him find some sort of strength.

She stood and extended her hand to him. He took it and slowly sat back up, using his knees to support him. He watched her smile for a moment, staring at her for what seemed like hours, with longing and happiness on his face before he was almost knocked over by a small form. He looked down and saw the little Iis in his arms, hugging him gently.

"I want to see you again," he whispered. Kenny placed his

hand on the little boy's head and held him there, realizing it was now his turn to be the savior for them both.

"I want to see you too, Robert," Kenny whispered, closing his eyes. The only thing remaining in his vision was Robert now. The little boy grabbed his arm and looked up at him with question on his face.

"You'll come back, right?" he asked. "You promised you would!"

Kenny's eyes widened a bit then finally closed, he held onto him, trying to make sure this moment would last for as long as it could. He shook his head, tears almost rushing out of his eyes. He bit his lip, trying to stop himself from showing this fear to Iis.

Tooka pulled Iis away from Kenny and began to walk off with him into the distance, Blueweed and Bloodwite followed, all of them becoming surrounded by the white lights.

"Wait, what should I do?" he shouted, halting all of their movements.

All of them watched him sit there for a moment, wondering if he had found the strength and hope he had lost. He looked down in shame, feeling as if this entire thing was his fault now, that all of those people who put so much trust into him and those who died for him were putting their trust into a failure. *I can't do it. I'm not strong enough, not like this*, he thought.

"Giving up already? I'm disappointed."

Kenny's head shot back up to the group of people. There stood Robert, smiling widely, his arms were crossed, and he had a cocky look in his eyes. He raised an eyebrow and laughed.

"Go get him," he ordered. "This is that fairytale ending you wanted, are you just going to give it all up now? C'mon, I'm waiting."

Chapter Forty-three:

THE BATTLE

WITH HUNGRY, POSSESSED eyes, Kenny once again turned to face O'Reilly, and soon he found himself diving in for the kill. Both beat on each other and slammed their bodies into the ground and the rushing waves of lava. Kenny felt his body become ten times stronger, ten times lighter. He could move freely and felt no stress in doing very athletic moves, ones which he could never have accomplished before. But with this, he knew O'Reilly had been given the same powers, the same curse.

Kenny was thrown back a bit, his feet driving into the pavement as he tried to stay steady. He quickly ran again and jumped in the air, thrusting his feet out in front of him. His stone plated boots collided with O'Reilly's chest and knocked him to the floor. But the moment he pushed himself away, O'Reilly had his ankle.

He quickly stood back up and swung Kenny's body around the arena. O'Reilly snickered and let go, leaving Kenny dizzy and unable to register what had happened, plus giving him little time to react. His body glided through the air, the rocky exterior covering his outsides dragging him down fast.

He grabbed a rock that was jammed into one of the still remaining pillars and swung his body back up onto its surface, using it as a platform to keep himself from being thrown into the lava. He scanned the area quickly, trying to find some other way out of this mess without getting himself killed in the process.

Kenny flipped himself around, grabbing the rock in his hands like a monkey-bar as he pushed his feet against the pillar, using his arms to defy gravity and keep himself held up in mid air. He pushed himself away, pulling the rock out of the pillar as he went. And then he launched his body in the direction of his enemy. O'Reilly was waiting for him, ready to continue this fight.

Kenny, only mere feet away, forced himself back onto the ground. He slid through the lava, right in between O'Reilly's legs. Startled, O'Reilly just stood there not knowing what to do. He quickly turned around to try and find his prey again. Kenny quickly slammed the rock into the ground and swung his body around back toward O'Reilly.

Before either had time to really register what had happened, Kenny had knocked O'Reilly to the floor, but it resulted with him losing his balance and being thrown very far away, almost into the lake of fire below. Kenny looked up. His vision caught a quick glimpse of O'Reilly diving in for the kill.

"Die!" O'Reilly shouted, slamming another dagger-like stone into Kenny's leg. He let out a cry of pain, kicking and screaming at the top of his lungs in attempts to get away. Red, crystallized blood was spewing from his leg where the dagger had been plunged into his flesh. Eventually he got O'Reilly kicked off of him and had him once again pinned to the ground, but his body was drained of energy, and he had barely enough strength to keep his larger foe on the floor.

Kenny found himself being punched in the face and beaten to death. He recoiled a bit and fell to the ground writhing in pain from the impact of the brutal beating. True most of him was covered in the stone exterior, but the impact of O'Reilly's large, stone fist against his still pounding head was painful. O'Reilly was standing above him again, hissing loudly like a cobra ready to devour a small rat.

O'Reilly kicked Kenny harshly. He flew across the floor over to the wall. He took a short breath before he felt heavy pain shoot into his shoulder. He opened his eyes again and saw another rock driven into his shoulder and O'Reilly's face very few inches away from his own.

"Tell me what you cherish most," he hissed. "Give me the pleasure of taking that away from you as well. I'd just adore seeing you cry again, you pathetic little worm."

Kenny's eyes narrowed. "You've already taken everything from me. There's nothing left...all of them are gone, I have nothing."

O'Reilly smirked widely, watching as Kenny lowered his head in fear and defeat. He laughed coldly, all of Kenny's muscles tightened, his fists clenched and his eyes narrowed. He looked back up at O'Reilly with a smirk of his own planted on his face.

"But there's not a thing I didn't, that I don't cherish! You can take them away, but you can't ever kill their spirits!" Kenny shouted.

He threw his fist up into O'Reilly's face.

He recoiled. Spit was sent flying from his now cracked mouth. A large chunk of his face fell onto the floor, revealing his jawbone. Kenny pulled himself away from the wall and went to run away, blood running from his shoulder as he removed the rock from his body.

In one swift motion, Kenny was knocked back onto the ground. O'Reilly grabbed Kenny's neck and pulled him up, a smile only the devil could produce on his face and pure hatred in his eyes. Kenny hacked a wheezed in pain, trying to get free from the man's brutal grip. O'Reilly slammed him down onto the ground, Kenny feeling his back snap upon the impact. He grabbed O'Reilly's hands weakly, trying to push him away somehow.

The ground beneath them was shattering from the attacks, lava was covering most of the area now, and the stairs back to the outside were crumbling. Kenny pressed his feet against the floor, slowly sliding himself backward toward the ledge. O'Reilly paid very little attention to what Kenny was planning; he almost had the remaining life choked out of him now, and the motions were almost stopped completely.

Now's my chance! Kenny thought, swallowing. He pressed his foot lightly against O'Reilly's chest and shot it upward and back harshly. O'Reilly coughed loudly as Kenny flew him up and over his body. He was sent flying over to the end of the battlefield. Kenny watched as he vanished beneath the rocky edge of the platform, nothing was heard after.

He slowly stood back up again and walked over to the ledge, looking down upon O'Reilly with anger in his expression. He was hanging on with one hand, the ground beneath his fingers steadily crumbling.

O'Reilly watched as chunks of the wall fell down into the lava next to him. His head shot back up to Kenny and he scowled, hissing loudly. He saw Kenny move his foot over to his hand, and his expression changed to a fearful one.

"Stop, I have family, they need me!" he spat.

"I missed the part where that's my problem," Kenny said coldly.

O'Reilly stayed still in shock as Kenny slid his foot on top of his hand. With a smirk he began to press down, the ground beginning to crumble.

"This is for the years you, your ancestors, and your spawns that still walk the earth have and will no longer torture Robert's family, my family! I'll make sure of it!" he shouted, pressing down harder. O'Reilly gasped and tried to slide his other hand back up onto the floor, but Kenny stopped that motion by pressing his other foot on it.

"This is for Bloodwite!" he shouted, putting all of his weight onto his enemy's hand.

"And this is for Robert!"

Kenny finally shot down so hard the ground shattered. O'Reilly screamed loudly as he plummeted to his death. The moment he hit the fire, he went up in flames, the lava roaring and snapping like an angry dragon that had just swallowed its prey. Kenny stared on into the inferno, watching as he finally completed his goal and finally was allowed to rest.

He felt the stones around his body crack and fall off, all sliding into the lava one by one, letting his battered skin finally breathe and his body un-tense. He wiped some sweat from his head and turned around, heading back over to the entrance with a limp in his step. He was teetering on the edge of death without realizing it. He used what little strength he had left to hurry to the door before the lava completely devoured his only means of escape. He pressed his hand against the door and tried to open it but couldn't. He stood there for a moment, unable to open it, until he felt another hand on his own. He looked back and saw the man who had continuously spoken to him before in the mazes, the one who had finally showed him the light and the way to communicate with the creatures around him. The pale white enigma who had opened his eyes to the truth.

"Join him," he said kindly.

He spread his fingers apart to become even with Kenny's. With a small smile, he nodded. Kenny felt the dried blood from Robert's face on his hands begin to moisten and a white light radiated from his palm. It overtook the door and soon the locks re-opened and Kenny was allowed back outside.

"Why?" Kenny asked.

The man shook his head. "It is not yet time to learn that," he replied, pushing Kenny back outside. He walked down the stairs until he was at the bottom then looked back at the man. He watched as the entire inside of the Grave started to crumble. Kenny went to go back inside to save him, but the man raised his hand. The door began to close again, leaving him inside to die with the other fallen ones.

"Go on," he whispered, just as the door concealed him from Kenny's gaze. The door closed and all was silent again. He just stood there, wondering what he meant, questioning everything again. It seemed, even at the end of all this madness he still didn't have any answers. For a moment, he remained calm, until he realized Robert was lying behind him, almost at his feet.

He turned around and walked over to his friend with a small

smile, knowing it was what Robert wanted him to do. Robert was motionless and the blood had stopped flowing from his body, and his back wasn't rising, which meant no breath was entering his lungs.

With closed eyes, Kenny went to kneel down next to him, to get one last look at his face. He was stopped when he heard a gunshot and felt his heart stop beating. He looked down and saw blood flowing from his heart and he struggled to breathe. *This is...not happening!*

Chapter Forty-four:

THE DANCE

KENNY FELL FLAT on the ground next to Robert, both lying there, breathless, bloody messes. The last vision he would ever see was Fireflood, standing there at the top of the stairs in the same state he was, lifeless. And then Robert at his side, his face filled with confusion. A small, sadistic smile was on Fireflood's face. *How...did he get away?* Kenny thought. He watched Fireflood's hand shake, the gun becoming a silver blur from his uneven movements.

"Bloodwite...Blueweed...I'll have my revenge, our revenge," he moaned, letting his body fall to the ground.

The gun flew from his hands into a small puddle of water on the platform below, his body landing on the entry way of the Grave. The three men, Fireflood, Robert, and Kenny, all laid there motionless, without a single breath entering or escaping their lips and blood rushing across the floor from the bodies. The area surrounding them was nothing but a bloody battlefield, one which no eyes would ever see again.

"Sorry...Robert," Kenny whispered. He grabbed his friend's

hand and held it, the memory of the car accident flooding back into his head for a last time. This was always how he sometimes had wanted it to end, the same way it started, but he never wanted Robert to be the one to go first. His tears covered his face and the ground below as he reached up to touch Robert's face. He gently brushed his hand against his eyes to help them close. With one deep, final breath, he too closed his eyes and lay there on the ground, whispering 'I'm sorry' to his friend.

The area was silent; it seemed the Grave had lived up to its name. Kenny, dying on the floor, Robert's blood spilled all across the area, Bloodwite lying in the lower chamber beneath where they were, and Fireflood lifeless on the stairs. This sacred place had claimed so many so quickly, with so little remorse. It seemed unfair yet destined to happen from the very beginning. Utter silence reigned in the night, gentle melodies rushing from everything, almost as if the Grave itself was speaking to them, trying to say something to the lives it had claimed.

A few rustling noises echoed inside and soon tiny little fireflies flew from the bushes around the room. They dashed over to the bodies of Kenny and Robert, looking on at them in question and wonder, words in their native tongue quickly spreading amongst themselves. Few stayed where they had stopped, most rushed to the bodies to see if any life remained in them but to their great disarray nothing was there. A few of them made noises to each other; others flickered their lights. The conversation went on for some time, arguing over something no ears were allowed to hear. Some bobbled up and down as if to answer "yes, yes we should"! Others rocked back and forth, small hissing noises coming from their tiny bodies in reply to their excited friends.

But then it was decided, and those small bugs, those little fairies, began to dance. The empty torches around the platform were set ablaze in a mass fury, the fireflies danced across the water and the land in circles and patterns like a beautiful painting. The lights grew and almost consumed everything in its mass furry and wonder.

This little dance was glorious; it would have made Kenny's eyes shine with tears and happiness. More than ten thousands fireflies were dancing around their bodies. This dance was to symbolize something, their great respect for the bodies of the fallen one would have guessed, but no. This dance was of a much greater cause.

The light was almost too intense to be able to block out, and soon it almost consumed everything in sight, the wet leaves around that were covered in dew looked as if they were on fire. Kenny's bloody body looked like a clay figure on the ground due to the lighting, one that was purposely made to stay there on the ground, as a monument of what had been a great fight, one that should never be forgotten in that sacred place. That boy, that strong-willed man, smiled until the end, keeping memories of everything he knew in his heart. That memory of a life that had now passed stayed still in the heart of one.

Chapter Forty-five:

THE SMILE

TOOKA STOOD ON the rock where she had first kissed Kenny. She stood watching the water calmly. In the crystal pond she saw her lonesome reflection. Someone had brought her back home while she was unconscious in the cavern in the rock slide. Tears fell from her eyes, but a smile was on her face, a large one, one of pure joy and happiness. She knew, somewhere, somehow Kenny was still alive.

"Ancients, please be kind to Kenny," she said quietly, sitting down on the stone. "He come back, he said he would. So I wait."

The rustling of the trees, the sound of rushing water, the howling of the wind, all reminded her of Kenny's smiling face. Every moment she had spent with him had been permanently etched into her mind; she would never forget any of it, the adventure she had always dreamed of going on, the prince she always wanted to be rescued by, and the love that she would never let die. It was all so wonderful. She turned around and saw her grandmother walking toward her, a smile on her wrinkled face.

THE GRAVE OF THE FIREFLIES

"Yes, I believe you're right child," she said. "He will come back."

Rui's head was lifted to the blue sky; she watched some large birds fly above her, making shadows all across the trees. Tooka's eyes followed; she watched on in silence, still dreaming like she had been.

"The ancients are not done with him. I think he has quite some time before he is ready to be set free," she said smiling.

Tooka's face was filled with joy as she stepped down onto the ground again, her face practically glowing from excitement.

"I happy," she said laughing.

"As you should be, child, as you should be," Rui replied, nodding gently in reply.

Tooka looked up at the sky again, watching the clouds rolling over the area gently like the waves across the bay. It was quiet for a moment, just her standing there in the middle of the small sanctuary. She turned to face her grandmother again.

"Robert?" she asked. Rui's smile faded and was replaced with a sadden look.

"The heir was still living, that means our lord is not fully gone. The Gohmas and The Uty's may come to war again in our near future; Iis may be our only hope," she replied quietly.

"Robert will stop fighting," Tooka said proudly. "He will bring peace, I feel it. We may finally smile forever."

The smile was still planted on her face, the thought of peace and Kenny, and even Robert, was all she needed. Her mind was resting easily now that she knew everything would be okay and nothing bad would happen. *We smile forever, together*, she thought. *Kenny and I.*

"But I have a question," Tooka said, raising a finger in the air.

Rui looked on at her, inquiring what Tooka was about to ask her.

"Kenny was beaten and battered almost to death many times. Yet he survived, like we could. He is not...human, is he?"

Rui laughed. "My child, you haven't figured it out yet? Well then, I guess that gives you a reason to find him, doesn't it?"

Chapter forty-six:
THE END

IT WAS WARM and dry in Heather Field now during the evening; the rain storms had stopped, and the sun was basking everything in a heavy but gentle heat as it was setting in the far distance. A body was lying in a sweat drenched bed, dried blood was all across his face, but a smile was planted there too. Two brown eyes opened slowly and a heavy yawn escaped his lips. He rubbed his eyes and sat up, holding onto his growling stomach in agony.

"Man, being dead doesn't feel much better than being alive," he moaned, yawning again. He looked at his hands, seeing the blood running through all of the indents of his skin. With a large, ear to ear smile and a loud, joyous laugh, he hugged himself and cried there, feeling the pangs of immense joy run through his sides as he collapsed backwards on the bed.

"I'm alive," he stammered, staring at his hands with glee. "Hear that, O'Reilly? Kenny Mathis still walks this earth!"

Kenny pushed himself from the bed and stretched, feeling completely rejuvenated and free. He walked over to the old mirror in the corner of the room and brushed back his bangs, looking at the large cuts all over his forehead that were slowly healing. He scanned himself thoroughly, not too pleased with his still bloody, mangled, dead skin covering body. But still, he felt happy to be alive and well and not dead in the middle of nowhere. He grabbed a sweater from the top of the old chest that was beneath the mirror and wrapped his mangled body in it. It had bizarrely become very cold and he wasn't overly pleased with how he looked. As he was staring over his body, his eyes gazed up to the top of the mirror. He saw a small note had been slid into the frame. Carefully, he pulled it out and opened it, wondering what it said.

"We, the holders of the Grave, have decided only you to save. Be strong, be brave, and be nice, for only you are allowed to live twice." Kenny looked it over and smiled and bit. *Twice those things have had to save my life*, he thought, folding the note, finally figuring out the reason why they had saved him the night he and Robert first met. He slid it into his pocket and turned to face the doorway. For a moment he just stood there until he realized that Robert might be in his room.

He smiled and ran out the door, heading into the hallway, then into Robert's room. He burst inside, the large smile still on his face. It faded quickly as the sight of the sleeping, unmoving Robert appeared. He was lying still on the bed, his hands over his stomach, and still no breath entered his lungs.

Kenny crept over to the bed and kneeled down on the floor next to Robert's head; he held Robert's hand and waited, praying he would wake up if he felt some sort of contact but his skin was cold to the touch. He pressed his head against Robert's bloody chest and listened, praying for a steady heartbeat, but nothing was heard except his own crying.

He stood back up and loomed over him for a moment, his hand lying still on his friend's chest. Silence filled the entire room for some time, only the weeping and gasping of Kenny remaining which soon turned into an almost heavy screaming and hyperventilation. He shook his head and cried, mentally re-reading the note. *We the holders of the Grave have decided only you to save. Be strong, be brave and be nice, for only you are allowed to live twice.*

They could only save me, he thought sadly as he embraced Robert's body gently, trying to wake him up even though he knew that it wouldn't work, no matter how much he struggled to get him to open his eyes. He let his hand come back to him. He looked at it, watching the blood drip from his fingers. He shook his head harshly and ran out of the room, back into his bedroom, feeling too guilty to look at his face anymore.

"It's not fair!" he shouted, slamming his hands on the wall. He heard a loud click and quickly re-opened his eyes. The tears stopped flowing, and his eyes became wide in shock. He saw a door, one he had never noticed. It was the one he had revealed when the bookcase had fallen, yet he hadn't been able to see it. It looked so interesting and untouched to him, so untainted and pure.

Kenny reached for the handle and jiggled it a bit. The door instantly unlatched itself and opened. Hesitant, Kenny went inside, creeping into the dark of the room that had stayed hidden for who knows how long. The further inside he went, the more he started to question if he really was awake now. The room was so large, it could never have fit in this little house, yet somehow it seemed so right to him and so perfect.

His eyes remained on the floor for most of the trip until he stopped at a shinning object on the ground. He knelt down and looked at it, rubbing the dust from its exterior gently with his shirt. It revealed itself to be a coin, a gold coin. He looked up, seeing an entire trail of them running across the floor.

He picked them all up as he went, trying to make sure he wasn't hallucinating, and slid them into his pocket for safe keeping. Also picking up rubies and some other odd jewels he had never seen before, ones of a purplish onyx color and another that was almost a pure pumpkin orange. It seemed like an endless trail of golden coins and unnatural stones, a smile was on his face, but it vanished and was replaced with a look of pure awe as he finally came to the end of the room.

From the floor to the ceiling was nothing but large piles of gold and rubies, treasure from every corner of the world was sitting there, all basking in the light from a crack in the ceiling. Kenny pinched himself to make sure it wasn't a dream and that he really was standing in front of this huge room of treasure. He took a torch from the wall and set it down in a small canal like area.

Soon the whole room was sent ablaze, a trail of light running all across the large treasury until it made the shape of circle, in the middle stood three lines running both up and down and across, creating a latch effect of six perfectly straight lines. Kenny just stood there, gazing over all of the treasure that had been right under his nose the entire time.

"All of that, and I could've slammed my fist on the wall, walked into a room, found the stupid money, and never left the house," he said sarcastically. But the sarcasm soon disappeared. He ran and dove into a pile of money, almost laughing as he went. Laying in it like it was his bed, his body sinking into it quickly like a cloud. He let himself be surrounded by the untouched golden items for a moment as he tried to register this newfound discovery in his head. It made no sense to him; he thought back as far as he could. Trying to find out what he could've missed. And then the poem, from the *Untitled* book was sent back into his head, and everything became so clear he almost was ready to kill himself over it. It was too easy. The door didn't open because he had slammed his fist against it. It opened because he had smeared Robert's blood across it. The Grave was there all the time.

"From the heavens beyond the vast lands of sea, through thicket, vine, and within every tree, a house, a home, a humble abode, that is what you *Mortals* are told. Will you dare seek? Will you dare follow? Follow them into the overshadowing hollow? A treasure, a myth, a legend you will find, hidden deep in the fiery land of vine. Go seek it, embrace it, find it, and then, you shall be given the treasure of *Men*.

I went through all of that and came back to the house. Robert was always told never to go past the fence, but they meant never to go past it into the house. The biggest legend of the fairies was of the heir, Robert. I embraced the things I couldn't understand, then came back here and opened the door. It makes perfect sense now."

Tears were running from his cheeks so heavily his shirt was almost completely drenched. The whole journey, everything he had done, seemed to be in vain now. With a heavy heart, Kenny walked back outside and headed downstairs; he needed some fresh air, some time to think and cool off a bit, some time to just sit and think.

The trip to the front door seemed to take forever, the creaking and cracking of the floorboards not even affecting him. Even the dog almost knocking him down the stairs did nothing to make him even move. He opened the door and felt himself being surrounded by fresh autumn air. It felt nice yet saddening at the same time. This was hard to deal with, this loss and this great discovery.

He sat down in one of the chairs and placed his head in his hands, tears running through his fingers onto the table. The old, rotting wood dampened where the tears hit it; the entire left side of the table almost thoroughly wet within the hour. He just sat there and let himself vent a bit, tears flowing until no more could come out.

And then there was nothing left to do again. He wondered something, replaying the events in his head, and re-reading the poem that started the whole thing. He also remembered the poem about the 'ark' in the fireplace which he never really found. The light that had led him to the faux grave provided him a guide, but he found nothing ark-like. Was he missing something? That puzzled him; it felt like something wasn't right. Something was incomplete.

It had grown dark, and he was sitting out there alone, listening to the crickets howling in the background, playing with the tiny golden coins and all the jewels he had found. Completely oblivious to the sound of tires on the road, his vision was suddenly blurred by a bright light as they swooped in on him. He rubbed his eyes a bit and looked out into the horizon, trying to figure out what the lights were.

As it grew closer, it turned out to be the headlights of an old car. A very plump man got out and headed in Kenny's direction. He went on the offensive and grabbed an old wooden plank that was just lying next to the door.

"Ho ho, settle down there, boy," he said, his voice gruff and old sounding. Kenny rubbed his eyes and looked at him again, trying to see who it was. He soon came up the stairs and was standing in front of Kenny with an outstretched hand.

"My name is William H. Kerry, Mayor of Heather Field," he said.

Kenny blinked and dropped the plank. He dusted his hands off and shook his hand, blushing slightly in embarrassment.

"Hi, I'm Kenny Mathis, I live here with Robert," he said smiling.

"Ah, good, where is the chap? Haven't seen him in some time," he said smiling.

"He's...sleeping. Uh, I'm not sure if you take gold coins and jewels, but I'm pretty sure the value of these things are more than what you were asking," he said, pointing to the small glistening objects on the table.

The mayor was in complete awe over the sight of these rare treasures; he pushed his glasses up further on his nose and picked some of the gems up.

He closely examined them one at a time, making sure they were all real, almost in complete awe at the wonderful items he was holding in his hands. Kenny stared off into the distance, not paying much attention to the odd man who had seemingly appeared out of thin air.

"If you're here to get the payment that means it's the thirtieth, right?" he asked quietly.

The mayor nodded a bit, not taking his eyes from the gems. *I was sleeping for four days?* he asked himself as he rubbed his eyes.

"My boy, I don't know where you got these fine artifacts, but thank you, the payment is accepted. Actually, I really couldn't bear to rip this house from its rightful owner, but that horrid

O'Reilly just kept insisting. If I would have had my way, you wouldn't have needed to gather these things, but I thank you.

"And I promise you, that O'Reilly and his family will not bother you at all, I swear, you have the rest of the town on your side," he said, bundling the gems up into a cloth. He folded it and slid it into his pocket.

Kenny watched in utter silence. *That's awful reassuring*, he thought. *At least I know I won't be bothered by anything else for a while.*

The man tipped his hat to him and smiled. "I must be off. Tell Robert I said hello, would you?" he asked.

"I will," he replied, nodding.

The mayor smiled and walked down the stairs to his car, Kenny watching his every movement until he left and his car was completely out of view. With a heavy sigh, he headed back up to Robert's room.

He slowly walked in, trying hard not to cry anymore. Robert always had hated to see him cry; he knew it would make him upset if he was watching over him. With a smile, he sat at Robert's side. He let his head hang down and his body loosened. He knew that he had nothing to be upset or nervous about now, so it was no use to continue racking himself with pain like he had been, especially when it was all over now.

Gently, Kenny placed his hand on Robert's and sat there before he began to speak to him, trying to get unspoken things off of his chest.

"I'm sorry," he began. "You know I was always jealous of you. I never knew why, but now that I found out the truth, I know, and I feel stupid. I was jealous of myself, you were leading my life, and I was leading yours. I always just wanted to be me, to be the way you portrayed me. Perfect.

"I want to keep smiling for you, but I'm not sure I can. I have so many wonderful things I want to tell you, and I may never get to now. You're probably saying the same thing now, laughing at me ranting here from wherever you are. You don't know how much that hurts me, Robert. I feel pathetic for not being able to get to you in time, for not having the strength needed to save you.

"My heart just aches at the thought of a life without you. Man, I sound selfish; pretty pathetic for a guy who just walked through hell and back, huh?" Kenny laughed a bit and closed his eyes. His rant was interrupted by another laugh. Kenny's eyes burst back open. He saw Robert lying there with his eyes open and a smile on his face.

"No, I can see it in your eyes. You grew up on me. I'm not looking at that same juvenile delinquent that I used to call my brother," he said, making Kenny's face become flustered. "No, I'm looking at a man, one who braved so many dangers to save my hide. I'm proud of you."

Robert sat up, groaning a bit in pain from the sudden movements. Kenny went to protest him moving so much, but Robert stopped him by embracing him in a hug. Kenny returned it and listened to him cry, a small smile on his face. Both sat there, tears rolling from their eyes, laughter coming from their lips.

Kenny gasped in realization, looked at Robert, and slammed his hand into his sore friend's chest. Robert let out a cry of pain and looked at him, hissing angrily.

"What was that for?" Robert hissed.

Kenny growled. "Don't do that! I thought you were dead. Don't stop breathing and then suddenly start again and then sit up and start talking and...you scared the living daylights out of me! I swear I'll kill you if you do that again; I'll kill you and drag your sorry rump back from the grave and kill you again—"

Robert stopped him by holding onto him. "Shut up, you moron," he whispered.

"Don't do that," Kenny mumbled. His voice muted as he buried his face into Robert's chest. "I thought you were dead," he whispered.

"I missed you, welcome home," Robert said, smiling.

Kenny pushed himself away and looked at Robert. "You don't know how long I've waited to hear you say that," he said smiling.

Both started to laugh, feeling relief and happiness for once in a long time. Robert felt exhausted and had to lie back down and let his body rest, still not fully recovered from everything. With a smile he looked at Kenny who was still wiping many tears from his eyes, almost in question at why he was so upset.

"Is everything all right?" Robert asked.

Kenny blinked a bit and nodded, a very large, very happy smile on his face and tears still gushing from his eyes.

"Tell me, tell me everything," Robert said with a wide grin on his face.

Kenny laughed. "It's kind of a long story."

"Does it look like I have anything better to do right now?" he asked. "Now get to it; I want to hear it from the beginning to the end, no details left out."

Kenny sat there for a moment, thinking hard about where to begin. He heard a giggle in the background.

"Don't forget me," the female's voice said. Kenny looked up and almost saw a flash of Tooka standing in front of him.

"I won't," he whispered.

Robert looked at him. "What?"

Kenny laughed, shaking his head. Robert sat there, watching him in question and wonder.

"What's so funny?" he asked.

"There's no end," he said.

Robert's smile faded; he looked at him with serious question on his face and pure confusion in his eyes.

Kenny smirked a bit. "This story is far from over."

EPILOGUE

ON A COOL November's eve, early evening around five, Kenny was fixing a busted part in the pick-up's engine. He was greasy and sweat-covered. He held a wrench in one hand and a washcloth in the other. He had his mp3 player strapped to his belt, cranked on high, and a random tune slipping from his lips.

"Kenny...Kenny!" Robert shouted from the porch.

Kenny still stood oblivious, whistling loudly as he wiped some sweat from his head.

Robert placed his hands on his hips, shook his head, and rolled his eyes. *Oblivious, as always, yeah he grew up, but his mind is still stuck in its awkward phase*, he thought as he trekked his way down toward the old car.

Kenny still focused on the broken engine. Robert sidled up to the car, hands in his pockets, and eyes filled with wonder. Kenny's eyes wandered across the top of the engine multiple times, scanning its surface like a typewriter. He looked from left to right, until he caught a glimpse of Robert swiftly and looked up. He removed his headphones and smiled.

"Hey, Rob. I thought you were asleep," he stated, setting his wrench down.

"I was, but I woke up," he replied. "How's it coming?"

"Not too bad, but not too good," Kenny replied, wiping his

hands on his pants. He stared at Robert who was staring around the lawn with worry. Kenny walked around the car to Robert's side.

"You okay? You look panicked," Kenny stated.

"Yeah, I just don't feel safe with you out here by yourself...you know," Robert stated.

"No, I don't know. Look, O'Reilly's been missing for a long time now, and the house is ours. We're millions of miles away from civilization, and we're totally secluded from everything...calm down!" Kenny said. *I can't believe I lied to him...again*, he sighed, but he knew it was for the best.

Robert hadn't remembered anything that happened, so Kenny kept it that way. He thought it best to keep those horrid memories locked away. Keep the heartache far away from Robert's mind. He wasn't faring well as it was; he was weak, and the doctor said he was going to be very frail for the rest of his life. Kenny was determined to keep him protected.

"Like I said, Rob, I'm not leaving your side, and I'm going to keep you protected, so just calm down," Kenny stated as he went back to work.

Robert sighed a bit and crossed his arms. He continued to stare off into the distance with little to say.

Kenny looked up at him in wonder. "Rob, something else is bothering you, isn't it? What is it?"

"I feel empty, like something is missing," Robert stated.

Kenny raised an eyebrow in question. "Like what? Food or something, or like that hunk out of the back of your head?"

Robert laughed. "No...like *someone* is missing," He stated.

He leaned on the car and stared at Kenny in a bit of wonder, almost asking "do you get what I'm saying?"

Kenny yawned a bit and thought, trying to consider all possibilities of what could have changed. *Maybe he...maybe he can feel Iis inside? Maybe he needs to know who he is.*

"Well, I guess I should let you get back to work. I need to get some sleep anyway," Robert said, almost a faint tone of disappointment in his voice from still standing answerless.

"Okay, goodnight Rob," Kenny replied. "If you need something, let me know."

Robert nodded and left without another word. Kenny watched him, knowing he was too consumed in his thoughts to think clearly. He waited until Robert was out of sight, and then he went back to work, cranking his headphones back on high.

The sun was setting over the horizon by the time Kenny was done. He closed the lid on the old red truck and sighed in exhaustion, eyes closed tightly and his arms outstretched in the air.

He slowly opened his eyes, and in amazement, he saw a man wander his way toward him through the hazy mist. He blinked and took a deep breath, feeling a familiar presence loom over his body. For the longest time, it seemed, he felt a longing to be surrounded by the auras of the creatures he had been in contact with. Kenny could barely feel Robert's connection with his alter, Iis; it was faint and wasn't enough. Kenny felt uneasy from being in this normal setting for too long.

The form of this man was eerily familiar. He had hair of black, eyes of pure white with orange swirling inside, like marbles. He was tall, thin, and young.

"Human named Kenny," he said, "child of the humans who released me from my prison. I come to give you my utmost thanks."

"Um, you're welcome?" Kenny said, raising eyebrows in wonder.

"You do not know of me?" he asked, his form becoming very clear in the fading sunlight. He was soon standing at least ten feet from Kenny. He waved him to his side with a gentle gesture. Kenny nodded and wandered in that direction little fear.

"I am the one called M'nep. My guardians probably spoke of me, no?" he stated.

Kenny's eyes widened. "*The* M'nep, the lord of the forest? You are...the original king, you, the one who's supposed to be dead?"

M'nep raised a gentle hand to silence him. "Yes and no. I was in a state of comatose, awaiting the heir who resembled me in perfect likeness, the only one who could open the lock I had placed on the Grave door. He is my reincarnation...my son, Iis," he stated.

Kenny gasped and backed away, shaking his head in confusion. Of all the things he had heard, this was the most shocking. Robert was indeed the heir. That he could comprehend, but a perfect reincarnation of M'nep, that was something he was never told.

"Why are you here, what do you need now? You're supposed to be dead, why when Iis was found do you suddenly wake up?" Kenny asked.

"Two races live in my world, The Uty—my people. And the Gohma, you have seen them. If it becomes known that Iis has been found, war is unavoidable, people will die trying to claim him for their own," M'nep stated. "He must be hidden."

Kenny cocked his head to the side in utter question. "I don't understand why you came here ..."

M'nep closed his eyes. "It's inevitable. I'm sorry, Kenny. I have to take Iis home with me. He can't be here any longer."